IVY SMOAK

This book is a work of fiction. Names, characters, places, and incidents are fictitious. Any resemblance to actual persons, living or dead, events, or locales is purely coincidental.

ISBN: 978-1542616768

2020 Edition

I didn't realize I was missing anything in my life until I started writing.

So thank you for giving my books a chance. Thank you for caring about the characters that I've laughed, cried, and grown with.

Just like every book I write, this one is a piece of me.

CHAPTER 1

Hailey

Friday

I glanced once more at the closed door of my father's office. He wouldn't be coming back to the bar for another 30 minutes, but I was still nervous. If he caught me snooping, he'd have a fit. I quickly opened the last drawer and found what I had hoped I wouldn't. I pulled out the stack of envelopes and spread them out on the desk.

All I could do was stare in silence. I was stunned. Final notices of payments due were staring back at me. They matched the one that had arrived in the mail that afternoon. There were half a dozen from different suppliers and even one for the electricity. I swallowed hard when I lifted up the envelope at the bottom of the stack. A notice of foreclosure.

A knock on the door made me jump.

"Jeff, you in there?" someone said from the other side of the door.

"No, it's just Hailey," I called to the closed door as I shoved all the bills back into the drawer and slammed it shut.

The door immediately opened. Anna, our assistant manager, stepped into the office with a huge smile on her face. "Hails!" She ran over to me and embraced me in a hug. "I didn't know you were going to start work quite yet." She held me at arm's length.

"Yeah, I just got home a few days ago, but I wanted to get back in the swing of things."

"It's so good to have you back, hon," she said. "With your fancy new management degree, I bet you have a ton of ideas for the bar."

"Mhm," I said. But the realization had already hit me. My new degree wasn't going to be able to fix anything. It just added to the debt that was already hanging over our heads. The bar was failing. Why hadn't my dad told me?

"Do you know when your dad will be in?"

"He said he'd be here by 8."

"Great. I was hoping to have a quick word with him. Are you helping behind the bar tonight? The regulars are starting to come in already."

"Sure," I said with a small smile. We needed as much help as possible. "What did you need to talk to my dad about?"

"Oh, well, a few months ago he promised me he'd give me a raise if Billy got into college. And we just got the acceptance letter this morning!" Her smile seemed to grow tenfold. "He'll be heading off to school in the fall."

I tried to hide my grimace. If anyone deserved a raise, it was Anna. She had been working here for as long as I could remember. She was basically a part of the family. All my dad's employees were. But my dad was also drowning in debt. I was drowning in debt. He couldn't afford to give her a raise. What had he been thinking?

"Tell Billy congrats from me," I said with as much positivity as I could muster. "I'm going to go get to work."

"It's great to have you back, Hails," she said.

I walked out into the hall, leaving Anna behind. When I had visited during winter break, business was booming. Well, as booming as it had ever been. Things had been good. And I was excited to come home and help the bar grow even more. But now there was a lump in my throat and tears prickling the corners of my eyes. How long had the bar been in trouble? My dad and I never hid things from each other. Ever. So why had he hidden this from me?

I walked behind the bar and grabbed an apron off the hook. This business was everything my dad had. It was his baby. And it was supposed to be my future. I had plans. Suddenly I felt so incredibly naive. I had gone off to college with hopes and dreams on how we could expand. Coming home to this wasn't what I expected. This bar didn't just mean everything to my father. It meant everything to me too.

I tied the apron around my waist and looked out at the patrons. Like Anna had said, the regulars had started to filter in. Even though I hadn't been here in months, the regulars were all the same. Our small town was notorious for never having any newcomers. But that was probably an exaggeration, because in order to be notorious, outsiders needed to know our town existed, which they did not.

At first I kept glancing at the clock, waiting for my dad to arrive. As everyone started coming up to me and welcoming me home, though, I quickly forgot about the time. It was so great to see everyone. I was happy to be home. And with how packed the bar was, I felt optimistic. We could turn this around. I came home with ideas and I could still implement them. Maybe they wouldn't help us grow, but they could help save the bar. My dad and I would get out of this mess. We always found a way.

I started to wipe down the bar counter during a down moment.

"As beautiful as ever," said a deep voice.

I rolled my eyes and glanced up at my ex boyfriend from high school. "It's good to see you too, Jack."

He smiled.

His smile used to make my legs feel like jelly. It hadn't had that effect in a long time though. I had learned the hard way that all relationships were fleeting. And I could thank Jack for part of that. He had cheated on me with my best friend, Claire, my senior year of high school. I hadn't been in a serious relationship since. Besides, I was too busy with my classes. I was happy to see that his smile no longer affected me though.

"I'm surprised to see you back here," he said.

"I was always coming back, I told you that. Can I get you a refill?"

"Sure." He slid his empty glass to me.

I refilled it a little lower than the brim. We were going to have to make some conscious cuts. And I certainly didn't mind making Jack pay for that. I placed the glass down in front of him. "How's Claire doing?"

"Good. She's pregnant."

"Wow, congratulations." I tried to make myself sound enthusiastic. Most people in this town did stay together. Jack and I were probably the exception. And most of them got pregnant young. Now that I was back, maybe I'd try to talk to Claire again. She had apologized to me right after she had kissed Jack, and I forgave her. But it still felt like a stab in the back when they started dating after I went off to school.

"Thanks, Hailey."

"Do you know if it's a boy or a girl?" I casually glanced around the bar, hoping that someone might need a refill. I maybe wasn't affected by Jack anymore, but I didn't want to be stuck talking to him about his wife and future child all night.

"A girl."

"That's wonderful." What was the appropriate question to ask next? Do you have any names picked out? Out of the corner of my eye I saw someone lift up an empty glass and wave at me. *Thank God.* "Table seven needs another round," I said. "It was great talking to you, Jack. And congrats on the baby," I added over my shoulder.

CHAPTER 2

Tyler

Friday

A beeping noise made me glance down at the dashboard. My gas light had just turned on. "Shit." I hit my turn signal and took the first exit off the highway. There was no sign of a gas station despite what the sign on the interstate had promised. Actually, there was no sign of anything. Just dark building after dark building. And a ton of farmland.

The beeping noise sounded again. I should have been paying better attention. I squinted at a cluster of lights in the distance. Maybe that was it. As I got closer, I quickly noticed that it was not a gas station. The lit up sign said Hails' Bar. One glance at my dashboard told me that if I didn't stop for directions now, I'd end up on the side of the road in the middle of nowhere.

I turned into the small parking lot. There were only a few cars besides my own. I pulled my phone out of my pocket, but it was dead. I had no reason to charge it. But maybe it would have helped me find a gas station. I grabbed my charger and slipped it and my phone into my pocket. It seemed like a small town. Maybe they'd be nice enough to let me charge my phone.

When I pushed through the door of the bar, I was surprised to see that the place was pretty packed. It must have been filled with locals who lived close enough to walk. It reminded me a little of the bars at the University of New Castle. Although, if this was their Main Street, this town did not have much going on. Some of the best nights in college had been walking back home with my friends after a night at the bar. That was one of the upsides of living in New York too. Everything was within walking distance. Apparently it was a perk of wherever the hell I currently was too.

I glanced over at the bar. Despite all the patrons, there was only one girl behind the counter. Which probably made sense. She was gorgeous. She had long brunette hair and a smile that lit up the room. They probably made a killing in tips with her working. I'd ask for directions in a bit. First I could really use a drink. I made my way over to the bar and sat down on an empty stool.

The bartender didn't even glance at me. She was talking to some guy on the other side of the bar. I leaned down and started searching the side of the bar for an outlet.

"Looking for something in particular?"

I sat back up. A few years ago I might have answered her with some line about looking for her number. But that was a long time ago. It wasn't like I wanted to hook up with a girl from the middle of nowhere and never see her again. I had no idea what I wanted, but I didn't want that. Even if she was gorgeous. I lifted up my charger. "An outlet. My phone's dead."

"Ah." She bit her lower lip, as if she was thinking over something. "It costs $5 to charge your phone."

I laughed.

But she didn't seem to think it was funny.

"Seriously?"

She shrugged. "New policy."

I shook my head and reached into my pocket for my wallet. "Okay. One charged cell phone and whatever you have on draft." I slid her a ten dollar bill.

"That I can do." She pocketed the money and grabbed my cell and charger. She walked past the bar and disappeared down a long hallway.

For a second I thought she may have just stolen my cell phone. But she came back in a minute.

She looked around the bar as she filled up a glass and then walked back over to me and set it down. She put her elbows on the edge of the counter and leaned toward me slightly. "So, what brings you here? Are you lost?"

"Not lost. Just looking for a gas station."

"So you meant to come here?"

"Not exactly."

"That means you're lost," she said with a laugh. "Where are you heading?"

I shrugged. "California. Eventually."

"Eventually?" She smiled.

Yeah, that smile could undo someone. But not me. I was already undone. I sighed. "I'm on a road trip of sorts."

"Really? I've always wanted to do that. Where are you from?"

"New York."

"The city?" Her eyes lit up.

"Yeah." People seemed to be easily excited by the idea of NYC. Little did they know that it was dirty and crowded and filled with people you couldn't bear to see anymore. I took a sip of my beer.

"What's it like?"

"You've never been?"

"It's like twelve hours away from here. So no, I've never been." She smiled again.

"Hails, can you grab Nathan another scotch?" said some lady who had just walked behind the bar. She was balancing a tray of empty glasses on one hand.

"Yeah, I've got it, Anna," she said. She tapped the bar in front of me. "Make a right out of the parking lot and drive about a mile down the road. The gas station will be on your left. Even though the lights aren't on, you can still pump the gas. Just let me know if you need a refill."

"Hails as in Hails' Bar?" I asked.

"That's me," she said over her shoulder.

I watched her pour a scotch. It looked like she had done it a million times. She was awfully young to own a bar. I started to wonder how old she was. I watched her as she gracefully walked over to Nathan. She laughed at something he said and touched his shoulder. She was definitely good at getting tips. I turned back to my beer.

I was twelve hours away from New York. So why did it feel like I was still there? Maybe when I got to California I'd finally feel the distance between Penny and me. I was doing my best to pretend I never knew her, hoping that it would make it easier to forget. But it wasn't working. I took another sip of the beer, suddenly wishing it was something stronger. *Three years.* I had been hung up on Penny for almost three years. What the hell was wrong with me? I downed the rest of my beer.

CHAPTER 3

Hailey

Friday

I glanced back over at the stranger as I wiped up a spill on the counter. For some reason, I wanted to know his story. I wasn't sure if it was because of the odd way he had answered my questions or because of his baby blue eyes. Maybe I didn't feel anything when I looked at Jack, but I felt something when I looked at him. I was currently holding his phone hostage, so it wasn't like he could just walk away into the night. Plus he had just downed a whole beer. He wouldn't be going anywhere for a while. I smiled. He needed a refill. I walked back over to him. "Need a refill?"

"No, I'm okay."

Crap. "Are you sure?"

He looked up at me. There was something else in his blue eyes I hadn't seen before. He looked sad. He gave me a small smile. "Yeah, I'm sure. I need to go find that gas station."

Now all I wanted to do was comfort him. I leaned on the counter and tried to hide my smile when I caught him steal a glance at my cleavage. Growing up working at this bar had taught me how to flirt at an early age. I was almost positive I could lighten his mood. "I really have always wanted to go on a road trip across the country. Are you taking any hitchhikers?"

He laughed.

I leaned slightly toward the sound. I had known he wasn't from around here as soon as I laid eyes on him. He was dressed a little more sleek than the men from town. I wasn't at all surprised that he had said he was from NYC. And I couldn't deny that he was handsome. Even though I didn't actually want to hitchhike with him, a little flirting never hurt anyone. "Is that a yes?"

"I'm pretty sure hitchhiking is illegal."

"Not one to break the rules?"

He smiled out of the corner of his mouth. "I didn't say that."

I laughed. "Well it wouldn't be hitchhiking if we knew each other." I stuck my hand out for him. "I'm Hailey."

He stared at my hand for a second before grabbing it. "Tyler."

"Nice to meet you, Tyler. So, why exactly are you going to California?"

He scratched the back of his neck. For some reason I found it incredibly sexy. "I just needed a change," he said.

"How mysterious."

He smiled again.

"Do you have a bunch of stops planned? I've always wanted to see the Grand Canyon."

"Not really. I'm just...driving." He shrugged his shoulders.

I could tell he was running from something. He didn't need to say it.

"But if you're coming along, I guess I could make a stop there."

I smiled. He was finally flirting back. I had successfully cheered him up.

His eyes left mine.

I turned around to see that he was staring at the TV screen behind me. There was a news broadcast on about the tech mogul, James Hunter, and his new wife. He had gotten shot on their wedding night. It wasn't looking like he was going to make it. They had been reporting on it for the past several days. "It's tragic. Aren't they the sweetest couple? I really hope he pulls through."

"Yeah. Yeah, me too. I should probably get going. Could you check on my phone?"

I turned back to him. Like a switch, he looked grim again. "Yeah, sure. Let me go check."

As I walked down the hall I heard my dad coughing in his office. It probably wasn't the best time to have the conversation we needed to have. But I couldn't stand the thought of him lying to me. Just the thought made my blood boil. I needed to know why he didn't tell me about the bar failing. I needed to clear the air between us. I knocked on his door and poked my head in. "Hey, Dad."

"Hi, honey. How's business tonight?"

I bit my lip. Anna could handle everyone for a second. I stepped into his office and closed the door. "Good." I took a deep breath. "Dad, I saw the bills."

He raised his eyebrows. "What bills?"

I put my hands on my hips. "The overdue notices. The foreclosure."

His pretend shocked face disappeared. He nodded.

"Why didn't you tell me?"

"I was waiting for you to finish school. I didn't want..."

"The bank is taking back the bar at the end of next month? We barely have any time to fix this. You should have told me."

"I didn't tell you because there's nothing we can do."

"Of course there is. I don't even understand what happened. Everything seemed fine over winter break. And there's tons of people out there right now. It doesn't add up. We should be cash flow positive."

"We are. I've...been using the money."

"For what?"

He sighed and leaned back in his chair. "I didn't want you to find out like this."

"Find out what?"

"All the money has been going to my chemo treatments."

My whole body suddenly felt cold. "Chemo? What are you talking about?"

His eyes looked slightly teary. He clasped his hands together on the top of his desk, like this was just a normal business meeting. "I have lung cancer."

I shook my head. "No. Dad. You can't..." I put my hand over my mouth.

"I do."

"No. We have to go get a second opinion. That's impossible. You've never even smoked."

He shook his head. "I've gotten a second opinion."

"Okay, so what can we do next?"

"Nothing. I'm dying, Hails."

"But can't you get treatment? Can't..."

"We can't afford to try anything else."

"Of course we can. We can figure it out. Just like we always have."

"I borrowed money against the bar. Against our house. Against my car. There's nothing left."

I shook my head.

"And we have your college loans to think about now."

"Screw that. There has to be something else we can do."

"Insurance won't cover any of the experimental treatments that my doctor has recommended. There is nothing else. Chemo didn't work. Radiation didn't work. It's the end of the road for me. We just have to use the time we've been given."

I tried to blink away the tears. "How much time?" My voice came out as a whisper.

"Four months."

I shook my head as the tears started to spill down my cheeks. "You can't just give up."

"I'm not giving up." He stood up and put his hand on my shoulder. "I'm choosing to enjoy my last few months with my girl."

"Dad." My voice cracked. I couldn't lose him. He was the only family I had.

"Chin up," he said and lightly tapped under my chin. He used to do that whenever I was upset growing up. It reminded me to be brave. It reminded me to be strong.

And I needed to be brave for the next thing I had to say to him. "What about Elena?"

He sighed. "She won't help us. And I don't want her to."

"Dad, I know she has the money."

"And she has no reason to give it to us."

"I've never asked her for anything. I could..."

"No. I don't want a cent from her. We've never needed a thing from her and we don't now either."

I pressed my lips together. How could he not want to try? How could he be giving up? And then I realized that maybe he had been fighting this for longer than I knew. Maybe he had been fighting alone the whole time I had been away. "When did you get diagnosed?"

"Halfway through your junior year."

"Why didn't you tell me?" For a year and a half he had been suffering alone. We told each other everything. At least, we used to.

"Because I knew you'd come home to help. I wanted you to finish school."

"You should have told me, Dad."

"And wouldn't you have come back?"

"Of course."

"Then I made the right decision."

"We're supposed to be a team, Dad."

"We are a team. But being a parent is also about making sacrifices for your child."

"I didn't ask you to do that."

"You being born asked that of me." He touched the bottom of my chin again. "I'm sorry I didn't tell you. But I'm glad you're home now. I could use the extra help around the bar. I haven't been feeling up to it."

I nodded. I suddenly saw the wrinkles around his mouth and the hollow look of his eyes. He looked sick. He looked like a shadow of the man I had left behind to go to college. And he was telling me not to feel guilty about that. But I felt horrible. Had I really been so self centered that I hadn't noticed he was hurting?

"I'm sorry about the bar. I thought...well, I thought I'd get better."

I shook my head. "Don't worry about the bar, Dad." I embraced him in a hug. I didn't give a shit about the bar. All I really cared about in this whole world was him. He was it. I had to figure out a way to get the money for his treatment.

"Now get back to work, your old man needs to sit down."

"Okay." I wiped away my tears. All I could think about was that he'd never get a chance to truly grow old. I watched him sit down. He coughed again. How had I not realized he was sick?

"It's going to be okay, hon. You're going to be okay."

Without you? No, I wasn't. I nodded my head, but it was more of a reflex than an actual agreement. I wasn't a child. I knew that life wasn't fair. But this? My dad didn't deserve this. I swallowed down the lump in my throat as I made my way back to the bar. If the bar did well the next month, that wasn't going to change anything. That wasn't going to be enough money.

"Here," I said and put Tyler's phone and charger down on the counter.

"Are you okay?" he asked.

"I'm fine." I put on my fake smile. The one I so often used around customers. The one I so often used around campus. The one I seemed to use way more than my real smile.

"Thanks for this," he said and grabbed his phone. For a brief second his fingers brushed against mine.

I felt a spark. This tiny spark that suddenly made me not feel like crawling under the bar and crying my eyes out. I frowned.

He immediately moved his hand away. "And for the directions," Tyler said. "I owe you one."

I stared at him. He owed me one? I'd never see him again. "Have a safe drive." I folded my arms across my chest.

"Thanks." He hopped off the bar stool and walked out the door where he had come.

I glanced back toward my dad's office. I wasn't ready to give up like he was. And staying here wasn't going to fix anything. I needed to see Elena. Despite what he said, she owed me. She owed me this one thing.

I couldn't let my dad die. I couldn't. I untied my apron, threw it on the bar counter, and ran after Tyler. He was just climbing into his car.

"Let me come with you!"

He turned his head toward me. "Um...what? I didn't think you were serious about wanting to hitchhike."

"You said you owed me one. Let me come with you."

"That's just an expression."

"Please." I could hear the exasperation in my voice. He was going to think I was completely crazy.

"Look, I don't even know where I'm going."

"It doesn't matter. As long as you end up in California."

"Why don't you just take a flight?"

"I don't have the money. But, I mean, I have some. I can help pay for gas. Or whatever you need."

"I don't know if..."

I grabbed the handle of the passenger side door and climbed into his car. He was taking me to California whether he wanted to or not.

CHAPTER 4

Tyler

Friday

I glanced back at the bar and then back at the girl that had just climbed into my car. Who the hell did she think she was? I leaned down and ducked my head into my car. "I really don't think..."

"I'm not crazy or anything, I swear. It's not like I'm going to kill you. I just need a ride. And you're going to California anyway. And there's an empty seat here."

This girl was out of her mind. So why did I not feel like protesting? Maybe it was her long legs. Or her dark brown eyes. Or the energy that seemed to radiate off of her. I had been driving aimlessly for a week. I was going crazy. Maybe it would be nice to have some company.

Her eyes met mine. It looked like she had been crying.

"Are you in some sort of trouble or something?"

"No. Please, Tyler. I just need a ride."

Fuck. How was I supposed to say no to that face?

"If you want, I won't say a word. You can just pretend I'm not here. Please." She was blinking hard and she subtly wiped a tear from her cheek.

"You're sure you're not running from the cops or anything?" I tried not to laugh at the irony of my question. Technically I was kind of guilty of that.

"No. I just need a ride. That's it."

"You're not going to rape me or anything?" Now I was just teasing her. I didn't want her to cry anymore.

She laughed. "No, I promise I won't rape you. We can even just agree to keep it platonic. Deal?" She put her hand out for me.

I really didn't have anything to lose anymore anyway. "Yeah, okay. Why not?" I climbed into the car.

"Thank you, Tyler. You have no idea how much this means to me." She put her hand on my shoulder.

It shouldn't have affected me. I had just seen her do it with a few patrons of her bar. It was a trick to get more tips. But for some reason, it did. Like this tiny little spark that I hadn't felt in so long. For three years I had been hung up on a girl that never needed me back, chasing a spark we had only gotten to act upon once. It felt nice to be needed for a change. I put my key into the ignition. "So where's this gas station?"

"Just down the road. Why weren't you just using your car charger?" she asked as she attached my phone to the chord.

"I haven't needed it." I turned out of the parking lot.

"You weren't using a GPS?"

"Like I said, I was just driving toward California. The signs on the highway were enough."

She nodded. "My house is right by the gas station. I just need to grab a few things."

"Okay," I said as I pulled into the gas station. "I can drive you there when I'm done filling up."

"Oh, that's not necessary. I promised not to inconvenience you at all. I'll just be right back." She quickly climbed out of the car and started sprinting down the street.

What she didn't seem to realize was that she really wasn't inconveniencing me. I literally had nothing to do for a week. It should have felt like I was driving toward my future, but it felt a lot more like I was running away from my past. My roots had been cut out from underneath of me in New York. I was barely holding on. And maybe if I hadn't wound up in bumblefuck, Indiana, I would have fallen. And this time, I wasn't sure I would have been able to get back up.

I watched her disappear into the darkness.

CHAPTER 5

Hailey
Friday

I grabbed a pen and looked down at the blank piece of paper. There were a million things I wanted to say to my dad. I wanted to tell him how much I loved him and how sorry I was for not being there for him. But I refused to start getting sentimental and giving up. My dad wasn't going to die anytime soon if I could help it. I quickly wrote him a note so that he'd at least know where I was.

Dad,
I'm going to find Elena. I'll be back soon.
Love,
Hails

I knew he'd freak out when he saw it. He had survived for four years on his own without me, though. He could survive another week or so. He was the strongest person I knew. I grabbed my duffel bag and hoisted it over my shoulder. I was going to fix this.

***

Tyler was leaning against his car, staring down at his phone. His blonde hair fell onto his forehead and I watched him absentmindedly push it away. He had scruff on his chin, like he hadn't shaved in a few days. The look worked for him. Any look would probably work for him, really. He was very handsome. And not in the way like the guys from town. He looked more distinguished even though he was just wearing khaki shorts and a t-shirt. I would have bet that he wore a suit to some fancy job in NYC. He'd probably look really good in a suit. When he noticed me approaching, he quickly slid his phone back into his pocket.

"That was fast," he said.

"I was kind of packed already."

"Do you always carry a go-bag or something? Now I'm starting to think you really are a criminal."

I laughed. "No, I just moved back here from college and hadn't unpacked yet." I opened up the back seat and tossed my bag into the car. There were two plastic bags already on the seat, but no luggage. "Is your stuff in the trunk? Would you prefer I put my bag back there?"

"No, that's actually all of it."

I closed the door and looked up at him. "You're telling me you're traveling across the country with two shopping bags and nothing else?"

"I left unexpectedly."

"Are you homeless or something?" I said with a laugh.

He climbed into the car, completely ignoring my question.

Weird. I opened up the passenger side door and got in too.

"How do you get back on the highway?" he asked as he started the car.

"Make a right and just keep going straight. There will be a sign in a few miles."

We were both silent as he pulled back onto the road. I studied him out of the corner of my eye. I should have been a little scared. I knew nothing about him besides for his first name and the fact that he was from NYC. But I wasn't scared. He seemed nice enough. A little closed off, but nice. Who cared if he was homeless? And as long as he wasn't running from the cops, what did it matter what he was running from?

He cleared his throat as he got back onto the highway. "So, you're in school?"

"Not anymore. I just graduated from Purdue."

"Good school."

Expensive school. "Yeah, I guess. What about you?"

"I graduated from the University of New Castle a couple years ago."

"Where is that?"

"Delaware."

"And I thought I was from a small town."

He smiled, but didn't say anything.

"So, you graduated from college a few years ago and now you roam around the country with two shopping bags?"

He laughed.

"But seriously, what did you do in New York?"

"I'm a business reporter."

"Oh, so you're going back?"

He was silent for a moment. "No. I don't know. Maybe eventually, but not anytime soon."

Yup, definitely running from something. "What does a business reporter do?"

"It's like business journalism. I write a lot. Sometimes I give speeches. I've even been on TV a few times."

"Really? I didn't realize you were famous." He definitely had a face for TV. I'd watch him any day.

He laughed. "No, it's not as glamorous as it sounds. What did you study in school?"

"Management."

"That's a good major for your business. How did someone in their early twenties acquire a bar anyway?"

"It's actually my dad's. He named it after me." I turned to look out the window. Guilt had suddenly decided to creep up on me. *What the hell was I doing?* My father was dying. And I had just abandoned him. *Again.*

"That makes a little more sense. Did you major in management to help out then?"

"I majored in management because one day I was supposed to take it over."

"Was? Are you not anymore?"

"Honestly, I don't really know. Nothing in life is certain." I kept my head turned toward the window. Tears were started to pool in my eyes. I blinked hard. I wasn't going to cry in front of a stranger. Part of me wanted to tell him to turn around. If I really only had four months to spend with my dad, I didn't want to spend a week traveling to California. I bit my lip. But if I didn't try to save him, I'd regret it for the rest of my life. I'd be home soon. Hopefully with enough money for some experimental treatments.

"You can say that again."

I turned back to him. "Why'd you need a change from New York?"

"Why'd you hop in my car and demand to be taken to California?"

CHAPTER 6

Tyler

Friday

She stared at me in silence for a second. "Touché. How long is it going to take to get there?"

"I have no idea."

"Can we start following a GPS?"

"I'd rather not."

"Why?"

"Because the voice is annoying and I don't exactly feel like being told what to do right now. Besides, I'm not in any rush."

"I know I'm good company and everything, but I am kind of in a rush. I thought that maybe when you get tired I could drive? That way we don't have to stop at all except for food and bathroom breaks."

"Yeah...not happening."

"Why?"

"Because I'm not letting a stranger drive my car."

"Then ask me a few questions so that I'm not a stranger anymore."

He laughed. "Look, you seem normal enough. But I was kind of doing my own thing and you hijacked that. I'm not changing what I'm doing just because you decided to come along."

"Fine." She kicked off her flip flops and pulled her legs up onto the seat, sitting cross-legged. "We'll do it your way then. Just don't stop at every tourist location on the way or anything."

"I wasn't planning on it." I could feel her eyes on me, but she wasn't saying anything.

"How long have you been driving?" she eventually said.

"A week."

"Okay. And where have you been so far?"

"Umm. Maryland, Pennsylvania, Ohio, and Indiana."

"It's taken you a week to drive through four states? It's going to take a month to get to California at this rate."

"I wasn't driving the whole time. I stopped at a motel in rural Pennsylvania for a few days."

"Why?"

"Because I didn't feel like doing anything." That was a lie. I had probably made one of the biggest decisions of my life earlier this week. When I was little, I always had a blast visiting my grandfather in Shippensburg. I hadn't been back since he had died when I was in college. So I drove aimlessly until I found the right church and then walked to his grave. It felt strange being back without him there. I just stared at his grave for hours. I had looked up to him. And it wasn't just because he was my grandfather. It was because he had made an actual difference, fighting for our country. He was proud of his time in the Marine Corps, and I was proud of him. The longer I had stood there, the more it seemed like I should be doing that too. Something I could be proud of. Something he would have been proud of me for. In my head it seemed like some monumental decision, but it wasn't. It was the only choice, really. What the hell else was I going to do? Go back to New York? *No fucking way.* I wanted to eventually look back and know that I had done something meaningful with my life. So I enlisted. I passed the physical and I requested to be as far away from the east coast as possible.

I was happy with my decision. The only thing that prevented me from being all in was the fact that my mom was so upset with me. I called her right after I signed the papers and she wouldn't stop crying. But I refused to feel guilty about enlisting. I needed to do this for me. It just sucked that an act that seemed selfless was maybe actually selfish on my part. If anything did happen to me, my mom would be alone. And I hated the thought of leaving her. I tried to focus on the road.

"Why didn't you feel like doing anything?"

This girl was starting to drive me crazy. "I think you mentioned that you wouldn't talk at all if I wanted that?"

She pressed her lips together. "Fine. I won't say another word." She hit the button for the radio and rap music blared loudly through the speakers. She didn't turn the volume down or ask to change the channel. Instead she just folded her arms across her chest and looked out the window.

The loud music made the car shake slightly. When I first left New York, I had been depressed. I had listened to old love ballads and sang at the top of my lungs like a little girl. But now? Now I was pissed. I was pissed for wasting so much time. Hailey was right. Nothing in life was certain. And I had thrown all my eggs into one basket like a fucking idiot. So I had turned to rap music because it seemed just as angry as me. But it didn't help soothe my soul. I was sick of being sad and I was sick of being angry. I just wasn't sure if I remembered how to feel normal anymore.

I sighed and turned down the volume. "I didn't mean that. I just don't want to talk about why I'm here. And I won't ask you. Deal?"

"Deal."

But we didn't start talking again. We drove in silence for hours until my eyelids started to grow heavy. When I saw an exit sign with a motel, I hit my turn signal.

"Are we stopping?" she asked.

I jumped a little when she spoke. I thought she was sound asleep. "Yeah."

She yawned and stretched her hands over her head. "You're sure you don't want me to just drive?"

"I'm sure."

We pulled into a gravelly parking lot and I put the car into park.

"Home sweet home," I said as I climbed out of the car. The night air was crisp, despite the fact that it was the middle of summer. I looked up at the stars. For some reason, they made me feel grounded. No matter how far I drove, the stars were always the same. They made me feel like one day I could be the same too. The way I was before Penny. Before she ever crawled under my skin. I opened up the back door and grabbed my two bags along with Hailey's duffel.

"I can get that," she said.

"It's fine." I pulled it over my shoulder. "Let's go check in."

She quickly followed me into the entrance. There was an old man sitting behind the desk sleeping. I cleared my throat and his eyes immediately opened. A smile spread across his face.

"Welcome to the Indy Inn. How many nights will you be staying with us?"

"One night. And two rooms please."

He looked back and forth between me and Hailey. "Alrighty." He grabbed two keys from behind his desk. "Room 202 and 203. Are adjoining rooms okay?" He set the keys down on the counter.

"That'll be fine."

"Are you paying separately?"

"Yes," Hailey quickly said from behind me.

"Okay, I just need a method of payment for your room first then," he said to me.

I pulled out my wallet and handed him my credit card.

He slid the card into the reader. "Alrighty, Mr. Stevens. I hope you enjoy your stay. Check out is at 9 a.m."

"Great. Thanks." I picked up one of the keys off the counter and stepped to the side to wait for Hailey.

"And I'll need a method of payment for you as well, ma'am," he said.

"Of course." She rummaged around in her purse and pulled out a wallet. "You can go ahead, Tyler."

"It's okay, I can wait."

"No, it's fine. I left my phone in the car anyway so I have to go back and grab it."

"I can go get it for you while you check in."

"No, really, it's okay. It's late. Go get some sleep."

I wasn't going to fight with her. She was right, I was exhausted. I pulled the duffel bag off my shoulder and set it on the ground. "See you in the morning, then, Hailey."

"Mhm."

I walked back out into the parking lot. I hit the button to unlock the car and made my way up the stairs to my room. Before I went into my room, I looked back over my shoulder. She hadn't come back out yet. I went into the room, switched on the lights, and closed the door behind me.

It looked like any other motel I had ever been in. A little dingy and a little musty smelling. It was becoming homey to me. I pulled my toothbrush and toothpaste out of one of the plastic bags and quickly got ready. Before I climbed into bed, I stared at the door between our adjoining rooms. I opened up the door on my side. Hers was still closed.

I wasn't exactly sure what I was doing. But it felt strange not saying goodnight to her. I tapped on the door. "Hailey?"

There was no answer. She must have already fallen asleep.

"Goodnight," I whispered to no one in particular.

***

I knocked on her door again. "Hailey?"

I had tried her when I had come back after my run to let her know I'd be ready to get going again soon. But she had still been sleeping. Check out was in ten minutes now. I knocked on the door a little louder. "Hailey?"

No answer.

I'd try again in a few minutes. I carried my bags down the stairs and walked over to the car. And that's when I saw her. She was curled up in the back seat of my car, her head resting on her duffel bag. It felt like I was seeing something I wasn't supposed to see, like I was intruding.

She had slept in the car? I scratched the back of my neck. *Shit.* I had let her spend the night in the car.

I thought back to when I had told her she should just fly to California. She said she didn't have the money. Why hadn't I offered to share a room with her? What was wrong with me?

CHAPTER 7

Hailey

Saturday

A tapping sound made me open up my eyes. I wiped the drool off the side of my face. For a second I forgot where I was. I looked out the window of the car to see a handsome face with the most breathtaking blue eyes staring back at me. And then I remembered where I was. And I remembered who that face belonged to. *Crap.* I quickly sat up and ran my fingers through my hair.

Tyler opened up the door. His lips parted like he was about to say something, but he immediately closed them again.

I plastered a fake smile to my face. "It took you long enough," I said with a laugh. "I was hoping to get on the road early."

"What?"

"I came down here hours ago hoping you'd be ready soon. I must have fallen asleep waiting."

He frowned. "Hailey, if you..."

"What?" I laughed again. "Now I know you like to sleep late. Give me one second, though, I need to use the bathroom before we head out."

He didn't say anything as I stepped out of the car. I felt my cheeks burning as I quickly walked toward the entrance of the motel. *He knows.* It was all over his face.

And despite the fact that I had done some quality acting, he didn't seem to believe me. I didn't need his pity. I could afford to stay in a motel if I really wanted. But it wasn't just about me. Money was literally the key to life and death right now. I wasn't going to waste it on some crappy room in a motel that was just as good as the back seat of a car.

The man behind the front desk lifted his head as I made my way inside. "Was he happy that you ended up wanting to share a room? I'm sure he was glad you changed your mind."

I was so relieved Tyler hadn't followed me in to hear the lie I had told the owner last night. "Yup," I said. "Do you have a restroom I could use?"

"Second door on the left."

"Thanks."

I hurried into the bathroom and closed the door behind me. My reflection gave it all away. My makeup was smudged and my hair was a mess. I splashed water on my face and pulled my toothbrush out of my purse. I needed to be more careful next time. Tyler was already driving me across the country. I didn't need him to give me any more handouts. Maybe I'd offer to pay for breakfast just to prove I had money. That was a solid idea. I flushed the toilet and washed my hands. I applied a little makeup and then made my way out of the restroom.

"Have a good day, ma'am," the man at the front desk said.

"You too." I made my way back outside.

Tyler was leaning against his car with his hands in his pockets. He looked up at me as I approached. "You could have told me." He pushed himself off the car and stared at me. There was something accusatory in his gaze. He had no right to accuse me of something he knew nothing about.

"Told you what?" I climbed into the car and closed the door before I could hear his response.

He sat down in the driver's seat, but didn't start the car.

"I really don't know what you're talking about," I said.

"Hailey..."

"Look, I'm starving. Let's go get something to eat. I'm paying."

"I would have paid for your room."

"Jesus, Tyler, get over yourself. I'm not asking for your help, okay? I'm not a charity case. Please can we just go eat?" I bit the inside of my cheek. I didn't mean to snap at him. But I didn't need anything from him. I didn't need anything from anybody. And it was starting to eat away at me that I was on my way to California to beg for money. I wasn't a beggar. This wasn't me.

He didn't look at me as he started the ignition.

I turned away from him and pulled my feet up onto the seat as I wrapped my arms around my shins. The last thing I needed was some beautiful stranger judging my choices. I already felt guilty enough for leaving my dad.

He let me silently fume as he drove back toward the highway. He pulled over to a diner near the end of the road.

"Is this okay?" he asked gently.

"Yeah, this is great."

He got out of the car before I could say anything else. I scurried out behind him. He held the door of the restaurant open for me. I tried to ignore the fact that no one had done that for me in years. It's not like this was a date. He was basically my chauffeur for the next few days, nothing more.

"Table for two?" the woman asked. She seemed bored out of her mind. The diner looked like it hadn't had its decor updated since the 60's. The floor was even black and white checkered. I was surprised the waitresses weren't rolling around on roller skates.

"Yes," I said cheerily.

She looked up at me like she was annoyed by my positive attitude. "Right this way." She grabbed two menus and showed us to a table. "Emery will be right with you."

I slid into the booth and Tyler slid into the seat across from me. He picked up his menu and scanned over the options.

Yesterday I felt like there was this flirtatious vibe between us. Today, not so much. I wanted to go back to that. I didn't want to drive across the country with someone who didn't even feel comfortable looking at me.

The waitress walked over. She was young, probably in high school, and her eyes were glued on Tyler like she had never seen anyone sexier in her life.

I rolled my eyes.

"Hi, I'm Emery and I'll be taking care of you today. Can I start you off with something to drink?"

"I'm ready to order if you are," Tyler said to me.

"Sure."

"Ladies first," he said.

"Could I just have an omelet with spinach and Swiss cheese. And a water."

Emery wrote it down in her notepad. "And for you?" She batted her eyelashes.

Tyler didn't seem to notice. Maybe he was gay.

"I'll just have a bagel with cream cheese. And some coffee, please."

"Sure thing. Just wave me down if you need anything else." She grabbed the menus and gave Tyler one last huge smile before she walked away with way too much shake in her hips.

"Who names their kid Emery?" I said. "It's basically like naming them Nail File."

Tyler laughed. "You sound jealous."

"Jealous of what? Some girl who works at a diner who wants in your pants? I don't think so."

He leaned back in the booth and stared at me.

"What are you looking at?" I awkwardly tucked a loose strand of hair behind my ear.

"Let's play 21 questions."

"What's that?"

"You've seriously never played 21 questions?"

I shook my head.

"We each get to ask each other 21 questions and we have to answer honestly no matter what. But we each get one pass."

"I don't know..."

"It's fun. I promise."

I stared at him skeptically. "Fine, you go first."

"Okay. What's your last name?"

"Shaw."

He nodded, as if satisfied by my answer. It seemed like a waste of a question if we only got 21, but it was better than him asking me why I had suddenly decided to become a hitchhiker.

"Thanks," he said to the waitress as she set down our drinks, without taking his eyes off me. "Your turn."

"Well I already know your last name, Tyler Stevens." If I asked him why he left New York, he'd certainly ask me the same thing. I needed to keep it safe too. "What's your favorite color?" Crap, that was just as lame as the question he asked me.

He smiled. "Green. What's your favorite food?"

"Pizza. Isn't it everyone's?"

"Is that your question to me?"

I shook my head. "No." I didn't want to repeat any of his questions.

Emery walked by again, clearly trying to get his attention, but he didn't even look toward her. I watched him pick up his coffee and take a sip, seemingly oblivious to her flirtations. Had he seemed oblivious to mine last night? I had kind of thought he seemed into me. But he had gotten distracted by the TV while we were talking. And it wasn't even because of a game. It was the news.

"Are you gay?"

He immediately spit the coffee back into the cup. "No. Why would you ask that?"

"You seem awfully defensive."

"I'm not gay." He lowered his voice slightly. "Seriously, why do you think I'm gay?"

I shrugged. "Don't get all upset about it. I was just wondering."

"Well, I'm not."

"Okay then. Question answered. Your turn."

He stared at me. He was even cuter when he was flustered. "Are you seeing anyone right now?"

"Are you trying to prove you're not gay or something?"

"It's not your turn for a question, Hailey."

I sighed. "No, I'm not in a relationship. What about you?"

He took a sip of his coffee and then set it back down. "No. How many boyfriends have you had?"

I shrugged my shoulders. "Technically just one. Back in high school."

"That's a long time ago."

"Well, I'm not as old as you."

"Who's defensive now?" he said.

"I'm not being defensive. When was your last relationship, hotshot?"

He ignored me as the waitress put our food down in front of us.

"Is there anything else I can get for you?" she asked and batted her eyelashes at him again.

This time, he smiled at her. I knew he was just trying to prove something, but I couldn't deny that I was a little jealous.

"Not right now," Tyler said. "Thanks, Emery."

"Sure thing." She smiled at him before walking away.

"Such a dumb name," I said under my breath.

CHAPTER 8

Tyler

Saturday

Things had just taken an unexpected turn. Yes, Hailey had flirted with me last night. But that was her job. It was a tip game. She was so hot and cold that half the time it seemed like she hated me and the other half of the time it seemed like she wanted to jump me. Right now she was acting like the latter, and I wasn't going to deny that I was flattered. Although my lack of game had made her think I was gay, which didn't really help my current mood.

The fact was that Hailey was gorgeous. Did I dream about what her tits looked like beneath her tight tank top? Yeah. But anyone who met her would probably dream of that. It didn't mean anything. The more jealous she seemed to get, the more appealing I found her pout, though. But I wasn't going to try to sleep with her. The last thing I needed was a random lay to get over my own problems. I had tried that before. It didn't work. And anything with Hailey would be meaningless, because in a few days I'd be dropping her off in California and I'd be heading to basic training. I'd never see her again.

But it didn't mean we couldn't both tiptoe around the idea of something more. It didn't mean I had to avoid staring at her long legs as she climbed in the car. Or her breasts when she leaned close to me. I was just going to enjoy this. Because even though I had set out to be alone on this trip and think, I was enjoying myself much more now that I had company.

"You didn't answer my question," she said and took a bite of her omelet. "When was your last relationship?"

"How long does it have to last in order to be considered a relationship?"

"The length doesn't matter. But it only counts if you had the girlfriend, boyfriend talk. The labels and everything."

"Yeah. Gotcha. My last relationship ended one week ago."

She nodded like she suddenly understood me completely. "Sorry," she said.

"Yeah. I feel bad about the way I left things, but I'm not really that upset about it. She was a great girl, but we weren't really that compatible."

"So why the sudden need to drive to California, then?"

"It's not your turn. How many guys have you slept with?"

She stopped chewing mid-bite. "That's a really personal question."

"It can be your pass."

She shook her head and set down her fork. "Um." She scrunched her lips to the side as she thought. "Does hand stuff count?"

I laughed. "No."

"Right. Well, three then."

I nodded. "Okay, your turn."

She leaned forward slightly. She did that a lot. It seemed like a habit from working at a bar. But I wasn't complaining. It allowed me to see down her shirt without being too obvious.

"How many girlfriends have you had total?" Hailey asked.

"With the same rules about labels and the talk?"

"Yeah."

"Four. Why did you break up with your only boyfriend?" I asked.

She didn't look excited by the question. "He cheated on me."

"Sounds like a quality guy."

"Absolutely. He cheated on me with my best friend at the time. And now they're married and expecting their first child."

Damn. "Ouch."

"It doesn't bother me anymore," she said with a shrug. "Honestly it's like you said...we weren't really compatible. How many girls have you slept with?"

I thought about it for a second. "Nine."

"You have triple my experience then." Her eyes stayed locked on mine. She was basically a professional flirter. But her gaze still affected me.

"I guess so," I said.

She looked back down at her half-eaten omelet.

"Why didn't you just ask to share a room with me last night?" I asked.

"Because I don't know you."

"That didn't stop you from climbing in my car."

"That's different. I was awake. Who knows what you'd do to me if I was sleeping with you. I mean, in the same room. Not having sex with you. Obviously." She laughed and her cheeks got slightly rosy.

I wanted to do all sorts of things to her. But not when she was sleeping. Maybe I was wrong. Maybe she was exactly what I needed to move on. It was pretty obvious that she wanted me. The way she was making fun of the waitress who was clearly flirting with me. But she also didn't seem to realize that I didn't give a shit about the waitress because I only wanted to look at the girl across from me. Didn't she know how pretty she was?

"My turn, right?" Hailey asked.

I nodded and pushed aside my empty coffee glass.

"How many men have you slept with?" she said with a smile.

I laughed. "I'm not gay."

"If you say so." She pulled out a 20 dollar bill and set it on the table. "Come on, we need to put a few states behind us today."

"I got this," I said and pulled out my wallet.

"Despite what you think, I don't actually need your help, Tyler."

And just like a switch, it seemed like she hated me again. "I wasn't trying to..."

"You can pay next time." She slid out of the booth. "We'll take turns."

I stood up and stretched. "Okay. If that's what you want."

"Like I said, I'm not going to inconvenience you at all. I'm just going to encourage you to get to California as fast as humanly possible so that I can get back home." She walked out of the restaurant without waiting for me.

I had been wallowing for a whole week. I was sick of my own thoughts. The toxicity that seemed to pour off of Hailey was somehow just what I needed. And I wanted to know more about her. I slid out of the booth and quickly followed her outside. That had always been part of my problem. I liked the chase. I liked when girls made me work for it. Apparently I was a glutton for punishment.

"So, how many girls have you slept with?" I asked as I unlocked the car.

She laughed. "Wouldn't you like to know?"

I'm sure I had a shocked look on my face.

She laughed again. "I'm just kidding. You wish." She got in the car.

When I sat down she was holding my phone in her hand. I tried to reach for it, but she held it out at arm's length.

"Can we please use the GPS now?" she said. "We need to figure out the best way to get there."

"Just use your phone then."

"It doesn't connect to your car charger and I didn't bring an adapter." She swiped her finger across my screen. "Do you know you have 23 missed calls?"

God this girl was infuriating. "Yes. Can I please have my phone back?"

"Who's trying to get a hold of you?"

"No one important." I snatched it out of her hand.

"Are you in some sort of trouble?"

"Are you?"

She bit her lower lip. "When life gives you lemons, make lemonade, right?"

I slid my phone into my pocket. "Yeah. I guess." That didn't really answer my question, but in a way it did. Something bad had happened to her and she was trying to fix it. I could relate to that. I started the engine and pulled out of the parking lot. If she googled that number, she'd find out who was calling me. She'd jump to conclusions about why I had left New York. It wasn't something I wanted to talk to her about. I wanted to go back to the light, flirtatious banter.

CHAPTER 9

Hailey

Saturday

If I had a photographic memory, I would have been able to memorize the number. As it was, I only got the first three digits. 212. I'd look it up later. It was most likely a NYC area code, which really meant nothing. But it was odd that all the calls were from the same number, which showed up as unknown on his phone. So it wasn't someone who he knew. Maybe it was his ex girlfriend, though. He could have deleted her number. 23 missed calls was a lot. Maybe she was a stalker.

I stole a glance at him. He was switching lanes on the interstate, going into the passing lane as he started to accelerate.

"It's my question, right?" I asked.

"Yeah." Tyler seemed distracted. Maybe he was just concentrating on the road.

"Why did you break up with your girlfriend?"

He thought about it for a minute. "Because I wasn't in love with her," he finally said.

"How are you so sure? Love is rather complicated. Maybe you just didn't give it enough time."

"No, I'm sure."

"How?" I asked.

He shook his head. "Because I was in love with someone else." He hit his turn signal again and sped by someone who was probably already going over the speed limit.

"Is that who you're driving toward? Does the girl you actually love live in California?" Suddenly it felt like I had just been transported into a romantic comedy. I was part of an epic love chase.

He laughed. It sounded strangled. "No."

"Why aren't you going to her? This could be your chance at true love."

"It's complicated."

"But..."

"As far as I'm concerned, true love doesn't exist. Look, I really don't want to talk about this. And haven't you asked like five questions in a row?"

"Okay, then ask me one."

He shook his head. "What's your favorite color?" He clearly wanted to go back to simple questions.

"Actually, it's quite the coincidence. Mine's green too. So, where does the girl you do love live?"

"Pass."

"But maybe that's where you should be driving, Tyler."

"Trust me, it's not."

"Why?"

"Please stop pushing this."

"You have to tell her how you feel. You don't want to go through your whole life regretting this missed opportunity."

"I did tell her, okay?! Happy?" He pulled back into the passing lane again.

His tone sent goose bumps up my arms. I bit my lip. So, maybe it wasn't a romantic comedy. Maybe it was more like a Shakespearean tragedy. "I'm sorry."

"Great. Thanks for your pity."

"I didn't say I pitied you."

"Can you please just stop talking for five seconds?" He hit the button to turn the radio on with his fist. Rap music blared through the car.

Whatever he was going through, I knew he'd feel better if he got it off his chest. But I wasn't going to force it. He'd tell me when he was ready.

Besides, the rap music fit my current mood. I had never been good at hiding my emotions. I wore them on my sleeve. Apparently Tyler did too. Maybe that's why we were butting heads so much. Or maybe it was the fact that we were stuck in a car together and barely knew each other. And clearly we were both going through some stuff.

Hell, maybe I'd feel better if I got my problems off my chest too. But not right now. Right now I just wanted to listen to angry rap music and curse the world.

***

"Seriously, I don't mind sleeping on the cot," I said for what felt like the hundredth time.

"I already left you to sleep in the car one night. Would you please just get in the bed?"

I put my hands on my hips. "Tyler, you're paying for the room. You wouldn't even let me split it with you. So I'm taking the cot." I sat down on it. The thin mattress felt like a brick.

The hotel only had king beds left, or else we could have just gotten two queens. As it was, there was one huge king sized bed in the room and a cot made out of stones. He scratched the back of his neck.

Why do I find that so sexy? "Or we could just share the bed," I said. "It's huge. We could just stay on opposite sides."

I thought he would continue to protest, but instead he shrugged his shoulders.

"Fine. We're both exhausted. Let's just call it a night." He grabbed his shirt by the nape of its collar and pulled it off over his head.

I tried not to stare, but it was hard to move my eyes away from him. I knew that he was in shape from the muscles in his arms. But I hadn't been expecting the perfectly sculpted six pack that was currently staring back at me. I made myself turn away as he started to unbutton his shorts. I fidgeted with the hem of my baggy t-shirt. Suddenly I wished that I owned sexy lingerie. I had noticed how his eyes had lingered on my legs, but he had quickly looked away when I caught him staring. I had been completely off base before. There was no way that Tyler Stevens the business reporter from New York City was gay. He was just heartbroken. He was in pain. And I felt like I could understand that. I knew what it felt like to live in pain. I knew what it felt like to want something so badly that I couldn't have. At the moment, I kind of wanted him. I rolled my eyes at myself.

The bed squeaked and I turned around. He had pulled the covers up to his neck and the light next to his side had already been switched off. I awkwardly climbed into my side, trying hard not to reveal my underwear. Not that he was looking. I switched the light off on my side and the room was bathed in darkness. My body hugged the edge of the bed like it was my anchor.

"Do you prefer Hailey or Hails?" Tyler said into the darkness.

"You can call me Hails," I whispered back.

"Okay. Goodnight, Hails."

"Goodnight, Tyler." For some reason I wanted to cry. It had been over four years since a boy I was attracted to had called me by my nickname. It made my whole body feel weirdly warm. I pushed the blankets off of me. Maybe I was still pissed about my ex cheating on me. If I didn't start letting go of some of this anger, I was worried I'd start to feel like I was drowning in it.

***

I woke up to the smell of freshly cut grass and mint. I took a deep breath. It smelled heavenly. For the second morning in a row, I had completely forgotten where I was. But unlike last night, where I had fallen asleep shivering, this morning I had woken up because I was overheated. I slowly opened my eyes to Tyler's face just inches from my own.

I immediately held my breath, worried I had been caught in a compromising situation. But we were almost exactly in the center of the bed. It's like we had both gravitated toward each other in the middle of the night. Neither one of us could be blamed more than the other.

His arm was slung protectively around me and I could feel his fingers pressed against my skin right above my underwear. Which meant his hand had pushed up the baggy t-shirt I was sleeping in. But it wasn't any worse than what I was doing to him. My leg was resting across his thighs and my hand was pressed against his abs. *God, his abs.* I exhaled slowly, trying hard not to disturb him. I felt completely frozen. Part of me wanted to roll away from him before he realized that I was snuggled up against him, but the other part of me wanted to kiss his beautiful face. I wanted to be able to forget about my worries and fears. I wanted to be able to run away from my problems like he was running away from his. But his arms weren't the ones I needed to run into. He was in love with someone else.

I ducked out from under his arm as slowly as possible and climbed out of bed. For some reason, I couldn't take my eyes off him though. During the day I was always captivated by his bright blue eyes. Right now, it was something completely different. There was something so peaceful about the way he slept. And his strong shoulders and chest were all I could seem to focus on. I should have relished how his skin had felt against mine instead of immediately climbing out of bed.

He was as angry at life as I was. Life had chewed us both up and spit us back out. And for some reason we had run into each other. Maybe I was over thinking things. Maybe he was exactly what I needed. Besides, I wasn't looking for something that lasted forever. Nothing lasted forever anyway.

He groaned in his sleep and placed his hand where I had been lying. It was like he could feel my absence. I knew he wanted me too. I knew that his heart was broken. Maybe I could help mend it. Maybe I could show him that there was more to life than whatever girl he had just left behind.

He groaned again.

No one should look sexy while they slept, but somehow Tyler did. I needed to stop staring at him before he caught me. I tucked a loose strand of hair behind my ear as I rummaged through my purse for my cell. I had two missed calls from my dad and a voicemail. I glanced once more at Tyler and made my way into the hall. I closed the door as quietly as possible behind me and dialed my voicemail.

"Hails." My dad's breathing sounded slightly labored. "I know you're trying to help. But this isn't helping anyone. Especially not me. Come back. Honey, please come home." He coughed and then the message beeped, signaling that it was over.

I held the phone to my chest and blinked away the tears that were threatening to fall. I'd call him back later. He'd be sleeping right now. He needed his rest. And despite what he thought, what I was doing was going to help. It had to.

CHAPTER 10

Tyler
Sunday

The sound of a shower running made me slowly open my eyes. *Fuck.* I was hard. I had dreamt of Hailey again. More vivid than the night before. Maybe it was because I had seen her in barely anything last night before bed. I was tempted to whack one off real quick, but I didn't want her to walk out of the bathroom and see me doing that. *Shit.* I ran my hands down my face as I tried to think of something else. Anything else. But when I closed my eyes I just saw her long legs stretching out beneath her baggy t-shirt. All I could think about was them straddling me.

When I opened my eyes she was standing in front of me in nothing but a towel. I blinked, thinking it was just my imagination. But no, she was really there. Beads of water rolled down her chest and disappeared beneath the knot in her towel. This was not helping my boner situation.

A smile spread across her face. "Take a picture, it'll last longer."

I laughed. "How did you sleep?"

Her cheeks looked flushed. Probably from the shower. "Really well, actually. How about you?" She leaned over to grab something from her duffel and nearly exposed her ass to me.

I forced myself to look away. "Good."

"Thanks again for letting me stay in the room with you. And for letting me share the bed."

"Yeah, of course."

She nodded. "Okay. I'm going to go change." She disappeared back into the bathroom.

I quickly got out of bed and pulled on a pair of shorts to hide the evidence of how badly I wanted her. I was just pulling on a shirt when she walked back into the room.

"So, I mapped out the best route to Pasadena," she said.

"Pasadena?"

"Yeah. Well, I know I said California, which was rather vague since it's such a huge state. And really you can just drop me off anywhere. Pasadena is where I eventually need to end up though. But if you..."

"I can take you to Pasadena." It was only a few hours away from the Marine Corps Recruit Depot in San Diego. Thinking about it gave me a pit in my stomach. I knew I was doing the right thing. But it didn't mean I wasn't terrified.

She looked relieved. "Great. I got this map from downstairs." She opened it up and spread it across the bed. "I really wouldn't mind seeing the Grand Canyon. I know I was just joking around about hitchhiking when we first met. But here I am. I'm officially a hitchhiker. I might as well see the Grand Canyon while I'm at it. It's kind of on the way." She pointed at a dot on the map.

"Yeah, sure."

"And if we start going south now, kind of cut through Missouri and then head west, I think that's probably the fastest route. We basically just follow Route 66, so we don't even need a GPS, because I know you hate those."

I picked up the map. "Ever been to Vegas?"

She laughed. "No. I've actually never even left Indiana before."

"Seriously?"

She shrugged.

"You do realize that we're in Illinois right now? You've officially left your home state."

"I know." She smiled. "It's pretty exhilarating. Is Vegas on the way too?"

"Kind of. Just like the Grand Canyon is kind of on the way."

"I guess we'll see if we're sick of each other by then."

I knew she was in a rush to get to Pasadena for some reason. I looked back down at the map. I had more than half a country to figure out why. "Mhm."

"Are you hungry?" she asked. "It's your turn to buy breakfast."

"Yeah, just let me go brush my teeth." I quickly freshened up. When I walked back out, the TV was on. Hails was watching a news reporter outside of a hospital. An image flashed across the screen with the caption "Mr. and Mrs. Hunter moments before the shooting." She was in a wedding dress and he was in a tux. They looked so happy. I swallowed down the lump in my throat.

Hails turned around to look at me. "They just had an exclusive with one of the doctors from the hospital where James Hunter is. They said that each day that goes by he gets less and less likely to wake up. It's not looking good. I can't even imagine what his family is going through. And his new wife? It's heartbreaking."

"It really is." *Heartbreaking.* I couldn't think of any other way to describe it. I looked away from the image and grabbed my bags and her duffel. "You ready to go?"

"Yeah." She turned off the TV. "I can carry that, you know."

"I got it."

"Do you want me to take a turn driving today?"

"Nope."

"Oh, come on," she protested as she followed me out of the room.

***

"I thought Kansas would be more...magical," Hailey said.

I laughed. "Why did you think that?"

"Well, because of Wizard of Oz and everything. But really it's almost exactly the same as Indiana."

"The Wizard of Oz isn't magical until Dorothy leaves Kansas."

"Still." She shrugged her shoulders.

The more time I spent with her, the more I liked her. She had these cute little freckles underneath her eyes and across the bridge of her nose. And her eyes lit up whenever she spotted something half interesting on our drive. Earlier today she had freaked out because she swore she saw a buffalo. I'm pretty sure she hadn't. She had even made me pull over and stop so that she could stare at nothing.

Half the time it seemed like she smiled as a defense mechanism. But when she laughed, her smile really showed. I liked seeing her real smile. We had stopped asking each other tough questions, and somehow that made it easier. It didn't mean I didn't want to know more though. I had been thinking about it a lot. Why would she just suddenly come home from college and leave immediately? What drove her away?

"I need to make a quick phone call," she said. "If the waiter comes, can you just order me a cheeseburger with fries?"

"Gladly." Yup, the more time I spent with her, the more I liked her. Any girl who ordered real food instead of a salad won my heart a little. I pulled my phone out of my pocket and clicked on one of my many new voicemails.

"Tyler Stevens, this is Officer Daugherty with the NYPD. We talked on the phone the other day..." I pulled the phone away from my ear and pressed the delete button.

Penny told me she'd take care of it. And despite everything, I trusted her with my life. She'd fix this. She'd fix this and probably forget I ever existed. I was easier to cast aside than she was to me.

I clicked on the next voicemail. "Tyler Stevens, this is Officer Daugherty with the NYPD. We need you to come in for questioning..." I deleted the message before I heard the whole thing again and clicked on the final voicemail. "Mr. Stevens, this is Officer Daugherty with the NYPD. We've already arrested your accomplice and we're going to be issuing a warrant for your arrest if you do not come in for your..." I pulled the phone away from my ear and pressed the delete button.

Accomplice? Penny told me to ignore their calls. She told me she'd fix it. So why the fuck were they still hounding me? I blocked the number from my phone. It didn't matter if they arrested me. I didn't have enough energy left to care.

CHAPTER 11

Hailey
Sunday

I knew my dad would be sitting in his office. I could picture him there. It was easy to see an image I had seen so many times in my life. But now he looked frail. He looked sick. I closed my eyes as the phone started to ring.

"Hello?" said a raspy voice.

"Hi, Dad." I leaned my back against the brick wall outside the restaurant.

"Hails, where are you? I've been worried sick. You can't just..."

"I'm in Kansas."

There was a pause. "What are you doing in Kansas?"

"I got a ride to California."

"With who?"

I bit my lip. I didn't want him to worry. "A friend."

There was another long pause. "You're still going to see her?"

I already felt guilty for leaving him. And now I felt like I was betraying his wishes too. "It's our only option."

"I want you to come home." His cough made me wince.

"I'll be home soon. I'm going to fix this."

"There's nothing for you to fix. I'm the adult. I'm the one..."

"I'm an adult now too, Dad. Please. I have to do this."

"She'll turn you away."

"Then at least I'll know I tried everything I could."

"I don't like the idea of you seeing her. Last time you two..."

"I'll be fine, Dad. I'm not a kid anymore."

He sighed. "I know, honey."

I swallowed hard and looked up at the stars. Whenever I saw the stars I felt close to him. For some reason I felt the distance tonight, though. And for some reason I knew he wasn't outside looking up at the same stars as me anymore. He was inside. He was sick. I felt like he was slipping away. "How are you feeling?"

"The same."

I put my face in my hand. It was hard talking to him like this, knowing that he had already given up. Knowing that he was angry at me. "I have to go. I love you, Dad."

"I love you too, Hails."

I pressed the end call button and kept my face in my hand. Again I wondered what the fuck I was doing. My dad didn't want me to go see Elena. So why was I disregarding his wishes when he had four months to live? I wiped away my angry tears and pushed off the wall.

Fuck this. Fuck everything. Just for one night I wanted not to think. I wanted not to feel like shit for being so blind. I took a deep breath and made my way back into the restaurant. I walked over to the bar and ordered two shots of tequila. Before the bartender even had a chance to walk away, I downed both of them.

"Two more, please."

He laughed. "Preparing for karaoke night?"

"It's karaoke night?"

"Yup, it starts in ten minutes."

"Then yes, I'm absolutely preparing for karaoke night." I picked up the two shot glasses he had just poured and walked back over to our table. I slid one of the shots over to Tyler.

"I thought you wanted us to keep driving after dinner?"

"That was before I found out that it was karaoke night." I lifted up my glass.

Tyler smiled. "How about you sing and I'll watch?" He slid the shot back over to me.

"Duets always get a better response. Please." I hated the desperation in my voice. And for some reason I felt like I was going to start crying again. "For one night I just want to forget about all my problems. I need this."

His tongue darted across his lower lip as he considered my idea.

I was already feeling the buzz of the tequila. And all I could think about was how good it would feel for his tongue to dart across my lips. I pressed my thighs together. Maybe this was a bad idea. I was so attracted to him. If I drank much more I'd probably throw myself at him.

"Let's both forget," I said before I could overthink it.

"I'll do one song. But that's it." He lifted up his glass, clinked it against mine, and downed his shot.

I smiled as I followed suit. I waved to the bartender and pointed to our shot glasses. "This is going to be so much fun, I promise." I reached across the table and placed my hand on his. The same spark I felt back in Indiana shot up my arm and I immediately removed my hand. *God, I was in so much trouble.*

***

"Ah, it's our turn!" I grabbed his hand and pulled him up out of his seat.

"You should just go."

"I already signed us both up. We're singing Near Me by the Cigarsmoakers."

He looked so reluctant, despite the fact that I had been forcing shots on him for half an hour.

"There's a boy and a girl part. I can't do it by myself." I gave him an exaggerated frown.

"Fine."

I grabbed his hand and we walked up to the stage together. I was surprised when he kept his fingers intertwined with mine until we got up on the stage. As soon as he dropped my hand to grab his mic, my hand felt cold. I liked the feeling of his skin against mine. I stared at him as he cleared his throat. The music started blaring through the restaurant.

"Babe, I thought I was good before I met you," he sang and pointed at me.

I laughed.

"I drink a lot which is an issue, but I'm alright." He winked at me.

Why the hell had he not wanted to do this? He was such a good singer. So much better than me.

His eyes stayed locked on mine. It was like he was singing directly to me.

He pulled the mic off the stand and walked over to me. "Now you're looking sexy in a dingy bar." He lightly touched a strand of my hair.

I felt frozen in place. Was this really happening? It felt like he was serenading me.

"Lick the tattoo on your shoulder," he sang and lightly touched my shoulder.

Chills ran down my spine.

He pulled the mic away from his face and I realized that it was almost my turn to sing.

I wanted to sing to him too. I wanted him to know how attracted I was to him. I wanted him to want me back. "You look better than the day I met you," I sang and touched his chest with my index finger.

The fire in his eyes made my throat feel dry.

"Stay, and blast that Wink-183 song, that we played to death in Tucson, alright." Looking at him made me nervous. But I needed to go for it. This seemed like the best possible moment. " So, baby, get beside me in the backseat of your Audi." I grabbed the front of his t-shirt and pulled him closer to me, before turning around and pressing my ass against him.

"Fuck."

Oh my God, had he really just said that out loud? Or had I imagined it? Why had I drank so much? I tried to focus on the lyrics but all I wanted to do was dance with him. I wanted to feel his hands on my hips. I wanted him to literally get beside me, just like the song said. Or maybe all up on me.

"Baby get beside me," he sang and grabbed my hips, pulling me more firmly against him.

And I could feel him. He was hard. Really hard. God, he wanted me too. I grinded against him.

" Pull those sheets right off the bed," I sang as I dipped low against him.

His fingers definitely tightened on my waist.

"We're never getting older!" I stood up straight and reached behind me, running my fingers down the back of his neck.

"We're never getting older," he whispered in my ear.

I laughed and turned around, spreading my arms in the air. "We're never getting older!" I sang at the top of my lungs and spun around in a circle. "No, we're never getting older!"

The music stopped and we were both staring at each other on the stage.

People in the audience clapped and a few patrons whistled.

I laughed and grabbed Tyler's hand, pulling him off the stage. I dragged him to the side of the bar, away from the speakers, hooking my hands behind his neck.

"Let's get out of here." Yes, I had consumed a lot of alcohol. But that wasn't what was making me feel the way I was right now. I was intoxicated by him.

"I can't drive right now." He didn't try to pull away from me. He let me stay pressed against him.

"I know. Let's go to the hotel next door." I ran my thumb along the scruff on his jaw. "Maybe we could share a bed again?" I stared up at him. I had never been so forward in my life. Hopefully it was working.

He stared down at me and for a long time he didn't say anything. I watched his Adam's apple rise and fall.

"I don't think that's a good idea," he said, almost too low for me to hear over the music.

"Why? You could just pretend that I'm her." It spilled out of my mouth before I even realized what I was saying.

"Who?"

"The girl you're in love with."

His eyes suddenly looked sad. "I don't want to pretend with you."

"Then don't pretend." I stood on my tiptoes and placed a kiss against his lips.

He didn't pull back.

I let my tongue dart against his lips. But he didn't part his for me. He didn't let me in. Instead he took a step away from me, and my hands fell from his neck.

"You're drunk, Hails."

"But I wanted you before I even had one shot."

He shook his head.

God, I was so embarrassed. I put a smile on my face. I wanted to tell him to go fuck himself. And that it was his loss. But his rejection stung. I blinked away my tears. I didn't want to think about anything. My dad, the bar, *him*. Seriously, fuck him. I didn't need this. I already had enough shit to deal with without whatever the hell this was. "Awesome. So, I'm going to go drink more and sing another song without you." I turned away and then quickly turned back to him. "And you know what? Don't bother waiting for me, I'll find a ride with someone else. Just leave my bag at our table. I really hope you find whatever it is you're looking for. And just for the record? You're being a coward for not going after her. Grow a pair." I turned on my heel and walked away from him.

CHAPTER 12

Tyler

Sunday

I watched her walk away from me and tried to swallow down the anger brewing inside of me. She was drunk. She was slurring her words. She didn't walk in a straight line up to the stage, despite there being a clear path. What did she want me to do? I wasn't going to take advantage of her. Of course I wanted her. But not like this. Not when she thought I was only doing it to forget about someone else. Not when she was drunk out of her mind.

She didn't really mean anything she said, but it still made my blood boil. She didn't know shit about me. I pushed my hair out of my face. Didn't she realize that I was being the bigger person? All I wanted to do was push her up against the wall and fuck her. I didn't care about the people around us. But I did care about her. Which is exactly why I didn't do that. I was trying to be respectful. And her reaction? To throw accusations at me.

So, fuck her. I didn't need this. Forgetting for one night had seemed like a good idea. But there was no forgetting. I turned away from the stage.

I had given up because I did love Penny. Not because I was a coward. Not because I needed to grow a pair. But because I wanted Penny to be happy. And she was happier without me. No one needed me. Hailey certainly didn't need me.

The beat to Poisonous by Britt Spearson started pumping through the restaurant. I let my eyes gravitate to the stage. Hailey was swaying her hips to the music staring directly at me.

"Baby, you can see, I want you," she sang with a flip of her hair. "A stud like you needs a warning. It's hazardous, I'm falling."

She was definitely wasted. But I couldn't seem to look away. Not when she was so blatantly singing at me. Albeit angrily, still directed at me. She dipped her hips low and shook her ass at the crowd. What was she trying to do to me?

"With one taste of your skin, I'm on a slide. You're poisonous, I'm slipping under." She Shimmied. "With one taste of toxic paradise." Her hips swayed again.

She was the sexiest girl I had ever laid eyes on. And for a second I did forget about Penny. I let myself get completely lost in the beautiful brunette running her fingers through her hair in the most sexual way possible.

"You're my addiction, don't you know that you're poisonous?" She ran her fingers down her neck and between her breasts. "Get me drunk right now. With your loving now."

She was wrong. She was the poisonous one. And I was in a little over my head.

She dropped the mic on the ground and threw her hands up in the air to the sound of the roaring applause. She slowly made her way back over to me. The flirtatious nature of the song was over. She was now giving me death stares.

"I told you to go get my bag. We're done." She gestured between the two of us as she sat down in the booth.

"How about you sleep on it?"

"Tyler Stevens, you're poisonous and I want nothing to do with you."

"That's not what the lyrics mean."

"Yes it is."

"No. They're about how you love the poison. About how badly you want it."

"You're so full of yourself." She closed her eyes and leaned her head on the back of the booth. "I don't want you. I was trying to make you feel better."

I ignored her comment. She had definitely wanted me a few minutes ago. Maybe it was the tequila talking, or maybe it was something more. Either way, tonight was definitely not the night to talk about it.

"Let's go sleep off the alcohol at the hotel," I said.

She groaned.

"Hails?"

Her head dropped slightly so that her chin was almost resting on her chest. I swore I heard a light snore.

I shook my head as I stood up. Despite what she thought, she did need me. I put my hand on her shoulder. "Hails?"

She snored again.

I leaned down and picked her up in my arms. She felt so light. I ignored the people staring at me as I carried her out of the restaurant. They had all seen me singing with her earlier. Besides, I had no intention of taking advantage of her. If I had, I would have given in when her lips were on mine. She snuggled her face against my chest.

***

I kicked the door of the hotel room open with my foot and turned the light switch on with my shoulder. I had told myself it made sense for us to share a room again. Just for the sake of safety. If she started throwing up, it would be better if I was with her. But I had at least gotten two beds this time.

She sighed against my chest. "You smell like freshly cut grass," she whispered. "And toothpaste."

I smiled as I carried her over to the first bed. I pulled the covers back and laid her down.

She moaned and rolled over. She was wearing a tank top and cutoff jean shorts. It probably wasn't the most comfortable outfit to sleep in, but I wasn't about to undress her. I grabbed her flip flops, tossed them on the floor, and pulled the covers up around her.

"Can you hold me?" she whispered. "Just for a second?"

Something constricted in my chest. I tucked a loose strand of hair behind her ear. "Get some sleep, Hails."

She closed her eyes tight and turned away from me.

I so badly wanted to give her what she wanted. When we had danced earlier, it felt like her body fit perfectly against mine. But if I climbed into that bed with her, I was afraid it would turn into something more. After one last glance at her, I went to the bathroom.

***

I put my hands on my knees as I tried to catch my breath. It had been a long time since I had run this early, but I couldn't sleep. All I could do was think about Hailey lying in the bed beside mine. I had gotten out of bed at five in the morning and had been running ever since. After several miles I realized I was trying to run off the sexual tension I felt. This whole situation was so frustrating.

I stared out at the field of grass. And that's when I saw it. A buffalo in the distance. Just like Hailey had said she saw yesterday. I held my breath as I watched it disappear into the sunrise. I hadn't believed her at all. Maybe she really had seen one too. I blinked and saw dots from staring into the sun. Or maybe I had imagined it too.

I turned back to the hotel and walked as slowly as possible, half trying to catch my breath, half delaying going back to the room. Hailey looked so peaceful while she slept. There was no pain or worry in her eyes. She just looked happy. And it made me realize just how much she was tormented while she was awake. She was dealing with something, and I wanted to know what it was. I wanted to help her. Maybe I could help fix whatever it was. But first, I probably had to open up to her. I just didn't know if I could.

I let myself into the room as quietly as possible so that I wouldn't wake her. But I was surprised to see that she was already up. She was sitting on the bed with her chin resting on her knee. Her hair was tied in a knot on the top of her head, giving me a view of her long neck. I felt like I was intruding on her privacy. She hadn't seemed to have heard me come in.

"I saw a buffalo," I said.

She turned toward me. "Did it stomp on my head?" She put her hand on her forehead.

I picked up the Advil I had placed on the nightstand for her and handed her it and the glass of water. "Here. And no, I saw it on my run while you were sleeping off your hangover."

"Ugh. That sounds rather majestic. Are you sure you didn't imagine it?" She put her chin in her hand and smiled at me.

That's what I had said to her yesterday. "No, it was there."

"Mhm." She downed the pill and took a huge gulp of the water. "What the hell happened last night?" She leaned back on the bed.

"You don't remember?"

She shook her head.

"You drank tequila like it was water and tried to seduce me."

She laughed. "I highly doubt that. Well, not the tequila part. That actually sounds like me." She sat back up and slid off the bed. "You should probably go take a shower so you don't stink up the whole car."

"I thought you liked the way I smelled?"

She drew her eyebrows together. "What?"

"Nothing." It really seemed like she didn't remember last night. Maybe that was for the best. Unfortunately, I remembered every second. Especially the way her lips felt against mine. And now it seemed like I had missed my chance. I should have fucking kissed her back. "I'm gonna go take a shower real quick and we can get going."

CHAPTER 13

Hailey
Monday

Shit, shit, shit. I quickly got dressed while Tyler was in the shower. I didn't remember all of last night. But I did remember wanting him. Really, really wanting him. I remembered singing with him on stage. I remembered his fingers digging into my hips and the feeling of his erection pressed against me. I clearly remembered him wanting me back. But then I had kissed him. And he didn't kiss me back. So I had told him off. I had told him to drive away without me.

Everything else was a blur. How I had ended up in this hotel room was a mystery to me. I tried to put the pieces together, but I couldn't remember. All I knew was that we definitely hadn't slept together. If we had, I wouldn't still be so horny that I could barely think straight.

I didn't know what happened when I walked away from him in the restaurant. But it didn't matter. The only important thing about last night was that I had put myself out there and gotten rejected. So that was that. We were just friends. Which was perfectly fine with me. In a few days we'd be going our separate ways. It's not like it could have been anything more anyway.

I'd just keep pretending like I didn't remember the whole night. Then there wouldn't be anything awkward between us. It was better that way. I shoved my dirty clothes into my duffel and zipped it closed. There were four states between us and Pasadena. All I needed to do was keep my legs closed and not get shitfaced around him again. I had just wanted to forget for one night. And it had just created more things I needed to forget about.

And even though the rejection stung, I was glad nothing had happened between us. I didn't want to be the girl he fucked to forget about what he really wanted. For once in my life, I wanted to be the one that someone actually wanted. Me. Not my slut of an ex best friend. I just wanted to be wanted.

I slung my bag over my shoulder when Tyler emerged from the bathroom. He was fully clothed, thank God. I didn't want to be distracted by his abs ever again. I quickly looked away from him. "Do you want me to drive some today?"

"Nope."

It was worth asking. I felt useless. He hadn't even let me help pay for gas yesterday. I was the worst hitchhiker in the history of hitchhiking. And the worst daughter.

He followed me silently out to the car. I got in the passenger's seat, folded my arms across my chest, and stared out the window.

Neither one of us spoke or bothered to turn on the radio. There wasn't really anything to say. I was sick of small talk, and it wasn't like I was going to flirt with him anymore. Silence seemed the most fitting.

Fields of grass blew by us in a blur. Eventually I saw the sign for Oklahoma. Neither one of us said anything about leaving Kansas behind in the dust.

"She got married last weekend," Tyler said, breaking the spell of silence.

I turned toward him. "Who?"

"The girl I..." he let his voice trail off. "I told her how I felt and she didn't feel the same way. She married him anyway."

Now I understood. I swallowed hard. "I'm sorry."

He shrugged. "It doesn't matter."

But I could tell it did. The love of his life had gotten married and he had fled the state.

"What does she look like?"

He kept his eyes on the road. "She's beautiful."

"You can give me more than that."

He shook his head and was quiet for a moment. "Red hair, blue eyes, petite, a smile that can light up a room. And she gets the cutest little line in her forehead whenever she's upset." His eyebrows lowered as he stared straight ahead.

So that was his type. No wonder he didn't want me. A tall, tan brunette with brown eyes was basically the opposite of what he was attracted to. "She sounds stunning."

"Yeah." He shrugged. "But it wasn't really about that. At first maybe. But she was just really sweet and fun to be with. Our personalities just meshed really well. She was one of my best friends."

"That must have been hard...losing a friend too."

He didn't say anything.

"How long were you in love with her?"

"Almost three years."

"Were you ever more than friends?"

He laughed. "For about a week a little after we first met. Pathetic, right?"

"No. I don't think so." I pulled my feet up onto the seat and sat cross-legged. "At least you tried. At least you got it off your chest before it was too late."

He glanced at me for a second. "Yeah. I guess. But it was a shot in the dark. She's never liked me as much as I liked her. She never looked at me the way she looked at him."

"But now you don't have to regret never trying."

"Yeah, I just have to regret losing one of my best friends."

"Maybe it's for the best. You needed to get away from her in order to move on. So, screw her."

He lowered his eyebrows again. "I still care about her. I want her to be happy."

"You deserve to be happy too."

"I'm working on that."

I stared at him as he drove on in silence. Any girl that could turn him down must have been blind. He was seriously hot. Like straight out of the pictures of a magazine. And he had lips that were just begging to be kissed. By someone else. Not me. Some redhead he hadn't met yet probably. I turned away from him.

He had just opened up to me. It seemed wrong to leave him the only vulnerable one. His heart was broken. I could see the devastation on his face. He loved and lost. That's why it was never really worth taking the risk to love in the first place. I knew that. I had been burned too.

I took a deep breath and turned back to him. "I'm not just low on cash. I'm in debt. Awful debt, actually. The bar is failing. The bank is taking it back at the end of next month."

"What about your dad? Can't he help?"

I looked away from him again. "He's done everything he could think of." Maybe I could open up to him about the bar and my financial problems. But I couldn't talk about my dad. I couldn't say that he was dying out loud. It made it too real. It made it an actual possibility. I couldn't deal with that.

"So, why the sudden urge to go to Pasadena then? Didn't want to stick around to say goodbye to your bar?"

"No. I'm not giving up that easily. There's someone there that can hopefully give me a loan." I didn't feel like answering any more questions. "What about you? Why are you heading to California? Did you just want to be on the opposite side of the country as her?"

"Something like that. Really I just wanted to go somewhere...sunnier."

"I get that."

We sped down the highway in silence again. Maybe we could both leave the darkness behind.

CHAPTER 14

Tyler
Monday

"Really? They didn't have a single room with two queen beds? There are barely any cars here." I looked around the almost empty parking lot.

She shrugged her shoulders. "That's what the guy at the front desk said. Maybe all the rooms with queens are being renovated or something." She quickly looked away from me.

I smiled as I pulled her duffel bag over my shoulder. "Maybe." But it kind of just seemed like she wanted to sleep in the same bed as me again.

Today had been the easiest day between us. I had finally gotten her to open up. She was trying to save her father's business, which was admirable. I didn't really understand why she couldn't try to get a loan from a bank in Indiana, but I wasn't going to push the subject. I was grateful that she had told me what little she did.

And honestly, it felt good to get some stuff off my chest too. Hailey was understanding. She had made me feel a little better about everything. Unlike last night when she had told me to grow a pair.

I didn't avoid staring at her ass as I followed her up the stairs to our room. She had kissed me the other night.

She had definitely just requested a room with one bed. If she tried to kiss me again, this time I would kiss her back.

But nothing happened when we got into the room. We both got ready for bed and a silence fell over us again. Maybe I was wrong about the sleeping situation. Maybe they really were renovating all the rooms with queen beds. I climbed into the other side of the bed and turned off the light.

I hated going to sleep without saying anything. Really what I wanted to do was wrap my arms around her. I wanted her to know that she wasn't alone, despite what she thought. And maybe I needed to be reminded that I wasn't alone either. I stared at the ceiling, waiting for her to fall asleep, but her breathing never seemed to slow.

I rolled toward her. "Everything has a way of working out, you know."

For a second I thought she was asleep, but then she said, "Yeah? I'm not so sure."

"It does."

"How is the love of your life marrying someone else working out for you?"

I swallowed down the lump in my throat.

"I'm sorry," she whispered. "I don't know why I said that."

"Actually, it's working out okay. I got to meet you, didn't I?"

She didn't say anything for a long time. "Goodnight, Tyler." She rolled away from me.

***

I breathed in the sweetest smell. Roses and cinnamon maybe. I took another deep breath and my eyes flew open. My face was nuzzled in Hailey's hair. I stayed completely still. My arm was wrapped around her and my palm was flat against her stomach. I had pushed up her t-shirt and my skin was flush against hers. But her hand was on top of mine, holding me in place.

I slowly exhaled. We were in the middle of the bed. It's like we had both gravitated toward each other in the night. My knee was pressed between her thighs. And I was so fucking hard.

Shit. I couldn't let her wake up with me holding her like this with a hard on. She'd think I was perverted. But a small part of me didn't want to let go. I wanted to slide my knee higher up her thighs and see if she wanted me like I wanted her. I wanted her to be as wet as I was hard.

What the fuck am I doing? I very slowly slipped my hand out from underneath of hers, skating it down her firm stomach. I stopped right above her underwear line. I wanted to slip my fingers into her panties. I wanted to wake her up the way she deserved to be woken up every day. I could imagine how tight she would be. I swallowed hard.

What the hell is wrong with me? I removed my hand from her stomach and slowly rolled off the bed. The smell of roses and cinnamon seemed to completely surround me. She smelled amazing. I didn't want to leave the room. I didn't want that smell to fade.

At the rate we were going, we'd be in Pasadena in just a few days. I didn't want our time to end without exploring what could have been. In just a few days, I'd be in basic training. Then I'd be in the Marine Corps for three years of service. Another three years living in regret seemed like the worst possible thing. And for the first time in a long time, I wasn't thinking about what could have been. I was thinking about the girl sleeping in front of me. And how much I wanted her.

A run wasn't going to help me this morning. I needed a long, cold shower.

***

When I came back out of the bathroom, Hailey was lying on the bed with her head perched up on her hand as she stared at the TV.

I had purposefully left my change of clothes in the room so that I could come out in a towel just like she had done to me the other day. The room still smelled like her.

"You know, they're saying it was her ex boyfriend and best friend. Can you believe that? What assholes."

I glanced at the TV. She was watching the news about the shooting again. A caption was scrolling across the screen that said, "Suspects coming to light in the Hunter shooting." I looked away from the screen. "No, I can't actually. That doesn't even make any sense. Why would they do that?"

"Maybe her ex was jealous or something? And I'm sure her friend was too. James Hunter was the richest bachelor in the country before she won him over." She turned toward me and her eyes seemed to bulge slightly.

I tried to hide my smile.

"Either way, she's totally your type, right? Long red hair, blue eyes, and she looks short. She's absolutely gorgeous."

"I don't have a type."

"No?"

"No."

She immediately looked away from me and picked up the map that was next to her on the bed. "I was thinking maybe the Grand Canyon is too far out of the way. It'll add a few hours to the trip. We should probably just skip it, right?" She ran her fingers through her hair as she stared down at the map.

I sat down next to her on the bed, way too close for a normal conversation, but I didn't care. I swore I heard her gulp. Right now, I wasn't in any rush to make our trip together end any earlier. I was going to spend the day teasing her. And tonight? Well, tonight I was pretty sure she'd be begging me to take it further.

"Where's the Grand Canyon?"

"Here," she said and pointed to the map.

It was barely out of the way. "You know what, I was actually thinking it might be cool to stop here too," I said and pointed to where Colorado, Utah, Arizona, and New Mexico all met. "How cool would it be to stand in four states at once?"

"That would be pretty awesome. But that's even farther out of the way. I need to get to Pasadena as soon as possible." She bit her lip as she looked back down at the map.

I wanted to bite her lip for her. "You know, I've heard that lots of people try to have sex in that spot."

She laughed. "And I bet they all get arrested."

I shrugged. "It would be pretty fun to try though, wouldn't it?"

She looked up at me. "Have you never seen the movie Vacation? I was serious about everyone getting arrested who try it. Besides, there's other fun places to have sex that don't necessarily break the law."

"Give me one example."

"Well, with a new partner, isn't anywhere pretty memorable? Even in a random hotel in the middle of Oklahoma?"

Now I needed another cold shower.

She smiled at me and climbed off the bed. "Can I drive some today?" She pulled out a tank top from her suitcase.

"Sure."

She froze, staring at me. A smile spread across her face. "Really?"

It would be way easier to flirt with her if I didn't have to pay attention to the road. And this stretch of road was basically deserted. Not many people were traveling to some of the hottest places in the country in the middle of summer. Even if she was a terrible driver, she'd probably be fine. "Yeah, it's about time you pulled your weight. You do have a license, right?"

"Of course I do. I'm not some slick from NYC who takes the subway and taxis all the time."

"Very funny."

"Keys please." She held out her hand.

"Well, let me get dressed first."

"Oh, I didn't even notice that you weren't."

I was pretty sure she was better at playing this game than I was.

CHAPTER 15

Hailey
Monday

My plan last night had somehow worked. My lie about there only being king beds left in the hotel had gotten Tyler to wake up in a great mood. A great, very flirtatious mood. And he had even said that Mrs. Hunter wasn't his type. Not those exact words, but close enough. And if he didn't have eyes for her, then maybe he really didn't only chase redheads. Because I had never seen a redhead more gorgeous than her.

His good mood was contagious, but it didn't really take away from the fact that I had woken up with this awful feeling in my gut. I needed to focus on getting to Pasadena, despite how appealing stopping at the four corners monument and jumping Tyler's bones sounded. The longer I was away from my dad, the more guilty I felt. My mission was to get the money, not explore the Grand Canyon and Tyler's body. So why did I so badly want to do both? I glanced at Tyler out of the corner of my eye. He turned toward me at the same time and smiled. I immediately turned back to the road.

"Truth or dare?" he said.

I laughed. "I'm not playing truth or dare with you."

"Why not?"

"Because it's a game for kids."

"Sounds like you're chicken."

I laughed again. "I'm not chicken. Fine. Truth."

He put his left elbow on the center console and leaned closer to me. "On a scale of one to ten, how attracted are you to me?"

God, I should have picked dare. I kept my eyes glued to the road and tried to play it cool. "You're awfully conceited. Who says I'm attracted to you at all?"

"You seemed attracted to me when you kissed me the other night."

"Yeah, well, I wasn't thinking clearly. It just so happened that I hadn't had tequila in quite some time."

"Fair enough. You still have to answer the question, though."

"Fine. You're an attractive guy, sure. Like a seven."

Tyler laughed. "I'll take what I can get. Your turn."

"Truth or dare?"

"Definitely dare."

I pressed my lips together. I had wanted to ask him the same question. But I had lied. He was a ten. He probably would have just lied to me too. I said the first dare that popped into my head. "I dare you to moon the next car that passes us."

He laughed. "Fine." He started to unbutton his shorts.

"Oh my God, you're not seriously going to do that?" I put my hand out to block the view of him. Not that I really wanted to. It was just a reflex.

"You think I'd back down from a dare? Never." He pushed his shorts down his legs but kept his boxers on. "You're going to have to slow down if you want someone to pass us."

I took my foot off the gas. "You don't actually have to do this. Let me think of something else."

"No, this is perfect. Here comes someone now."

I watched him unbuckle his seatbelt and stand up in the moving car. He winked at me as he pulled down the back of his boxers, keeping the front of himself covered.

I stared past him at the van that was driving by. The couple in the front didn't seem to notice, but a little girl in the back looked like her jaw had hit the floor.

"Oh my God!" I pointed to the kid.

Tyler ducked down, peered through the front windshield, and started laughing hysterically.

Which made me start laughing hysterically. But I didn't miss the side view of his ass before he pulled his pants back up. His firm, perfectly squeezable ass. I gripped the wheel tighter than necessary and tried to push the image of his ass out of my mind.

"That was epic," he said and playfully shoved my shoulder.

And there was that spark again. That little indescribable burst of electricity that made my whole body feel alive.

He slowly let his hand fall from my shoulder. My heart was beating so loudly, I swore I thought he could hear it.

"Your turn," I quickly said.

"Truth or dare?"

"Truth."

"What's your greatest fear?"

I hadn't expected such a serious question after he had just mooned a ten year old girl. I bit the inside of my cheek. *Losing my dad.* That fear seemed to be seeping into my system. The farther I drove away from my hometown, the guiltier I felt. "Can I pass?" I could feel him staring at me.

"I'm just trying to get to know you."

Why was I trying to hide from him? Didn't I want him to know me? Didn't I want this to be more than whatever it was right now? "I'm terrified of being alone. Not in the physical sense. I'm fine being home alone and reading a book or whatever. That's fine. But I'm scared of not having anyone to count on." I swallowed hard.

"It seems like you and your dad are really close."

"We are."

"What happened to your mom?"

I wish he was still mooning strangers.

"I'm sorry, you don't have to answer that. I just..."

"No, it's fine. I don't have a mom. It's just my dad and me." I knew how weird that sounded. Everyone had a mother. Humans didn't just get dropped off by a stork. "I mean, of course I had a mom. I just...don't anymore."

"I'm sorry."

I knew what he probably thought that meant. And I didn't feel like correcting him. "No, it's fine. Truth or dare?"

"Truth."

"On a scale of one to ten, how attracted are you to me?" I smiled at him and then looked back at the road.

"You really can't tell?"

I shook my head. "Honestly, half the time I think you like me and the other half of the time it seems like you wish I had never gotten in your car."

"I'm really glad you climbed into my car."

"Yeah?" I tried to hide my smile. "Why is that?"

A big, fat raindrop fell against the windshield with a splat.

"I find you incredibly refreshing."

"Why, thank you, Tyler. But you didn't answer my question."

"You're a fucking ten, Hails."

I didn't dare turn my head toward him. I didn't want to see whether or not he was smiling and joking around with me. I wanted to believe he really did think I was attractive. And the way he had said it affected me in an embarrassing way. I pressed my thighs together.

"Not that it matters," he said. "Since you only think I'm a seven."

I didn't need to look at him to know that he was smiling now. It was strange how quickly you could feel like you really knew someone even after only a few days. I wanted to tell him that I was lying. Because Tyler Stevens was a fucking twelve.

The rain started to fall faster. I turned on the windshield wipers. The storm had come out of nowhere. It had been sunny five minutes ago.

"Do you want to switch with me? I don't mind driving."

"No, I got this." I leaned forward slightly. It was like someone was throwing buckets of water on our windshield.

"Really, I can..."

"I got this, Tyler. Don't you trust me?"

He laughed. "Not really."

I hit his arm and made sure not to wrap my fingers around his perfect biceps. "I just opened up to you about my biggest fears. Don't be an ass."

"My biggest fear currently is that you're going to drive us off the side of the road."

"I'm a good driver!" I leaned forward in my seat even more. It was almost impossible to see. But I refused to back down. All I could hear was the rain splattering against the car, making the whole thing shudder.

"Seriously, Hails, pull over. We can just wait out the storm. This is crazy." He put his hands on the dashboard and leaned forward to get a better look out the windshield.

And of course I stared at him. Because it was impossible for me to not stare. My eyes just loved gravitating toward him when he wasn't looking, when I couldn't be caught.

That's when the car slid. I slammed my foot on the brake but nothing happened. *Oh my God.*

"Hit the brake!" he yelled.

"I'm trying!" I tried to pump the brakes with my foot, but the car continued to swerve.

Tyler reached down and pulled the emergency brake and the car started to slow just in time for it to collide with something.

My body jolted forward, pressed hard against the seatbelt, and then jolted back. It felt like my heart was beating out of my chest. I had almost killed us.

"Are you okay?"

Crap. Fuck. Shit. God, what had I just done?

"Hails, are you okay?" He touched my cheek and turned my face toward his.

The concern in his eyes was almost palpable. And just for a second, I didn't feel like I had just royally fucked up. I felt safe. With his hand on me, I felt so content.

"I'm okay," I whispered.

He immediately dropped his hand from my cheek and opened up the door, stepping out into the torrential downpour.

"Tyler!" I yelled but he had already slammed the door.

I saw him run his hands through his wet hair as he looked at whatever damage I had caused to his car. He kept them on the top of his head like he had never seen something as horrible in his life.

I unbuckled my seatbelt and stepped out into the rain too. It was pouring so hard that the rain almost hurt my skin.

"Get back in the car, Hails!" he yelled over the sound of the splashing water.

"Let me help!" I stepped around the car and saw the huge dent in the front fender. The tire had a large gash in it and was already completely deflated. We had run straight into a small boulder. If Tyler hadn't pulled the emergency brake, the car probably would have been totaled. And we'd both be... I tried to ignore the thoughts floating around my head.

I looked over at Tyler. His t-shirt was completely soaked. It clung to his strong chest and biceps. I suddenly had no desire to help him put on a spare tire. All I wanted to do was touch him.

"You've already helped enough!" he said.

I had no idea how I could want to rip someone's clothes off at the same time I wanted to rip their throat. I stormed over to him. "You can't fix anything when it's pouring. You need to wait for the rain to let up."

"I can fix it. Would you just get back in the car?"

"No." I wasn't really angry. I was just completely focused on his baby blue eyes and I never wanted him to stop looking at me. I always wanted them on me.

CHAPTER 16

Tyler

Monday

I glared at her. But I wasn't actually angry. At first I had just been relieved that she wasn't hurt. And now? Now I was looking at the way her wet shirt clung to her body. The rain was cold and her nipples were starting to show through the thin fabric. I wanted to touch her. I wanted to run my fingers over every inch of her wet skin. But something was holding me back. Probably the fact that she looked like she wanted to take a swing at me.

"Are you always this stubborn?" I asked.

"Me?" She took another step toward me. "What about you?" She poked me in the middle of the chest. "Take a look in the mirror, Tyler. You're the most stubborn person I've ever met."

The only problem with what she was saying was the fact that her hand hadn't left my chest when she poked me. She spread her fingers out, laying her palm flat against my chest, right over my heart. When I left New York, I felt broken. But staring down into her eyes, I didn't feel that way anymore. I didn't care about anyone I used to like. I didn't care about the fucking car. All I cared about was the fact that she was standing in front of me, wanting me as badly as I wanted her.

I grabbed the back of her neck and pulled her face to mine. She didn't pull away, she simply melted into me. It was nothing like when she had kissed me before. This wasn't some drunk kiss that she wasn't going to remember in the morning. This kiss was everything.

A part of me had wanted her from the moment I saw her. But I was still holding on to something that didn't exist. For the first time in a long time, I didn't need to hold on anymore. I was all in. I was done living in the past. I just wanted to experience this moment. I stepped forward, pushing her backwards against the wet car.

She moaned into my mouth. If I wasn't already hard, that would have done it. This time I was the one pushing her forward, parting her lips, making her give into me. I fisted her hair in my hand, drawing her head back so that she could give herself completely to me. Hailey Shaw was finally going to be mine.

She grabbed my shirt in her hands, clinging to me like I was her fucking life preserver. I knew she was hurting. I knew she felt like the weight of the world was on her shoulders. Drinking wasn't the way to fix that. But getting lost in each other? That was an idea I could get behind.

The sound of a car speeding by made me reluctantly pull away from her far too soon.

I watched her catch her breath. The only thing separating us was the pounding rain and steam rising off the pavement. Her cheeks were flushed and her chest was rising and falling as fast as I'm sure mine was. A gentleman was supposed to end it right there. Just a kiss. But I wasn't a fucking gentleman.

"Get back in the car, Hailey." This was her one chance to get out. All she had to do was get back into the passenger's seat and this would be over. Just a kiss. *Please want more than just a kiss.*

She stared back at me defiantly. "Make me."

CHAPTER 17

Hailey
Monday

His lips crashed back down onto mine. I ran my fingers through his wet hair as he pulled my thighs around his waist, lifting me off the car. All I could focus on was that kiss. Suddenly nothing mattered but him. This moment was all I needed. He was all I needed.

I knew what was about to happen. And I didn't care if it was on the hood of his car or on the side of the road. All that mattered was that in a few seconds I'd be full of him. I heard the click of the car door opening.

I laughed as I pulled back from the kiss. "I don't actually want to get in the car. I want you. How much more obvious do I need to be?" I tightened my legs around his waist. He looked even more handsome when he was soaked. His shaggy hair was stuck to his forehead, and droplets of water hung seductively to his eyelashes. *God, I was in trouble.*

"That's why I'm coming in with you." He ducked down and suddenly the rain wasn't falling on us anymore. He laid me gently in the backseat and closed the door behind us.

I could still hear the rain falling against the roof but everything seemed muted now that we weren't standing in it.

It looked like he wanted to say something, but I was way past talking. I needed him to touch me. I needed his fingers, his mouth, his cock, whatever he was willing to give me. I spread my thighs apart, not embarrassed at all. Because I could tell his desires matched my own.

He put his hand on the inside of my thigh and slowly slid it up, stopping right below the hem of my jeans shorts. "You're beautiful, Hailey. Do you have any idea how gorgeous you are?"

"I don't need flattery." I grabbed the front of his shirt and pulled him toward me. "I need you to fuck me."

His lips crashed back down on mine. The hand that was on my thigh moved to the button of my shorts. In a matter of seconds he was pulling them down my legs. Without any hesitancy he thrust a finger deep inside of me.

Oh God.

He slid another one inside of me, stretching me wide. His fingers were amazing, but I wanted more. I needed him. I wanted all of him.

I reached for the button on his shorts, but he stopped my hand.

"I don't have a condom."

Shit. "I still want to please you." I could see the fabric straining around his erection. The evidence that he wanted me was all over his face too. I tried to reach for him again, but he stopped me.

He lifted my hand above my head, leaned over me, and lightly bit my earlobe.

Fuck yes.

"It's okay, Hails," he whispered in my ear. "I just want to see you come." He moved his thumb to my clit and started massaging it while his fingers started to thrust even faster.

And I wanted to let go. But not like this. I hadn't been dreaming of his fingers. I was so horny that I couldn't even be embarrassed by anything that spilled out of my mouth. "I'm on birth control. I'm clean. Please, Tyler, I need you."

"Are you sure?"

"If I don't feel you inside of me I'm going to internally combust."

He let go of my hand. This time when I started to unbutton his shorts he didn't stop me. I let my fingers run down his happy trail and dip beneath the waistline of his boxers. I wrapped my hand around his erection. God, he was huge. He was going to feel so amazing inside of me. I started to pump up and down his length with my hand.

"Fuck. This isn't going to work," he groaned.

"What?" For a second I thought I had done something wrong as he pulled away from me.

"The angle. Get on top of me, " he said as he shoved his boxers to the ground. His cock stood at attention, just waiting for me.

I had never had sex anywhere but a bed. I had never had sex with someone I had known less than a week. And I had never had sex without a condom. But no one had ever looked at me the way he was looking at me either. And I had never been this wet in my life. And I had never wanted something so badly before.

I sat up and lifted one of my thighs across his legs, straddling him in the backseat of a car on the side of a highway.

He pushed my wet tank top and bra up past my breasts and took one of my nipples in his mouth. It was like it had a direct line to my groin. I closed my eyes as I felt his hands grip my waist. He slowly lowered me onto him, sliding into me inch by inch.

"You're so fucking tight," he said against my breasts as his fingers tightened on my waist.

I had never felt this full. I let the sensation overcome me as I gripped his shoulders. God, I couldn't move. I couldn't even think. I let him guide my hips up and down, setting the pace. The wonderful, wonderful pace. Nothing had ever felt this amazing before. I dipped my fingers beneath the back of his wet shirt and down his muscular back. His skin was so smooth. We were a tangle of wet clothes and limbs. I had never experienced anything so sexy in my life.

His mouth moved to my other nipple. His tongue swirled around, teasing me, turning my nipples into hard peaks. I could feel myself tightening around him. *Oh God, not yet.* This couldn't end yet. "Stop, you're going to make me come." I felt him smile against my breast.

"I want you to come, Hailey. I want to make you come a thousand times."

Jesus Christ, where had his dirty mouth come from?

He guided my hips faster, fucking me the way I had demanded. Hard. Raw. Intense.

And I loved every second of it. I slammed my hand against the foggy window. It made a squeaking noise as he started to guide my hips even faster.

"I want to feel you come around my cock, Hails. Let me feel how much you love me inside of you, baby." He lightly bit down on my nipple.

And I completely unwound. I felt myself tightening around him. "Tyler," I panted as I grabbed a fistful of his hair. "Oh, God, Tyler!"

He grabbed the back of my neck and pulled my face down to his. I felt his cock start to pulse, pressing against my walls. A second later, his release shot up inside of me as he groaned into my mouth.

And he didn't stop kissing me when he finished cumming. We continued to make out like two kids in high school. One of his hands cupped my breast and the other was squeezing my ass.

"We should have been doing that this whole trip." He kissed the side of my neck. "That was amazing."

I had never felt this warm before. I had never felt this whole before. I swallowed hard. I was in trouble. Because this didn't feel like meaningless sex. It felt like the best sex of my life. He was still buried deep inside of me and I was already wondering when we were going to do this again.

"Are you okay?" He lightly touched the side of my face. A gentle touch. A loving touch.

Instead of answering, I kissed him again. I was okay when his lips were on mine. I was okay if we stayed in this moment for as long as possible. I was okay as long as I wasn't thinking about what this meant.

My hands disappeared into his hair. I needed to touch every inch of him before this spell was broken. If this was a onetime thing, I wanted to be able to remember it. I needed to remember it. I wasn't naive. I knew that our time together was limited. In a few days I'd be going back to Indiana. And even though he didn't seem eager to go back to New York right away, there was no way he'd ever come back with me to my small town when he was used to living in a city. There was no point in getting attached. So why were tears starting to prickle my eyes? Why did this feel like so much more than a summer fling?

"We should probably call a tow truck before it gets too late," he said as he kissed the side of my neck again.

"Mhm." My voice sounded strange. That was it. The moment was over. I climbed off his lap without looking at him and pulled my shorts back on. "I thought you said you could fix it?"

"I'm pretty sure the axle is bent. A new tire isn't going to fix anything. I was just...agitated."

I glanced back over at him as he buttoned his shorts back in place and reached for his phone in the front console. He didn't look agitated now. He looked relaxed, more relaxed than I had seen him since we met. And I did that. For a brief moment, I had helped him forget. He had made me forget too.

A second ago I had felt so warm. And now I was freezing cold. My clothes were soaked. The rain had somehow made the summer heat disappear. I folded my arms across my chest as Tyler started talking on the phone.

There was a lump in my throat that I couldn't seem to swallow away. What if I didn't want to just make him feel better for a few minutes? What if I wanted to do it again and again and again? I bit the inside of my cheek. What was wrong with me? I didn't do relationships. This certainly wasn't going to be an exception. If anything, our situation was just more of a reason to keep my distance. I pulled my arms tighter around myself.

"You're shivering," he said.

I turned toward him. I hadn't even realized he was off the phone. "I'm okay."

He smiled as he put his arm around me, pulling me close. And I was instantly warm again. How could he make me feel so secure with just one touch? He couldn't be the one to comfort me. I needed to be able to do it myself. I couldn't need him. I rested my head on his shoulder. Well, maybe I could need him for just a second.

CHAPTER 18

Tyler

Monday

I pushed a strand of hair out of Hails' face as I stared down at her. She had fallen asleep in my arms. Not like the other night, where we had both accidentally ended up in the middle of the bed. She was in my arms because she wanted to be.

Something in my chest felt tight. She said she didn't need flattery. But that's what she deserved. Maybe she was more broken than I even realized. And while I stared down at her, I knew that I wanted to help put the pieces of her back together. I didn't want her to be drowning in debt. I didn't want her to be wounded because of her cheating ex. I wanted to take care of her. I wanted to make everything right.

She sighed into my chest. Her breath was warm on my skin.

For three years I had let myself be second best. I wanted more than that. I needed more than that. It was pathetic, but that's what it really came down to. I wanted to be needed. Wanted. Loved.

I leaned my head against the back of the seat. I was chasing after something that I didn't even understand. No one had ever loved me. Like? Lust? Sure. But not love. And this wasn't exactly the best time to chase after it. I had just signed away three years of my life. I was proud of my decision, but the closer we got to California, the more nervous I got. If I had met Hailey a few days earlier, I honestly wasn't sure if I would have signed the papers. I wasn't anything like my grandfather. Maybe I was a coward, because I certainly wasn't ready to die.

I thought about the fact that I thought Hailey was broken. Maybe I was the broken one. Maybe I wanted her to put me back together one piece at a time. Because I always needed people more than they needed me. That was my life's fucking story.

A truck pulled to a stop in front of our car.

I looked down at Hailey sleeping. I truly was pathetic. Because I didn't want to wake her up. For just a few more minutes, I wanted to pretend that she needed me. I wanted to pretend that this was more than what I knew she thought it was.

Someone stepped out of the truck and slammed the door.

My time was up. "Hails," I whispered and lightly kissed her temple.

"Mmm."

I swallowed hard. That tiny little sound. I fucking wanted to hear that over and over again. I wanted her to wake up in my arms and moan into my chest. But I knew she'd never feel the same way.

I removed my arm from around her shoulders. "Hails, the tow truck is here."

She slowly opened up her eyes. Her hand clutched to my shirt as she looked out the window. "It stopped raining. How long have I been asleep?"

I waited for her to pull away, but she stayed pressed against me. "About an hour."

She nodded. "Tyler, I don't want..."

She was interrupted by the tow truck guy knocking on the window.

"Let me go see what the damage is," I said. I instantly felt cold when her hands fell from me. Maybe I was wrong about what she wanted. Maybe we both needed something to hold on to. I stepped out of the car.

"Looks like your axle is bent," the guy said when I joined him at the front of the car. "It's good you called. If you had driven on it, it would have done damage to your CV joints."

I nodded like I actually knew what that meant. I knew how to replace a tire and jumpstart a car, but that was about the extent of my mechanical prowess. "Is it easily fixable?"

"We'll need to take it into the shop. But I should have it fixed up by morning."

"What's the damage going to be?"

"If you want to replace the front bumper too, then..."

"No, just the axle and tire."

He nodded and glanced down at his clipboard. "Probably about $500 depending on how long labor takes. Do you two need a lift somewhere?"

"Yeah, wherever the nearest hotel is."

The guy laughed.

"What?"

"You're joking right? All the local hotels have been booked for months in advance."

"Seriously? Why?"

"That big music festival that all the kids are going to. Figured you two were on your way there. Have anywhere else to crash?"

Shit. I knew someone who lived nearby, but there was no way we were going there. I opened up the back door of the car and leaned down. "Know anyone who lives around here?"

She bit her lip. "Where are we exactly?"

The tow truck guy laughed. "About 10 miles out from Amarillo."

Hailey shrugged her shoulders.

"If you'd like to go farther, I can call you folks a taxi. But I'm telling you, the hotels are booked for miles. There are some camping sites set up for the festival though if you'd like to try one of them."

You've got to be shitting me. We were both soaked. We needed a hot shower.

"Should I call?"

I sighed. "No, I know someone."

"Even better. Just let me hook the car up and I'll drive you over."

CHAPTER 19

Hailey
Monday

"You don't seem particularly excited to go see whoever it is you know around here," I said as I stepped out of the car.

"No, it's fine."

"Mhm." I leaned back down to grab our bags out of the back seat. "Anything else you need from the car?" I turned around. He was staring directly at my ass. I didn't bother hiding my smile.

"What? No," he said with a laugh, knowing that I had caught him in the act. He grabbed his bags and my duffel out of my hands.

"I can carry..." I started.

"I got it."

At first him doing that had kind of bothered me. I was perfectly capable of carrying my own stuff. But now that we had had sex, it felt different. He was doing it because he didn't want me to have to. Really, that was the reason he had been doing it the whole time. And there was something really sweet about that. He was a gentleman. I pressed my lips together. *Kind of.* The way he had talked during sex was not gentlemanly. It was dirty. And hot. God, it was so hot. I wanted him to talk to me like that again. My heart rate started to accelerate at the thought of it.

His hand slipping into mine brought me back to reality. The flutter in my chest made me feel like a kid on the playground. I didn't want to overthink things. He had held me in the car, making sure I was warm. And now he was holding my hand. If those things didn't mean he wanted more, I didn't know what did. Well, it at least meant he wanted to have sex again, which I was more than fine with.

I let my fingers intertwine with his as we walked over to the truck. He helped me step up into it. As soon as he sat down beside me, I rested my head on his shoulder. I didn't feel self conscious around him. Actually, I never had. We just had this comfortable relationship. Everything just felt right. But as soon as I thought that, something twisted in my stomach.

I lifted my head off his shoulder. "How much are the repairs going to cost?"

"Not that much, don't worry about it."

"How much, Tyler? I have to pay you for it. It's my fault that..."

"Hails, it's okay," he said, cutting me off. "I'm just glad we're both alright." He lightly touched the side of my face. And the look in his eyes was so genuine that I knew he meant it. We were both lucky to have come out unscathed. Because of him. He had enough sense to pull the emergency brake. Really, he had saved my life.

I wasn't going to fight with him about this. I needed to keep my money. I couldn't afford to be prideful right now, and he was offering. He was taking care of me yet again.

He pulled me closer to him and rested his chin on the top of my head.

It was such a small gesture, but it warmed me to the core. If I wasn't careful, I was going to fall head over heels for this man.

CHAPTER 20

Tyler
Monday

"Are you sure this is okay?" Hailey asked. She looked up at me with her big brown eyes.

It didn't really feel okay. But we were kind of out of options. The car wouldn't be ready for us to pick up until tomorrow morning. We were both still soaked. We were in desperate need of a hot shower. And I didn't want her to feel bad about what had happened.

"Yeah, we were close in college. We lost touch, but I'm sure he'll be happy to see me." *Fat chance.* I grabbed her duffel bag out of her hand and walked toward the front door. I knew that Josh was doing well, but I hadn't been expecting this. His place looked like a Spanish villa. He had started an e-commerce business after graduation and it had exploded in a matter of months. He was probably the richest person from our class.

"Well, did you at least tell him we were coming?" she said as she followed me up the sidewalk.

"No. I think it's probably better this way." I pressed the doorbell and took a step back.

"Why would it be better like this?"

Luckily I didn't need to answer her question, because just at that moment, Josh opened the door. "Tyler Stevens." A smile spread across his face.

I was a little surprised. I was expecting more of a punch in the face, not a smile. "Great to see you too, Josh," I said. I stuck out my hand for him.

Instead of shaking my hand, he folded his arms across his chest. "Rumor has it that you're fucking my ex."

And there it is. I laughed awkwardly. "It's not what you think, we both..."

He laughed. "I'm just messing with you. You should have seen your face. I don't really care, man. We broke up forever ago." His smile was back again. "I'm just glad to see that you're finally over Penny." He stepped forward and slapped me on the back. "Who's your friend?"

"Hailey," she said and stuck out her hand before I could say anything.

"Nice to meet you, Hailey." He shook her hand and held on to it for way longer than he should have. She looked a little uncomfortable from the exchange.

"So, we were just passing through and got in a little accident during the storm," I said. "Apparently there's some music festival and all the hotels are full. I was hoping..."

"Say no more. Come on in." Josh put his hand on the inside of Hailey's wrist and guided her inside.

I clenched my fist by my side. I knew what Josh was doing. I had been his wingman enough in college to know his moves. Despite what he said, he was clearly pissed that I had been dating his ex. Now he was trying to screw me over. *Fuck this.*

"Your place is seriously amazing," Hailey said as she looked around the foyer.

And she was right. Everything was modern and sleek and spotless.

"Thanks," Josh said with a smile. "I have one guest room. Are you fine with staying on the couch, Tyler?"

I slipped my hand behind Hailey's back, trying to take control of the situation. "Hails and I can share a room, it's fine."

He shrugged his shoulders. "Sure, man. How long are you guys gonna be staying?"

"Just the night."

"Then we are definitely going out," said Josh.

"I don't know if..." I started.

"That sounds great," Hailey said.

Josh smiled. "There's a bathroom connected to the guest room. How about you two go get out of those wet clothes. Maybe we can leave in thirty? Dinner and drinks on me."

"Thanks. That's really generous," Hailey said.

But it wasn't really generous. He just wanted to show off how well he was doing. He had always seen women as a conquest. And I knew that's how he was looking at Hailey. I was surprised by how much it bothered me. Hails and I weren't a couple. We were friends who had just slept together. We hadn't talked about what that meant. But she was also the sexiest girl I had ever laid my hands on. She was strong willed and stubborn and so fucking gorgeous.

"I'm actually going to take you up on that hot shower, I'm freezing," she said with a smile.

"Let me show you to your room, then," Josh said. The two of them walked ahead of me. They laughed about something that I couldn't hear as they made their way up the stairs.

I tried to stay calm as I followed them.

The balcony upstairs looked out over his enormous family room. It was just as modern looking as the rest of the house. Josh opened up one of the doors in the long hallway and stepped aside.

"Thank you," Hailey said. "It's so nice of you to let us stay the night."

"Of course. Anything for Tyler," Josh said and clapped me on the back. He smiled at me. "I'll leave you guys to it. There's clean towels in the bathroom closet. Just let me know if you need anything else."

"This place is seriously amazing," Hailey said as I closed the door. "You didn't mention that your friend was rich." She ran her fingers across the pristine white comforter on the bed.

"I didn't think it mattered."

She gave me a weird look. "It doesn't. I was just making an observation."

I wasn't sure what I was so pissed off about. Josh flirted with everyone. I'm sure he didn't actually mean anything by it. And Hailey wasn't exactly flirting back. I sighed. Honestly, I did know why I was upset. It was because no matter how much I knew it wasn't true, there was always something nagging me in the back of my head. That suspicion that Penny hadn't chosen me because I wasn't rich like her husband. And I knew it was ridiculous. Penny wasn't a gold digger. I knew it was about more than that. But the issue of money was something that I could focus on instead of the fact that she just didn't like me for me.

And it wasn't like I didn't have any money. I was doing fine for myself. I had money in the bank. But I certainly wasn't rich. And I'd never be as rich as Penny's husband.

"Hey," Hailey said and put her hand on the center of my chest. "How about you come take a shower with me?" She raised both her eyebrows in the cutest way possible.

I wasn't even sure why I was thinking about Penny. I should have been focused on what was right in front of me. Why couldn't I let this go? Hailey deserved more than that. "I'm actually just going to change into dry clothes."

"Yeah, of course." She moved her hand off of me and laughed awkwardly. "No big. Just thought it would be good to save some water, that's all. Forget I even mentioned it." She grabbed her duffel bag out of my hand.

The last thing I wanted to do was upset her. I grabbed her arm and pulled her back to me. "It's just a rain check, Hails."

She smiled. She looked even more beautiful when she smiled.

I placed a soft kiss against her lips.

"I'm going to hold you to that, Tyler Stevens."

I watched her walk into the bathroom and close the door behind her. I quickly changed and walked back into the hall. I wanted to clear the air between Josh and me. He had been one of my best friends in school and I felt guilty about losing touch with him. It felt like I was busy all the time when I was in New York. But what the hell was I actually doing? I should have at least invited him to come visit. Even more than that, I felt guilty about dating his ex. It shouldn't have really mattered, but it did. I was the ass here, not him.

I looked out over the balcony. Josh was sitting on the couch in the living room. I made my way down the stairs and walked over to the couch. "It's really good to see you, man," I said to him.

He nodded. "Tonight's going to be awesome. It'll be like we're back in school again."

I laughed as I sat down beside him on the couch. "The good old days?"

"Something like that. So what are you doing here, Tyler?".

"My car ran off..."

"No. I mean, what are you doing here? I haven't heard from you in over a year. Why didn't you tell me you were coming to Texas?"

"I didn't really know until a few days ago."

"Does this have anything to do with Penny tying the knot?"

"I figured you had heard about it."

"Yeah, I don't exactly live under a rock." He gestured to his enormous living room.

"Your business must be booming."

"It is." He stared at me for a second. "Dude, I don't get it. What the hell were you thinking shacking up with Melissa? I mean, Penny's best friend of all people? You had to have known that it wouldn't end well. Especially since you were still clearly hung up on Penny."

"I don't know. Melissa and I have been friends for just as long. It just turned into something more. Neither of us meant for it to happen. I hope there's no hard feelings."

"Besides for the fact that you broke bro-code by banging my ex and cut me out of your life when I moved here? No, no hard feelings." He smiled.

I laughed. "It wasn't intentional."

"Well that's good to know. We're supposed to be brothers, man. It would be nice if you'd give me a call when you start fucking my ex. That's all I'm asking."

"Next time I'll be sure to do that," I said with a laugh.

"It's not really that funny. How is she, by the way?"

"She's waiting to hear back from a bunch of law schools."

"I'm sure she'll get in. That girl knows how to win an argument." Josh laughed. "Ugh. Do you sometimes miss it?"

"Miss what?"

"College? When everything was simple. And we all lived close together instead of spread out all over the country."

College had been simple for me. Until I met Penny. She had slammed into my life full force senior year and disappeared just as quickly as she had come. Honestly, she had probably brought me more pain than joy. But some of those moments with her had been the highlight of my college experience. That was the problem. I kind of stopped living after I met her. "I don't miss the tests. But I do miss hanging out with you all the time."

"I have an idea."

"And what's that?"

"Come work with me. Hell, you could actually do it anywhere, you wouldn't actually have to move here. It's all online. But we'd get to hang out again."

"As appealing as that sounds, I can't."

"Oh, right. How's your job going? Business analyst, right?"

I shook my head. "I quit."

Josh laughed. "Not great then. So why can't you come work with me? Really, I'll beat whatever salary you had."

"No, it's not that." I hadn't said this out loud to anyone but my mom. And she hadn't taken it well. "I joined the Marine Corps."

Josh laughed.

"No, I'm serious. I'm driving to basic training."

He just stared at me. "Why the fuck would you do that?"

"I want to make a difference. I want to do something I can be proud of. And I couldn't stay in New York. Not after what happened. Penny was the only reason why I was there."

"Damn." He shook his head. "So you only have a few days of freedom left?"

"That's one way to put it."

"I'm sorry, man."

"I'm not. I don't regret it."

"Still. What does that mean for you and Hailey? Does she know?"

"No, she doesn't know." *She doesn't need to know.* "She just needed a ride to Pasadena and I was heading out to California anyway. We're just...friends." It wasn't really true. To me we were way more than that. But our time was limited. It wasn't like I was going to ask her to put her life on hold for three years when I had only known her a few days. It was what it was.

"Oh. Sharing a bed type of friends?" He smiled.

I laughed. "Can you blame me?"

"No, she's fucking hot."

"Yeah. She is." I felt bad agreeing to that. Because it was so much more than just her looks that attracted me to her. But it wasn't like I was going to say, "No, Josh, I love her personality." He had already given me enough shit in college for being hung up on Penny.

"So how is she in the sack? Better than that torch you're holding?"

I laughed. Josh was right. I had been holding a torch for Penny ever since we had slept together. But I wasn't sure I needed to anymore. "Hails is definitely a ten in bed."

CHAPTER 21

Hailey
Monday

I wasn't intentionally eavesdropping. Well, not at first. But when I had opened up the door to my bedroom, their conversation spilled into my ears.

Normally I would have chimed in to let them know I could hear them, but something had caught my attention. It wasn't just the words that bothered me. It was the way that Josh had said them. *"So you only have a few days of freedom left?"*

What the hell did that mean? Tyler had joked around with me about being on the run. But maybe he was the one that was in actual trouble. I would have been hung up on the issue if their conversation hadn't taken a turn toward me.

"So what does that mean for you and Hailey? Does she know?" Josh asked.

"No, she doesn't know." He paused. "She just needed a ride to Pasadena and I was heading out to California anyway. We're just...friends."

I swallowed hard. Just friends? Maybe before this afternoon. But it didn't feel like just a friendship anymore to me. I really liked him.

"Oh. Sharing a bed type of friends?" Josh said.

Tyler laughed. "Can you blame me?"

That asshole!

"No, she's fucking hot," Josh said.

"Yeah. She is."

"So how is she in the sack? Better than that torch you're holding?"

Tyler laughed. "Hails is definitely a ten in bed."

My whole body felt cold. So that's all this was. A con quest? Why had I let myself think for a second it could be more? In just a few days he'd be dropping me off in Pasadena and heading back to New York. I shouldn't have been shocked by his words. But why had he let me fall asleep in his arms then? Why had he held my hand? Why did he tell me I was gorgeous? The answer was clear, but I didn't want to accept it. He did all that just to get in my pants. Like every other guy I had ever met, he was only after one thing...sex. I wanted to punch his stupid beautiful face.

I stood there for a second, trying to calm down. I closed the door hard to alert them that I was coming down. Tyler may have thought we were friends, but I certainly wasn't his friend now. As far as I was concerned, we were acquaintances that hated each other. Because I really, really loathed him right now.

I made my way down the stairs. I didn't want to be compared to the girl he was in love with. I didn't want to be second. There were enough times in my life where I was second best. I wasn't doing that again.

"Hey, guys," I said as cheerily as I could muster. "Ready for dinner?"

Tyler stood up and smiled his perfect smile. It was annoying how handsome he was.

"Yup." said Josh. "You guys are going to love this place."

***

The restaurant was covered in Texas longhorns skulls, whiskey bottles, and barrels of who knew what. We had passed a bunch of chain restaurants on the way out of the city, but I was happy to be in a place that screamed Texas. The odds of me ever coming back to this state were slim to none. And I wasn't going to let some lying ass-wipe ruin this adventure.

"I don't know many girls that drink whiskey," Josh said.

"I'm not most girls." I took a sip from my glass. It wasn't my drink of choice, but I was pretty used to drinking anything. We had gotten a crescent shaped booth and I was sitting between Josh and Tyler.

"I can tell." Josh smiled at me. "So what do you know about the stranger that you've been driving around with for the past few days?"

"Enough."

Tyler laughed. "What's that supposed to mean?"

I shrugged my shoulders and turned back to Josh. "Why? Do you have some incriminating stories you could tell me?"

Josh smiled. "Absolutely." He rubbed his hands together. "Where to begin? Well, there was that time that he got in a fist fight with a professor."

I glanced at Tyler. *Who the hell gets into a fist fight with their professor?* Lots of my lectures were so big that I never even spoke to the teacher, let alone got close enough to him to put my fist in his face. "Well that's dumb."

Josh laughed. "Yeah, it was a pretty stupid move."

Tyler clearly had anger problems or something. Plus he was a womanizer. And he just loved what he couldn't have. That's the only reason he had wanted to sleep with me. To prove that he could have me like he couldn't prove with Penny. *Well, fuck him.*

"It was warranted," Tyler said.

I completely ignored him. "Did you guys hang out a lot in college?"

"All the time. We were in the same frat."

In my mind, that literally explained everything. Of course Tyler had been in a fraternity. Most assholes were in fraternities. "I bet you guys threw amazing parties." I decided that I needed to completely shove it in Tyler's face. Not only was I going to completely ignore him, I was also going to flirt with his friend. Because Josh seemed a hell of a lot nicer than Tyler.

"Yeah, we did. Theme nights really were the best," Josh said with a laugh. "You should have seen some of the awesome themes we had."

"Like what?" I said. "I've been to a few frat parties and everyone always looked ridiculous."

Tyler laughed. "That about sums it up."

I ignored him and kept my eyes glued on Josh. He seemed to like the attention. He took another swig of his whiskey and leaned in a little closer to me.

"Well, the best one had to be our annual ABC party."

"Did you all wear a different letter or something?"

Josh laughed. "No. You've seriously never been to an ABC party?"

I shook my head.

"It's an Anything But Clothes party."

"So...it's just a bunch of naked dudes chillin' in the frat house? Sounds fun."

"What? No," Josh said. "First of all, there were always tons of girls at our parties. And second of all, we weren't naked. You just have to dress in anything but clothes. So like, aluminum foil, body paint, newspaper...that kind of thing."

"What did you guys wear?"

"Just plastic wrap," Tyler said. "We really wanted to show off our junk."

I laughed. *Damn it, don't laugh with him!* "Wait, seriously? That's disgusting."

Tyler shook his head. "Of course not. If we had done that, we probably wouldn't have had any girls show up."

"But one year Tyler did wear bubble wrap," Josh said. "And a few bubbles got popped...so..." he let his voice trail off.

I laughed. "Sounds wild."

"It was seriously the best. I'm sure you would have loved our parties." He smiled at me.

It finally seemed like Josh was fully flirting back. No more restraint whatsoever. I leaned forward and put my elbow on the table, effectively blocking Tyler out of our conversation. "I'm sure I would have. Did you have a girlfriend the whole time you were in school?"

He laughed. "No. I did date one girl pretty much my whole senior year. The one that Tyler was just sleeping with."

"Doesn't that break all sorts of bro-code? It definitely breaks girl-code."

"Nah, Tyler and I are cool."

"You don't want to get back at him? Even just a little?"

Tyler cleared his throat from behind me. "Hails, can I talk to you for a second?"

CHAPTER 22

Tyler
Monday

What the hell was going on? Before we had shown up at Josh's, Hailey was completely into me. We were in a good place. Yeah, we had a lot to talk about. But I never thought she'd be trying to hook up with my friend right in front of me. What was her problem?

"Just a second," she said. She leaned over and whispered something in Josh's ear and they both laughed.

If this was some kind of jealousy game, it was working. The problem was, I had no clue why she wanted to make me jealous. This afternoon I had thought we were on the same page. Clearly I was a few chapters behind her and I had some catching up to do.

I watched her put her hand on Josh's arm, just like she had with the guys at the bar the first night I met her. I didn't know what was real and what was fake. I slid out of the booth. There was no way I was going to ask her twice. Either she wanted to talk to me or she didn't. I walked toward the restroom. She didn't follow me.

I leaned against the wall. The fact was that I didn't really know Hailey. Really, one of the only things I did know about her was that she needed money. Could that be what this was? Was she really flirting with Josh because it would be convenient to fall for someone who could fix her problems with a snap of his fingers? Fuck that. I wasn't going to put myself in a situation again where I lost a game I couldn't win. Hailey wasn't Penny. But right now, it sure felt the same.

"What's up?" Hailey said.

I hadn't even heard her come over. Something about the casual way she asked me that made my blood boil. She had this way of crawling under my skin. I didn't need this right now.

"Never mind, it's nothing. I'm going to get an Uber back to Josh's. I'm beat. Have a good night." I brushed past her.

"Really? That's how you're going to play this?" she said to my back.

I turned around to face her. "Play what? I think it's pretty clear what's going on here."

"And what is that?"

"You know he's loaded. And you're in debt. It's easy to connect the dots."

She shook her head. "You think I'm hitting on Josh because he's rich?"

"Yeah. I do."

"God." She folded her arms across her chest. "I'm not a hooker. I don't need anyone's handouts. I'm flirting with him because you're an asshole!"

The people sitting near us were starting to stare. I walked back into the small hallway where the restroom was and pulled her with me. "I'm an asshole? You're the one flirting with my friend mere hours after we had sex. Take a look in the mirror, Hailey."

"And what will I see? The sharing a bed type of friend?" She put air quotes around the word friend. "A ten in bed? A conquest?"

Shit. So that's what this was about? She had overheard me talking to Josh? That was just guy talk. She had to know that.

"I was starting to really like you, Tyler. I thought that we could be more than whatever this stupid road trip is. But obviously I was wrong. I've always been a shitty judge of character. It's great to know that all you think I care about is money, though. I'm so glad you have such a high opinion of me." She stormed past me and into the women's bathroom.

Fuck. I glanced back toward the restaurant. No one was on their way over. I had just called Hailey a gold digger. I needed to clear the air. *Now.* But just because no one was on their way in, it didn't mean the bathroom wasn't already occupied by other women. *Damn it.*

I walked back over to our booth to prevent myself from following her.

"If you hadn't already slept with her, I'd totally call dibs," Josh said as I sat back down.

Every part of me wanted to punch him in the face. But this wasn't his fault. It was because Hailey had overheard a conversation between us.

"Could you back off a little?" I said.

"She's all over me. What do you want me to do? You know, you act like the world gave you a shitty hand. Hot girls line up for you and all you care about is the one you can't have. You dated Natalie when you were in love with Penny. You dated Melissa when you were still in love with

Penny. And who knows what you've done in between that, because you sure haven't been calling me with updates about your life. So the question is, what are you going to do to Hailey, huh?"

"It's not like that."

"Really? Because I think it's exactly like that. And maybe she sees it too. You're pissed about coming second in Penny's life and then you treat every girl you meet second best because of her."

Fuck. "I don't do that."

"You gave me so much shit for breaking up with Melissa before graduation. But I did that because I knew we couldn't make it work long distance. And I didn't want to hurt her. I did that because I respected her. I'm not the ass here, Tyler. You are."

"I'm not trying to hurt Hailey. She's different."

"But the situation isn't different. And if Penny calls you, I know you'll go running back to her. You always do."

I suddenly felt exhausted. "The situation *is* different. Penny's married." It sounded so weird saying it out loud. "There is no going back."

"I know, man. I'm sorry. But don't jump down my throat because some girl that you'll never actually commit to is being a little flirtatious. That's not on me."

I shook my head. He was right. Maybe I had been using Penny as an excuse. Maybe the problems were deeper than that. Commitment issues wouldn't be so off base. I was terrified of losing someone I loved. It had happened before and almost killed me. I was so sick of hurting.

"Did you at least tell Penny the truth?" Josh asked.

"Tell her what?"

Josh shook his head. "That you're still in love with her, man."

I folded my arms across my chest and leaned back in the booth. "The morning before their wedding, I told her how I felt. I actually told her I wanted to run away with her." I laughed, but it came out forced. "She didn't feel the same way."

"That's rough."

I shrugged my shoulders. "It is what it is. But I like Hailey. A lot." The whiskey was making me not quite as tight lipped as I usually was. "I don't have anything to go back to. That was part of the reason why I enlisted. But if I hadn't, I don't think I'd even hesitate to go back to Indiana with Hailey."

"Why are you telling me this instead of her?"

"Because I did enlist. I've only known her a few days. The whole thing is insane. Plus she's furious with me."

"What did you do?"

I wanted to say I didn't do anything, but that wasn't true. "She overheard the end of our conversation earlier. About her being a ten in bed and just a friend and shit."

"So that's why she's flirting with me? Well that's an ego boost for me. Not." He smiled.

"And I may have insinuated that she was a gold digger."

"Dude, chicks liked me before I was rich. Don't you forget it."

I laughed. "None of it really matters though. We barely know each other. Like you said about Melissa, long distance never works. And you two had been dating for months."

"It was more than that, though. We had fun, but I couldn't imagine being married to her. And I'm pretty sure she felt the same way. There was nothing for our relationship past college besides tons of fights on the phone. My advice to you is to tell Hailey the truth and let her help make the decision. Don't make it for her."

He had a point. But I would never ask Hailey to give up three years of her life waiting for me to be done with the marines. I had done it willingly for Penny, and I would never get that time back. That feeling of being stuck. That wasn't a way to live. I wouldn't wish it on anyone.

CHAPTER 23

Hailey

Monday

I grabbed the edge of the sink and closed my eyes. There was light music playing in the restroom and for some reason it made me even angrier. I needed the rap music that Tyler liked so much. I wanted it pumping through my veins. I wanted to throw things and curse and scream.

God, I felt like such an idiot. I shook my head and wiped my eyes. The reflection staring back at me in the mirror made me want to cry all over again. The extra mascara I had put on was smeared. I had been trying to look good for him. Now I just wanted to go home. I missed my dad. I had no idea what the hell I was doing anymore. I had almost died today. That gave me more clarity than I'd had in years. Life was too short. And my dad's days were numbered. I shouldn't be in a random restaurant in Texas. I should be with him.

I turned away from the mirror. We were only a two day drive away from Pasadena. I couldn't go back now. Not before I saw Elena. And I'd make it worth the trip. I'd get down on my hands and knees and beg her if I had to. My dad wasn't going to die. I'd get the money, go home, and everything would go back to the way it always was.

I swallowed hard. I just needed to get through two more days with Tyler. I could do that. With a deep breath,

I plastered on a fake smile and walked out of the restroom. Just two days. *I can do this.*

Josh was laughing at something Tyler had just said. I couldn't help but think they were probably laughing at me. The poor girl from Indiana who was dumb enough to sleep with a stranger. Laughter at my expense. I kept the smile on my face.

"Hey, boys, I'm probably ready to call it a night. I'm hoping we can head out pretty early tomorrow."

"Already? It's only eleven," Josh said. He glanced at Tyler and then quickly added, "Yeah, actually, I'm pretty tired too. Let's head out."

***

The whole way home was awkward. Josh kept trying to make small talk which I wasn't in any mood to participate in. And Tyler kept looking at me with those big puppy dog eyes. Those beautiful blue puppy dog eyes.

I shook the thought away as I walked up the stairs. I knew he was right behind me, even though I was hoping he'd stay up later hanging out with Josh.

"Hails," Tyler said right before we reached our room. He grabbed my wrist to stop me in my tracks.

Finally, I turned to look at him.

"Hails, I'm sorry."

An exasperated laugh escaped from my lips. "Tyler, you don't have to say anything. We're on the same page. Whatever happened between us this afternoon was a one-time thing. It's not like there's a future between us. We're both going home after we get to California. Really, don't worry about it. I don't know why I overreacted. It's fine."

"I'm sorry about what I said."

"Which time?"

He shook his head. "It was just guy talk with Josh. Of course we're more than friends."

"Are we though? I don't even know you. And you certainly don't know me. So don't pretend that you do." I was trying to stay level headed but the alcohol was making it hard.

"Hails." He looked at me pleadingly.

I wished I had never asked him to call me that. He didn't earn the right to call me by my nickname. And it seemed like everyone who ever did call me by my nickname ended up betraying me in some way. Why hadn't I learned from any of my mistakes?

He took a step toward me.

"Seriously, Tyler..."

He grabbed the back of my neck and pulled my face toward his. God, I wanted to kiss him back. Every inch of my body was telling me to. But my mind wasn't. And I wasn't going to give into stupid impulses anymore. Especially when it came to Tyler Stevens. I pushed him off of me. "I believe Josh said you could sleep on the couch." I closed the bedroom door in his perfect face.

I leaned my back against the door and closed my eyes tight. What I said was true. We barely knew each other. So why the hell did this hurt so much?

***

I pretty much stared at the ceiling the entire night. I seriously needed to stop drinking around Tyler. It made me do the stupidest stuff. More than anything, I was embarrassed. What had I wanted him to say to his friend? That we were boyfriend and girlfriend? That probably would have been even worse than him saying we were friends. Especially since we hadn't talked at all about where we stood. I would have thought he was crazy. Instead, I had come out looking like the crazy one.

I slowly sat up. And had I thought the sex was amazing too? *Hell yes.* So what was I doing? The problem was that once I was angry, it was really hard for me to calm down. I wanted to talk to him about what having sex with me meant to him without seeming like a lunatic. He'd had sex with nine other people. He was still in love with some girl from New York. So where did that leave me?

His rebound. Second place. I crawled out of bed. It was better if we went back to being friends. That way neither one of us would get hurt. I just needed to play it cool and brush off last night like it was no big deal.

I nodded my head to myself as I got dressed, as if that could convince me that I could play it cool. I opened the door and quickly closed it loudly to ensure that I wouldn't overhear any disgusting conversations this morning. When I got to the bottom of the stairs, I was surprised to see the couch exactly as it had been last night. I made my way into the kitchen. Josh was standing there in sweatpants and no shirt. It spoke volumes of Tyler that I felt literally nothing. Josh was good looking and fit, but I was pretty preoccupied by my feelings for his friend. Also, the kitchen itself was rather distracting. Like the rest of Josh's house it was perfectly pristine. The stainless steel appliances actually shimmered, as if they had never been used.

"Good morning." I said.

He turned around. "Hey. Do you want some coffee?"

"Absolutely." I slid into one of the stools at his counter.

"Milk or sugar?"

"Black is fine."

He handed me a cup.

"Where's Tyler?"

"I dropped him off at the repair shop a little while ago." He sat down in the seat next to mine.

I swallowed my sip. "Is he coming back?"

Josh laughed. "Of course. They just said it would be another hour. He should be back any minute."

"Oh, okay." I took another sip of my coffee.

"He's not going to leave without you, if that's what you're worried about." Josh smiled.

"Psh. No." I had been a little worried. For a second I had let myself think he had abandoned me in Texas.

"You know, he told me about your fight last night."

I shook my head. "I wouldn't really consider it a fight. Just a misunderstanding. It's not a big deal."

"Right, right. Well, maybe you should tell him that."

I laughed. "And why is that?"

"Because he's walking around like a sad puppy."

"Maybe he deserves to be."

"Or you could cut him a break," Josh said with a smile. "He's been through more than you probably realize."

I wanted to take this opportunity to learn about Tyler from his friend. It was probably wrong, but I couldn't resist. "You mean because of Penny?"

Josh shrugged. "Yeah that. And other stuff."

"What kind of other stuff?"

Josh got up and opened the fridge. "I don't know. The accident he was in messed him up pretty bad. Do you want some cereal or something?"

"What accident?"

"You should really be asking him about this stuff. How about a bagel?"

"Yeah, a bagel is fine." My head was spinning. What kind of accident? "How long have you two known each other?"

"Since freshman year of college. We rushed the same frat. We've been friends ever since."

"So, you know Penny?"

"Yeah. I know her." He popped a bagel in the toaster and leaned against the counter on his elbows.

"What's she like?"

Josh shrugged. "Nice. Too nice, really. I don't even think she realized she was leading him on. That's the kind of thing that messes with a guy's head." He grabbed the bagel when it popped out and handed it to me on a plate. "Cream cheese okay?" He slid a tub of it across the counter.

"Yeah, thanks." I stared down at my bagel as I spread cream cheese across it. My mind was going a million miles a minute. "Why do you think he's so hung up on her?"

"Because she's pretty and understanding and completely unavailable."

"Unavailable?"

"Yeah. He just needed something to hold on to when they met. If you ask me, he just liked the idea of her more than anything. She's always just been a distraction."

"Why did he need something to hold on to?"

"Because of everything he lost."

CHAPTER 24

Tyler

Tuesday

I pulled my phone out of my pocket. There were a dozen missed phone calls and two voicemails. I clicked on the first one.

"Mr. Stevens, this is Officer Daugherty from the NYPD. We haven't heard back from you regarding our case. We will be issuing a warrant for your arrest if you don't return to New York for..."

I pulled the phone away from my ear and pressed the delete button. Apparently blocking one number from the NYPD didn't block all of them. I blocked this number too. I wasn't going back to New York. Nothing could make me go back there.

I leaned against the brick wall of the repair shop and stared out at the barren street ahead of me as I pressed on the other voicemail.

"Sweetie, it's your mother. I just...I wanted to apologize about the other night." She cleared her throat. "Would you please give me a call? I love you."

The voicemail beeped, signaling the end of the message. I pressed on my mom's name in my phone and put it back to my ear. It only rang once before she answered.

"Hi, sweetie. How is your road trip going?"

The fake optimism in her voice didn't fool me at all. But I was going to let her pretend that everything was okay. I didn't need to second guess my decision. It was too late for that anyway. "It's good. I stopped at Josh's."

"In Texas? You're making good progress."

"Mhm."

"How is he doing? I haven't seen him since you two graduated."

"He's doing great. His business really took off." *He offered me a job that I would have accepted in a heartbeat a few days ago.*

"So, just a few more days now?"

I looked down at my shoes. "Yeah, Mom."

"You know, I was wondering, are you going to be able to call me during basic training?"

"I really don't know."

"Okay."

"I'll call you whenever I can, though. Don't worry about that."

"I know, sweetie." There was an awkward silence. "Are you driving safely?" She always asked me that whenever I went anywhere. Even if it was only a few miles away. And I wasn't about to tell her I had gotten in an accident yesterday. She'd freak out.

"Of course."

"Good. I worry about you, you know."

I nodded, as if she could see me. She was the only person in the world who worried about me. She was all I had. "I love you, Mom."

"I love you too." There was another awkward pause. "I'm sorry, but are you sure this is what you want? It just seems like you made this decision without really even thinking it through. It's not like you. I thought you loved your job. I thought..."

"Mom, we've already talked about this. It's done." There was a lump forming in my throat.

"But..."

"It's only for three years."

"Three years is a long time."

I knew that better than anyone. "I'm going to be okay."

"Just be careful. Promise me you'll be careful?"

I looked back out at the nothingness in front of me.

Someone cleared their throat from beside me. I turned to see the owner of the repair shop holding up a clipboard, trying to get my attention.

"I have to go. I'll call you again soon, okay?"

"Promise me, Tyler."

Instead of responding, I pulled the phone away from my ear and pressed the call end button. I wasn't going to make a promise I couldn't keep.

"We're all set," the man said. He looked down at the clipboard. "It took a little longer than we expected. It's going to be $750 for the repairs and labor."

"That's fine." I followed him back into the building. I wasn't going to haggle with him over a price. The only thing that mattered was that Hailey and I were both okay.

***

The voices I had heard when I opened the front door were suddenly hushed. I walked into the kitchen where I had originally heard them talking. Hailey and Josh both looked over at me. I'd have to be an idiot to think they hadn't just been talking about me.

"What's up, guys?" I said.

"Just telling Hailey your life story," Josh said with a smile.

I laughed it off. I wasn't that interesting. "You all set, Hailey?"

"Yeah." She didn't make eye contact with me at all. "Let me just go grab my stuff." She excused herself from the kitchen.

"Seriously, what were you two talking about?" I said and sat down next to Josh.

"She was asking why you were still hung up on Penny."

I found that interesting. I thought she wanted nothing to do with me. But now she was asking questions about me? "What did you tell her?"

"I said you liked Penny because she was unavailable and you just needed a distraction when you met her."

"That wasn't why." *Fuck, was that why?*

"Whatever you say, man." Josh placed his coffee cup down on the counter. "I think you two still have a lot to talk about."

"I don't think she's really that interested in talking to me anymore."

"Don't worry, I handled it."

I laughed. "Handled it? What is that supposed to mean?"

"It means I created a mystery for her. Now she's dying to talk to you again."

"What mystery?"

"I dropped the bomb about your accident. And how much you lost."

I shook my head. "That's not exactly a story that fixes the fact that she hates me. I doubt she cares anyway."

"Oh no, she definitely took the bait. You owe me one."

"I don't want her pity." Josh had always been good at playing the game. But I didn't want to play Hailey. Really, I just needed to keep it in my pants and drop her off in Pasadena and forget. Trying to make it more than that was just going to hurt both of us.

"Take what you can get, man," he said and clapped me on the back. "Anything else you need before you head out?"

"No, I'm good. Thanks for letting us crash here."

"Well, there is one thing you can do for me."

I laughed. "I didn't say I owed you one."

"But I say you do. I just fixed your relationship with Hailey plus I didn't let you sleep on the street last night. And I didn't get upset about you banging Melissa."

"Yeah, maybe I do owe you one. Or a few."

Josh smiled. "Then come work for me when you get out. It'll be just like old times."

"I might just take you up on that."

"Take him up on what?" Hailey said as she walked into the room.

"I was just offering your friend a job," Josh said.

"Oh?" She glanced at me and then immediately looked away. "Well, thanks for letting us stay here, Josh. I really appreciate it." She gave him what I thought was a pretty awkward hug. Maybe she was regretting being all over him last night at dinner. Thinking about it again made me feel sick to my stomach.

"Don't mention it," Josh said. "It was great meeting you."

"You too." She tucked a loose strand of hair behind her ear. "You ready?" she said to me without really looking at me.

"Yeah. It was great seeing you, Josh." I gave him a much less awkward hug.

"How about you don't wait over a year to talk to me next time?" he said as we all walked toward the door.

"I won't. Maybe I'll come visit you again soon too," I said. And I meant it. Out of everyone I know, Josh lived closest to the base.

"I'm holding you to that!" he yelled after me.

Hailey and I were both silent as we got into the car. I was pretty sure that's how it was going to be the rest of the way to Pasadena. As long as I didn't look at her. Because whenever I did that, I just wanted to rip all her clothes off again. I started the ignition and waved goodbye to Josh. In three years, I probably would take him up on his offer. Hopefully I'd make it till then.

"I'm sorry about last night," Hailey said as soon as I pulled onto the road.

I glanced at her out of the corner of my eye. "You don't have anything to apologize for."

"No, I do."

What the hell had Josh actually said to her? She seemed so calm and understanding today. I was the one that owed her an apology, not the other way around.

"I overreacted. You guys were just talking. And honestly, you're right. We are just friends."

Just friends. I shook my head. "Friends don't usually sleep together."

"Yeah, well, friends with benefits. Whatever you want to call it." She waved her arm dismissively. "And I'm sorry I flirted with Josh. I wanted to make you jealous and I don't know...I regret it is what I'm trying to say. I'm sorry."

"It's not a big deal. I get it. I shouldn't have talked about you like that. Especially when it's not even true."

She laughed. "You don't think I'm good in bed?"

"Oh no, I meant that." I smiled.

She laughed again.

"It was more than just physical for me, is what I meant."

CHAPTER 25

Hailey

Tuesday

Me too. Everything about Tyler was off the charts. Yes, I had finally given into his charm because he looked even better when he was completely soaked for some reason. But it was more than physical attraction for me too. I liked his personality. It's what drew me to him in the first place. So what the hell did that mean?

"We never got to our 21 questions, you know," I said.

"No? I didn't realize."

"Can I ask you one?"

He smiled at me out of the corner of his mouth. Just one look and my stomach seemed to flip over.

"Would you be open to maybe repeating what happened the other day?"

"Letting you drive and getting in an accident? I'm not sure I'm up for that," he said with a laugh.

"No, smart ass." I lightly hit his arm. I wanted to wrap my fingers around his biceps again. "The other thing."

"Crashing at a friend's house?"

I rolled my eyes.

"Or do you mean stepping over the line of just being friends?"

"Yeah." My voice sounded so small. "That one."

"I'm going to be honest, Hails, I'm not really in a place for a relationship right now."

I looked at his hands on the steering wheel. He was gripping it so tightly that his knuckles were turning white. Why was that? Because he was upset about what he just said? Because he wanted more? I still did. I didn't want us to be a onetime thing. We could at least be a three day thing. I bit the inside of my cheeks. Or maybe we could be more. I could convince him that he wanted more, couldn't I?

"Neither am I," I said. "But we're both adults. We both know what it would be. It doesn't have to be more than what it is."

"Maybe."

"Maybe it doesn't have to be more than what it is? Or maybe you're open to trying it again?"

He glanced at me and smiled. "I might be open to trying it again."

I laughed. "How eloquent."

"Your words, not mine."

"Let's just see where today goes. I just want things to be normal between us again." I stared at him, waiting for his reaction.

"Sounds good to me."

We passed a sign signaling that we had just entered New Mexico.

"Let's pretend Texas never happened," I said.

"Tell my wallet that."

I laughed. "You said you didn't mind. If you want I can pitch in. I'm really, really sorry about your car."

"I'm just messing with you. Really I'm just glad we're both okay." He gave me a small smile.

I bit my lip as I thought about what Josh had said. Some accident that he was in. He physically seemed okay. Like, really, really okay. Perfection in human form. But emotionally, it almost seemed like he was as messed up as I was. I knew he had lost something. I just wasn't sure what.

***

I stared out the window until it was completely dark. And then even a little longer before I turned my attention to Tyler. All day I had convinced myself that I shouldn't ask him any more questions. We were at peace. I didn't want to ruin that. But there were still so many things I was dying to know.

"I think I still have some more questions left in the game," I said.

"Probably a few, yeah."

"Okay." I shifted in my seat so I could look at him. "Josh mentioned that you were in an accident a while back. What happened?"

I watched his knuckles turn white again as he gripped the steering wheel tighter. I looked up at his face. He had lowered both his eyebrows and was staring straight ahead. Josh was right. I was right. Whatever had happened had really messed him up.

"Is it okay if I pass on that one?" His voice sounded strained.

I had definitely hit a nerve. "Yeah, of course." I continued to stare at him. His demeanor didn't change at all. "What's your biggest fear?" I asked instead.

"Dying." He didn't even hesitate. He said it like it was a matter of fact.

Someone so young would only be scared of death for one reason. He must have lost someone close to him in that accident. I knew better than anyone that life could take a sudden turn for the worst. Tyler knew that. His heart ached. Mine did too. I swallowed hard.

Tyler cleared his throat. "If you were given a choice of living in your hometown forever or anywhere else in the world forever, which would you choose?" He scratched the back of his neck when he asked. It almost seemed like he was nervous to hear my answer.

I wanted to lie. I so badly wanted to tell him I'd go wherever he was. But that wasn't true. It would also be crazy. "My hometown."

He nodded.

"Have you ever deliberately broken anyone's heart?" I asked.

"I don't think anyone's liked me enough to get their heart broken," he said.

"I'm sure that isn't true."

"I don't ever want to hurt someone. I'd never do it intentionally."

I folded my arms across my chest. *Just unintentionally.* Like Josh's ex girlfriend? Probably like any girl he had dated since meeting Penny?

"What's the strangest place you've ever had sex?" Tyler asked.

I laughed. "Hmm..." I bit my lip as if I actually needed to mull the answer over. "There was this one time where I had sex with a guy I had just met in his car on the side of Route 66."

Tyler smiled. "And how was that?"

Amazing. "It's not your turn for a question."

"Fair enough."

I liked that our conversation seemed easy again. I wanted to keep it that way. I didn't like seeing him upset. Despite how crazy it seemed, I cared about him. It hurt me to see him hurting. "If you were exhausted, hungry, and really dirty all at the same time, would you sleep, eat, or shower first?"

He laughed. "Probably eat."

"Yeah me too," I said.

He glanced at me out of the corner of his eye. "Why did you stoop to sleeping with someone you deemed a seven anyway?"

I laughed. "Because I lied. On a scale of one to ten, you're like a twelve, Tyler." I watched his lips curve into a smile. It made my insides flutter.

"Are you saying that you lied during truth or dare?"

"Was that when I told you that? I'm not so sure..."

"It was definitely during truth or dare."

"Hmm..."

"That's quite the offense."

"What, are you going to punish me or something?" I said with a laugh.

"I guess we'll see."

I swallowed hard.

CHAPTER 26

Tyler

Tuesday

I was done fighting it. As far as I was concerned, Hailey was mine. And right now, all I wanted to do was show her how true that was. A repeat of what had happened between us in the car yesterday was the best way to do that. I wanted to be inside of her again. I needed to hear her scream my name. So I was going to cash in on that rain check from yesterday. I just hoped she felt the same way as me.

"Really, they only had king beds left again?" Hailey asked as she stepped into the hotel room behind me.

As soon as she closed the door and turned around, my mouth was on hers. She clearly wanted the same thing as me because she didn't hesitate to kiss me back. She even grabbed my shirt and pushed the fabric up my abs. We were definitely on the same page. I grabbed my shirt by its collar and pulled it over my head.

She ran her fingers down my abs as she looked up at me with her big brown eyes. Everything about her was screaming, "Fuck me."

I pushed her back against the door and kissed the side of her neck.

"I was hoping..." she moaned, abandoning her thought, as I pushed her shirt up her torso.

"What were you hoping?" I pulled her shirt off and quickly unhooked her bra, exposing her perfect tits. God, it was like they were made for my hands. I unbuttoned her shorts and pushed them and her thong down her long legs. She was visibly panting as she stared up at me completely naked.

"I was hoping that it wasn't just going to be a onetime thing," she said.

"It couldn't possibly be." My lips were on hers again as she fumbled with the zipper of my shorts.

As soon as I had kicked them to the side in the heap of clothes, I grabbed her ass, lifting her up.

She immediately wrapped her legs around my waist as I carried her to the bathroom. I kicked the door open with my foot and turned on the shower. She was kissing me like I was the air she needed to breathe. And I felt the same way. I was quickly becoming addicted to this girl. She was worried I only wanted her once? There wasn't a plan in my head that involved quitting her anytime soon. We had both more or less said we were okay with whatever this was between us. Right now that had to be enough.

She squealed when I pressed her back against the cold tile. She grabbed my face in her hands, pulling me away from my assault down the front of her chest. "Tyler." Her face had suddenly grown serious. "After Pasadena I have to go back to Indiana."

"I know." I didn't care about the future right now. All I could think about was this moment. I could stay here forever with her in my arms.

She stared back at me. "I don't have red hair and blue eyes." Now her serious face looked sad. Like she knew she wasn't what I wanted.

But she was dead wrong. I was only thinking about her.

"And I definitely wouldn't consider myself sweet." She pressed her lips together.

God she was beautiful. "I know. You're not anything like her. And all I want is you." I kissed her slowly this time, savoring the feeling of her soft lips. I carried her into the shower, letting the hot water fall on us. But the water didn't come in between us at all. It drew us closer together. Wet kisses. Slick skin. And more heat than I could handle.

My hands cupped her firm ass, sliding over her slippery skin. "I need you. Now." I stepped forward, pressing her back against the tile wall.

"Then take me."

CHAPTER 27

Hailey

Tuesday

God, that dirty mouth. He thinks he needs me? I'm the one that needs him.

I gripped his shoulders as he slowly slid his length inside of me. *Fuck.* I was still sore from yesterday, but I didn't care. I wanted every inch of him.

He sighed against my neck. "You're so fucking tight."

My. God. What was he trying to do to me? His hot breath and his even hotter words sent a chill down my spine. I ran my fingers down his muscular shoulders and back. They were slippery from the water, and it somehow made it that much more erotic. I wanted to explore his perfect body.

But as if he could hear my thoughts and disagreed, he pulled my hands from his skin and pushed the backs of them against the cold tile. *This is so much hotter.*

He held me in place as he began sliding slowly in and out of me. It only took me a few seconds to adjust to him, and then he picked up the pace. Yesterday I had asked him to fuck me. Now he was doing it again, but I wasn't on top. He was the one in control and he was fucking me hard. And I was loving every second of it.

I moaned as he began kissing my clavicle.

"You're the only vice I need," he groaned.

God, Tyler.

I closed my eyes as he picked up the pace even more. Each thrust slammed my ass against the wall. I could feel myself tightening around him.

"That's right, baby. Show me how much you love my cock inside of you." He bit down on my earlobe.

"Tyler," I moaned. I was almost embarrassed by how fast he was going to make me come. But the pleasure building in the pit of my stomach far outweighed my self-consciousness.

His tongue swirled around mine, somehow matching the rhythm of his relentless cock. *Fuck.* I had absolutely no willpower left. *God, yes.* I tightened my grip on his hands as I started to unravel.

He groaned in my mouth and I felt his warmth spread inside of me for the second time. It was my new favorite sensation. Nothing in the world beat that feeling.

When he let go of my hands, I immediately buried them in his hair. There was just something so sexy about the way he looked when he was completely soaked. I wasn't sure any of this would have ever happened if we didn't get stuck in that rainstorm yesterday. I needed to thank Mother Nature for this one.

He slowly pulled out of me and I slid down his hard body. My chest rose and fell against his as we both tried to catch our breaths. He dipped his fingers below my chin and tilted my face up to his. I thought he was going to say something, but instead he placed a soft kiss against my lips.

I couldn't help but melt into him. Our bodies just seemed to fit together.

"You're definitely all that I want," he whispered. "Don't second guess that, Hails."

How could he say that? In a few days we'd be going in different directions. We'd never see each other again. I swallowed hard. But I'd be lying if I said I didn't feel the same. I linked my hands behind his neck. "You're all that I want too."

He stepped back under the water, pulling me with him. I thought he was going to kiss me again, but instead he pressed his forehead against mine. We stood that way for a long time, with the water cascading down on us. It was like we both knew that this felt like something more, but at the same time realized that it could never be. But if we just stood here, everything was alright.

***

"They had to make Nick and Jess break up," I said and gestured to the TV screen. We were watching a rerun of New Girl. Somehow it had turned into an analysis of the characters. "The show wasn't as good when they finally got together."

"Of course it was," Tyler said. "That's what everyone was waiting for."

"Then they shouldn't have done such a crappy job at making them a couple. It was very anticlimactic when they finally got together. Didn't the show almost get canceled that season?"

"I don't think so."

"All I'm saying is that the tension between Nick and Jess is what made the show. They made them hook up way too fast."

"I wouldn't say a few years was too fast," Tyler said.

"In show terms it was."

He sighed. "You're ridiculous. You do know that, right?"

"Well, if I'm ridiculous, then you're stubborn and illogical."

Tyler laughed. "I just think it kind of sucks that they aren't together now. That's all."

I rolled over so that I could look up at him instead of facing the TV. I'm not sure how I ended up with my head on his lap, but it was so comfortable. I could easily get used to watching TV like this. "Don't project your own issues onto the characters." I lightly tapped his chest. He still wasn't wearing a shirt from earlier and I liked the way my fingers felt against his skin.

"I'm not. Actually, I'm perfectly content exactly where I am." He smiled down at me.

Something constricted in my throat. Why did he keep saying stuff like that? Was it because he wanted this to be more? He had to. I knew it in my heart that he had to be feeling the same way. So why were we fighting it? We should be making a plan about what was next. I so badly wanted to ask him, but I didn't want to break whatever spell we were currently under. I just wanted to stay in this hotel room forever, analyzing TV characters and having shower sex.

"What's wrong?" he asked.

Spell broken. I sat up and hugged my knees to my chest as I turned toward him. "I really like you, Tyler."

He smiled. "I really like you too, Hails."

I took a deep breath. We were on the same page. I just needed to ask him. "Can I ask you a question?"

"Of course."

"You said you quit your job in New York. Are you planning on going back right away?"

He leaned back on the bed on his elbows and stared back at me. "No, I'm not."

"Where are you going then?"

"California." He smiled at me. "I'm pretty sure I already told you that."

I laughed. "I know. But are you really planning on staying there? I know that Josh offered you a job and..."

"I already have something lined up in California."

"Oh." I looked down at my knees. "How committed are you to that, though? I mean, if you worked for Josh, you could work from anywhere in the world."

"I know." He sat up and scratched the back of his neck with his hand. "And I might take him up on it later down the road, but not anytime soon."

I didn't want to talk about someday. I wanted to talk about right now. And right now, it seemed like we were supposed to be together. I didn't feel so alone when I was with him. I didn't feel like doom was knocking at my door. This was a feeling I wanted to hold on to as long as possible. "I can't change your mind?" I straddled him on the bed and his hands gravitated to my hips. I stared down into his eyes. He looked like he was in pain. He looked...lost. I felt the same way, but not when I was with him. When I was with him, everything seemed okay. I didn't feel lost anymore.

"If anyone could change my mind, it would be you." He smiled at me, his hands still locked on my hips.

"What, do you want me to beg you?" I ran my fingers down his six pack.

His Adam's apple rose and fell.

I dipped my fingers slightly before his boxers. For the first time I noticed a small scar on his hip. I thought about the accident he had been in. I thought about the loss he must have experienced. "How did you get this?"

He grabbed my hand and didn't look down at his hip. "I got it a long time ago. It's nothing."

I could tell it wasn't nothing. But I also didn't want to talk about our issues. I wanted to convince him that it could be more than whatever it was right now. If I could convince him of that, then I'd have more time to learn about him. "Fine, I'll beg," I said, going back to our original conversation. "I want you to come back to Indiana with me."

"Hails..."

"I know it's not the big city, but you grew up in Delaware. You're used to small towns."

"It's not that. I..."

"Look, I've gotten used to falling asleep next to you. I don't want to stop doing that." I smiled at him as seductively as I could and unbuttoned his shorts.

"Hails, I can't..."

"I promise my town isn't as small and boring as you might guess." I kissed the side of his neck. "Plus, I'm pretty sure you enjoy my company."

His fingers dug into my hips.

"Come back with me," I whispered in his ear. "We can figure it out one step at a time."

He had stopped protesting. Instead, he tilted his head so that his lips met mine.

Silence was never consent. But I took his silence as a yes. I knew it was fast and crazy, but Tyler and I just seemed to fit. We were two pieces of a puzzle that used to be broken. Now it was whole again.

CHAPTER 28

Tyler
Wednesday

"Hailey," I whispered against the back of her neck. My stomach was twisted in knots. I tried to tell her I couldn't come back with her last night. The problem was that I wanted to. I wanted to go back to Indiana and figure it out one step at a time like she said. It wasn't an option though. Three years. I would never ask her to wait three years.

I breathed in the smell of her. Today she smelled more like roses than cinnamon. It was the sweetest smell in the world. I wanted to stop time. Somehow, I was always a little too late. With Penny I was too late. If I had met her a few days before her husband, maybe she would have ended up with me. With Hailey I was too late too. If I had met Hailey four days sooner, maybe I wouldn't have been motivated to suddenly change my whole life. I could have gone back with her. I wish it didn't feel like I was throwing my life away, but it did now, now that I didn't feel so alone.

I should have just told her about basic training. I didn't mean to lead her on, but I knew that I had. She thought I was thinking about coming back with her. When in reality, it wasn't even an option. I slipped my hand off her skin and rolled away from her in the bed.

I had royally fucked up. She had asked me if I had ever intentionally broken anyone's heart. Now I was worried that I was doing it to her. And that was the last thing I wanted to do. She deserved so much more than I could offer. She deserved better than me. It felt like I needed her though. Before we had run into each other, I had given up. She made me feel better. It was greedy of me to need her. It wasn't right. So why the hell did it feel so right?

Even though the sun hadn't risen yet, I climbed out of bed and pulled on a pair of athletic shorts.

Hailey moaned in her sleep. It was the softest, cutest noise in the world. Everything this girl did seemed to get to me. All I wanted to do was climb back in bed and hold her in my arms. But I couldn't get used to that. A future between us was never going to happen. I pulled on a pair of socks.

"What are you doing?"

I turned around. Hails was sitting up in bed, the sheets clutched in her hand, barely covering her naked breasts. She looked so beautiful. The moonlight streaming through the blinds made her eyes sparkle in the darkness. She was breathtaking.

I realized I had been staring at her and cleared my throat. "Going for a run. Go back to sleep."

She glanced out the window. "It's the middle of the night, Tyler."

I didn't really have anything to say to that. Telling her I was trying to run away from my feelings for her wasn't exactly a reason I felt like sharing. I turned away from her instead and picked up my sneakers. There was nothing to say. I needed to run because I was frustrated. And honestly, I was scared to death.

"Can you...come back to bed for just a few minutes?"

Reluctantly, I turned back toward her. I immediately realized that I had mistaken the sparkle in her eyes. It wasn't from the moonlight. She was crying. No one should look that beautiful when they were crying.

She wiped underneath her eyes. "Sorry, I just...I had a bad dream. And I thought...well, never mind." She wiped underneath her eyes again.

I dropped my sneakers on the floor and climbed back into bed. Seeing her cry made my chest ache. It completely trumped the twisted feeling in my stomach. I just wanted to make her happy. I wasn't sure when that had become the most important thing to me, but it was. I pulled her into my arms.

She immediately pressed her face against my chest as she wrapped her arms around me. She clung to me like she needed me. I closed my eyes. God, I needed her too.

"It's okay," I said and ran my fingers through her hair. "It was just a dream."

She shook her head. "I'm sorry, I just keep having it over and over again. And when I wake up I think it's real." Her cold tears trickled down my chest.

"What is the dream about?" I kissed the top of her head. I still wanted her to open up to me. Even though I knew how one sided that was, because I hadn't opened up to her either.

She didn't say anything for a few minutes.

I took her silence as her not wanting to talk about it. "It's okay, Hails. It was just a dream."

She shook her head again, smearing her tears against my chest. "You've never told me about your family. Tell me about them."

I pressed my lips together as I looked down at the top of her head. "It's just me and my mom."

She looked up at me. Her eyes were still teary. "Are your parents divorced?"

"Um...no." I ran my hand down her back. "My dad actually passed away a few years ago. Well, not really a few anymore. Five years ago."

She pulled away from me. "Shit, Tyler I'm so sorry."

"It's okay. You couldn't have known." *Because I don't talk about it.*

"I'm so sorry."

"It's fine, Hails."

"What happened? If you don't mind me asking, that is."

I didn't really want to talk about it. But she had stopped crying. I didn't want her to start again. "It was a car accident."

She nodded. "Were you two close?"

"Yeah, we were."

She was starting to blink fast, like she was about to cry again. She reached out and splayed her fingers against the left side of my chest, right on top of my heart. "Sometimes the worst things happen to the best people."

We just stared at each other. Something unspoken seemed to settle around us. She was everything good. I certainly didn't feel that way about myself. But she seemed to see it in me. That warmed me to the core.

She let her hand fall from my chest as she snuggled in close to me again. "Is that why you said your biggest fear was dying?" Her breath was warm against my skin.

"Yeah, I guess." The lie came out before I could even stop it. The truth was more complicated than that. I learned a lot from my dad's death. But it was mostly to live each day to the fullest. To go after what you really wanted. I looked down at the girl lying on my chest. Maybe that's why I was scared of death now. I couldn't go after what I really wanted. Because what I wanted was Hailey. I was terrified of dying in combat without ever knowing what my life with her could have been.

"Thank you for staying."

I wanted to tell her I wasn't going anywhere. That I could be there whenever she needed someone to catch her when she fell. But that couldn't be me. Instead, I just held her until she fell asleep again. Then I slipped back out of bed and went for a run while dawn was just starting to break.

CHAPTER 29

Hailey

Wednesday

I reached out my arm and felt the empty sheets beside me. I rolled over to Tyler's empty side of the bed and breathed in the smell of freshly cut grass and mint. It was the only thing that could seem to soothe me recently. I had woken up in the middle of the night in tears, dreaming about my father dying before I got a chance to say goodbye. It was ridiculous. He had at least four months to live. Longer after I talked to Elena.

The closer we got to Pasadena, the less I wanted to get there. A small part of me was terrified of seeing her. It had been 15 years since we had last spoken.

But now that I had a glimmer of hope that Tyler might come back with me to Indiana, nothing seemed quite so bad. With him, nothing seemed as daunting. I slowly opened my eyes and smoothed my fingers along his pillow. He knew what it was like to lose a parent. He knew how painful it was. Josh had told me that Tyler hadn't been the same after the accident. His dad's accident had to be what Josh was talking about. Tyler had been close to his dad. Maybe as close as I was to mine. Five years didn't change that. He was healing from heartache and healing from loss. I could make it better. I wanted to. Because he made me feel better than anyone else had in a long time.

I closed my eyes tight and breathed in Tyler's scent. This didn't have to be the end. It could be the beginning of something wonderful. And today I wasn't going to worry about seeing Elena. Today I was just going to focus on having fun with Tyler. We were less than two hours away from the Grand Canyon. This was the part of the road trip that I was most excited for.

A buzzing noise pulled me out of my thoughts. I yawned and grabbed my phone off the nightstand. I quickly slid my finger across the screen, but the call had already ended. It also wasn't my phone. I had accidentally picked up Tyler's. Before I set it back down on the nightstand, I stared at his home screen. There were a dozen missed calls from a blocked number as well as six missed calls from a different number. I glanced at the hotel door. I wasn't sure when Tyler was coming back. But I couldn't help how curious I was to see who was calling him nonstop.

At the same time, if we were going to be more than a summer fling, I needed to trust him. I placed his phone down on the nightstand and turned on the TV. It was another broadcast about James Hunter's shooting. His fate still looked bleak. It had been over a week since he had been in a coma. They showed a picture of James and his wife at their wedding, smiling. Normally I'd be sucked into the story, but I couldn't seem to focus on the news. I bit my lip as I stared back at Tyler's phone. Yes, I needed to trust him, but I also needed to know that he was trustworthy. Who would call him so many times? And why would a number be blocked?

Fuck it. I picked his phone up and typed in the number that had called him so many times into my phone. The first result in Google was a precinct for the New York City Police Department. I swallowed hard as I scrolled through the rest of the results. It was definitely the number for the NYPD. Why would the NYPD be calling Tyler?

We had both joked around about how we were running from the cops. But I never thought he really was. I stared down at the blocked number on his phone as my mind raced. What had he done? I tried to think of anything he might have said that would point to something. *God, is he really a criminal?* There was absolutely no way. Tyler was the sweetest guy I had ever met. A bit angry at the cards he'd been given maybe, but not a criminal.

All that I could think of was the fact that Josh said he had been in an accident that messed him up. But Tyler had said the accident that killed his dad was five years ago. That couldn't have anything to do with this.

And then it hit me. There was one more thing Josh had said. In the conversation that I had overheard between him and Tyler, Josh had said, "So you only have a few days of freedom left?" And I couldn't really remember the rest, except for the fact that Tyler had said, "I don't regret it."

Oh my God. What did he do? What horrible thing didn't he regret?

Tyler's phone buzzed again, signaling a voicemail. It was from the blocked number. Without hesitating at all, I clicked on it, thankful that it didn't require a password. I put the phone to my ear to listen to the voicemail.

"Mr. Stevens, this is Officer Daugherty with the NYPD. Penny has informed us that she wouldn't like you to be a part of the investigation, but since you did not report for questioning, we are issuing a warrant for your arrest. You are now officially our lead suspect for the shooting and attempted murder of James Hunter." The line went dead.

James Hunter? I stared at the television screen. *The* James Hunter? The one that was dying in a hospital bed in New York City while the whole country held their breath? A picture of James with his wife flashed across the screen again.

My hand shook as I removed the phone from my ear.

The caption on the screen read, "Penny and James Hunter, minutes before the shooting."

Penny. My heart seemed to stop beating. The red hair. The blue eyes. *That's Tyler's Penny?*

I was hitchhiking with a murderer.

CHAPTER 30

Tyler
Wednesday

I walked into the hotel room to see Hailey throwing her clothes into her duffel bag. She immediately turned her head to me. Her eyes seemed to grow when she saw me. Her hair was haphazard like she had just rolled out of bed. And I'm pretty sure her tank top was on backwards. She looked adorable, like she was rushing to make sure she wasn't going to delay our departure. I knew she was excit-ed to see the Grand Canyon, but now I just wanted to stay in the room as long as possible.

"Hey," I said. "Just let me take a shower real quick and we can get going. Unless you want to join me?" I walked over to her.

Her response was the harsh zippering of her duffel bag. She immediately pulled it off the bed and over her shoulder. "I actually have to go. I wanted to thank you for taking me as far as you did. I really do appreciate it more than I can say." She looked down at the ground as she tried to step around me.

"Hails, what are you talking about? We're almost there." I grabbed her shoulder before she could pass.

"Don't touch me, Tyler." She shifted her shoulder away from me.

I lifted my hand off of her. "What the hell is going on?"

"You lied to me." She looked so hurt.

"I never lied to you." *Fuck, that isn't true.* But I didn't mean to. I didn't want to anymore. I wanted to tell her about basic training. I needed to. Before I could say anything else, though, she tried to brush past me again, so I stepped in front of her.

She immediately took a step back. "Really? Well maybe people from the east coast have a different definition of lying. But from where I'm from, it's very simple. When you don't tell the truth, you're lying, asshole."

"Hails, I was going to tell you. If you'd just let me explain."

"Explain? You've had days to explain, Tyler. And I don't care that you didn't tell me. I just care that you lied about it."

I had withheld information from her. I hadn't let her in. But honestly, I had never lied. Was she talking about something else? "I don't know what you're talking about."

She pointed to something behind me. "You said that she wasn't your type."

Before I even turned around I had a sinking feeling in my stomach. Hails had been obsessed with the story of the shooting ever since I had met her. Sure enough, the TV was on mute, but there was a picture of James and Penny on the screen. *Oh, shit.* "I didn't lie, Hails. I said that I don't have a type. And I don't." Penny had come crashing into my life and I fell for her. I didn't have a thing for girls with blue eyes and red hair. I had a thing for Penny. *Had.* It was the first time I had used the past tense when thinking about my feelings for her. And I knew it was because of the girl standing in front of me seething. I was falling for her. I was falling for her when I couldn't have her.

She laughed, but it sounded forced. "Really? You're going to pretend she's not everything you ever wanted? God, something is seriously wrong with you. You've been watching me watch the news this whole time. And you never said a word. You know both of them. They're in pain and there is absolutely no emotion on your face. You're a monster."

"You think I'm not hurting for her? I am. Every day he doesn't wake up kills me."

"Why, Tyler? James is dying. Every doctor that they've interviewed thinks so. The girl that you love is about to be single. So what the hell are you doing in the middle of the desert with me? Go get your prize. You won."

"I didn't win." How could she think so little of me to believe that I'd find joy in someone suffering? Someone I care about deeply. I wasn't a monster. I was trying to move on. I was trying so hard to leave the past behind but it continued to follow me everywhere. "I don't want to go back to New York. You have to believe me. I'm where I want to be."

"Give me a break," she said under her breath.

"Hails, I want to be here with you. I do."

"Bullshit! Don't feed me some insincere line!"

"What do you want me to say? Penny was the love of my life? My best friend? What do you want from me?"

"Tell me the truth!"

"The truth is that our relationship is over. I told Penny I loved her and she told me she'd never feel the same way.

She told me she'd rather be alone than with me. She didn't even want me to come to her wedding. I meant nothing to her and she meant everything to me." I swallowed hard. "Everything." My whole body suddenly felt cold. "I can't even look at her without feeling like I lost. I'm just trying to figure out who I am without her."

"So that's why you did it?"

"Did what?" I didn't want to be talking about Penny with Hailey. I was trying to start over. I needed to start over.

"You're insane." She tried to walk past me again but I reached for her wrist. She immediately pulled away. "Touch me again and I'll scream. I swear to God, Tyler." Tears were streaming down her cheeks.

"Would you just talk to me? You knew all this already. You just didn't know it was Penny. Why does this change anything?"

Hailey shook her head like she couldn't believe what I was saying.

"If you're upset about Penny..."

"I don't even care about that! I knew you were still in love with her. I let you use me to help get over her because I can't seem to resist you. That's on me for being stupid. That's not why I'm upset."

"I didn't use you." I resisted reaching for her again. I so badly wanted to wrap my arms around her and console her. But she was being irrational.

"Just stop okay? Please just let me go."

"No. Hails, I don't want you to leave. Not like this. Please just talk to me."

"I won't tell anyone where you are if you let me go. I promise. Please, please just let me walk away from this."

"What the hell are you talking about? No one's looking for me."

"More lies. All you do is lie. You know what, it doesn't even matter. I'll never believe the excuse you give me anyway."

I shook my head. "I really have no idea what you're talking about."

"Officer Daugherty called," she said. "You should really put a password on your phone."

Oh, fuck. "Hails. Just let me explain."

"I don't want to know anything about it. I'm not being a part of this. You'll get me arrested for conspiracy or something. I'm getting as far away from you as possible."

"You don't understand."

"Of course I don't understand! How could you do something like that?" She shook her head back and forth. "And the truth is, you're not with Penny right now because if you go back to New York they'll arrest you. It has nothing to do with me. Admit it."

"That's not true."

"There was a police officer on your phone saying they're putting a warrant out for your arrest."

"So let them arrest me! I didn't do it. I wasn't even at the wedding. I wasn't even in the fucking state. Penny didn't want me there. No one wanted me there. I didn't shoot James. I would never do something like that."

"That's not what it looks like."

What it looks like? *Fuck that.* My patience was gone. Yes, I hadn't told Hailey a few things, but it wasn't because

I was trying to hurt her. I was just trying to protect myself from more pain. I was so sick of being cast aside. "They're just rumors, Hailey. Horrible and cruel and completely false. And if you believe it, get the fuck out."

She didn't say anything. She just blinked at me with her stupid big brown eyes.

"Seriously, go. I left New York because I had nothing left. I'm trying to start over. And I'm not going to spend another second with someone who is too hotheaded to even hear my side of the story. I'm so sick of people throwing accusations at me. I haven't done anything wrong. Welcome to my life's story. I'm just a good guy in a shitty situation. And I refuse to let anyone tell me otherwise. I'm done. Get out."

CHAPTER 31

Hailey

Wednesday

I wanted to believe him. But how could I trust him over a cop? Tyler was in trouble. He was on the run. And I should have been running away from him. My feet had an idea of their own though. They seemed frozen in place.

I knew grief. I knew suffering. And that's what was all over Tyler's face. Not guilt. I knew him. It was crazy and fast, but I did. Tyler wasn't capable of killing someone. He was good. He was so good.

"Can I hear the whole story?"

"I'm trying to forget, Hails." He turned away from me.

I dropped my duffel bag back on the ground and walked over to him. "It's easier to forget if you get it off your chest." I slipped my hand into his.

He looked down at my hand. For a second, he let his fingers intertwine with mine, but then he removed his hand and scratched the back of his neck. "It's simple, really. I fell in love with a girl. She fell in love with someone else."

"I don't think it's that simple."

He sighed. "Actually, it kind of is. Do you know their story at all?" He gestured toward the TV.

An image of Penny and James Hunter was still on the screen. I grabbed the remote and switched it off. "I know that he was her professor. That's pretty much it."

Tyler sat down on the edge of the bed. "Yeah, well, Penny and I met in his class. I was a senior, she was a sophomore. I had been going through some things and for some reason, she just made me smile. I needed that." He looked down at his hands, which were clasped together.

I wanted to know what things he had been going through, but I kept my lips sealed.

"She led me on. Or maybe I led myself on. I don't even know anymore. She kept telling me she was getting over her ex and that she just wanted to be friends. But she didn't act like she just wanted to be friends. It was always more than that." He shook his head. "She flirted back. It wasn't one sided. It never was. But the whole time I was falling for her, she was actually dating James. She was falling for James and lying to me about it. Lying to everyone. And when I found out, I was so pissed. I stopped talking to her. And it sucked. I was depressed again..." his voice trailed off.

Tyler was quiet for a moment. "They broke up a little while after that. She completely disappeared inside of herself. She was just this wisp of the person that I loved. And I couldn't stand it. I told her we could be friends. Because it killed me to see her hurting. I told myself that I could be okay with that. But then it was there again. That feeling that it was more. And it was. For one night, she validated all my thoughts. I let myself think that there really could be a future between us. That she'd get over him. That we could be together."

He shook his head. "The very next day, she got back together with James. And maybe I'm a fucking idiot for just letting it happen. But she was happy with him. He could give her a life I couldn't."

"You mean the money?" Suddenly it all made sense. Why Tyler seemed so upset that I was in awe of Josh's place.

Tyler looked up at me. "It was easy to fixate on that. But I know it was more than that. She just didn't like me." He looked away from me again. "No matter how much I liked her, it didn't change that fact. So I just accepted it. I told myself I had to move on. I applied for a job in New York and was excited to move away when I graduated. But then they fucking moved there too.

"Penny and I got into this routine of being just friends. It was easy. I just liked having her in my life. I guess I kind of repressed my true feelings for her for years, though, because when they called the wedding off, all I wanted to do was tell her."

I hadn't known that they had called the wedding off. I was surprised the tabloids hadn't picked up that story. I swallowed hard.

"I told her how I really felt. That I had always loved her and that I always would. She told me that she'd always love him."

I pressed my lips together. *He'd always love her?*

"Even if they never got back together, Penny said she'd never move on. She said she could never love me." He sighed. "That's it. I'm the biggest fucking joke."

I sat down next to him on the bed. To me it sounded like Penny was a tease. Running to him whenever there was the smallest problem in her relationship with James. Which was fine to do if they were just friends. But clearly it was more than that. She had to have known that. And I hated her for hurting him. Even if it wasn't intentional.

"But why are the cops coming after you?"

"Because James' ex wife is a psychopath. She's trying to set me up."

"Why?"

"I don't know. To break them up or something. She made it look like I stole money from them. And when that clearly didn't work, the psycho shot him. I have no idea why they're looking at me."

"So on the news when they said it was Penny's ex and best friend?"

Tyler shrugged. "Me and Melissa I guess. Which is crazy. I would never do anything to hurt Penny and neither would Melissa."

"And you broke up with Melissa because you realized you were still in love with Penny?"

"Yeah."

"And now you're traveling across the country to get away from all of it?"

Tyler didn't say anything.

"Why aren't you going back, though? If James dies..."

"I'm done being second. I'll be there for Penny as a friend if she wants, but nothing more. And I meant what I said before, Hails. I'm where I want to be. These past few days with you have been some of the best I've had in a long time."

"Me too." I took a deep breath. "I think I've been accidentally putting myself in a similar situation."

"What do you mean?"

I looked up into Tyler's baby blue eyes. "I'm falling for a guy that will never love me as much as he loves someone else." A tear trickled down my cheek. I lifted my hand to wipe it away, but his hand beat mine. He brushed away my tear with his thumb. It felt more intimate than any other moment between us before.

"I've been holding on to my feelings for Penny because it feels like I'm drowning when I don't have them. But it's not because of her. It's because of my own problems. I don't want to feel the way I do. I want to move on." His eyes searched mine.

"We can heal each other."

"That's the thing, Hails, I don't think you need healing. I think you need someone as whole and full of energy and life as you." He brushed away another of my tears.

"I think that maybe I just need you."

"You don't need me." He pressed his forehead against mine. His words and actions contradicted each other so fiercely. Like he was telling me no but beckoning me forward.

I breathed in his breaths. He tasted so sweet. Every second with him was better than any I had ever experienced before. "When I'm with you, I feel like everything's going to work out. Come back to Indiana with me. Please, I don't want this to end. Your heart is bigger than you realize. There's room for me too."

"I can't."

"Why?"

"When I left New York I felt like I needed something to hold on to."

"Hold on to me."

He brushed my tears away again. "If I could, I would. I'm falling for you. All I want to do is stay right here with you and forget the world."

That's what I wanted too. But the world wasn't stopping. And I was running out of time to save my dad. "Stop time back in Indiana."

"I joined the Marine Corps."

I lifted my forehead off his. "What?"

"I needed to make a change. It seemed like the right choice."

For some reason I couldn't process his words. "I don't understand. You joined the marines?"

"I'm heading to California because that's where basic training is."

Oh my God. It felt like my heart was beating out of my chest. "When do you have to report?"

"Friday."

I shook my head. "This Friday? As in two days from today?"

He nodded.

I was completely speechless. So that's what him and Josh were talking about when Josh said he only had a few days of freedom left.

"I'm sorry. I should have told you sooner. I've just been trying to clear my head on this trip. I needed to not think about it the whole time."

"But last night...it seemed like you were going to come back with me. Tyler, I meant what I said. I'm falling in love with you. I don't just say that all the time. I mean it."

"I'm falling for you too." He touched the side of my face. "For just a second I wanted to believe it could be more."

"This doesn't mean it can't be."

His hand fell from my cheek as he stood up. "It does."

I stood up too. "No, it doesn't."

"I signed up for three years. We've known each other five days. I'd never ask you to wait for me."

"Then don't ask me. Let me make my own decision."

"I wasted three years of my life pining over a girl who didn't reciprocate those feelings. I'm broken, Hails. You deserve so much more than that. I wouldn't let you wait. Not when we don't know what we even have. Three years is a long time. I would never do that to someone."

I know what we have. And I had two days to show him what I already knew. That we were two pieces of the same puzzle. Cast aside. Lost. Second. I knew how he felt. I knew what it was like to not be good enough for someone.

Proving to him that we could be more would take my mind off the nerves dancing around my stomach as we got closer and closer to Pasadena. It gave me something to hope for. Something big and scary and so wonderfully exciting. I hadn't had something like that in my life for a long time. "Okay."

"Okay?" he asked.

"Let's just enjoy our last few days together then. Let's make the most of it. A grand send off for you."

Tyler smiled sheepishly. It was probably the cutest thing I had ever seen.

"As long as you promise you're not a criminal."

He laughed as he stepped toward me. "Unless what I'm about to do to your body is criminal."

"It depends on what you're going to do."

I laughed as he picked me up over his shoulder and carried me toward the bathroom.

CHAPTER 32

Tyler

Wednesday

Every time I glanced at Hailey out of the corner of my eye, she somehow caught my gaze and smiled. I noticed everything now, like my senses were heightened. The freckles on her shoulders and across the bridge of her nose. The dimples she got when she smiled. The chestnut highlights in her hair when the sun shone through the car window. I wanted to remember everything before it was gone.

She was stubborn and feisty and so different from any other girl I had dated. I found her determination sexy. And the way she belted out the songs on the radio like she had no inhibitions. I hadn't realized I could fall for someone so quickly. It was going to be hard to say goodbye. My mind wouldn't stop thinking about that fact. In two days I'd be saying goodbye. I didn't want it to end.

"Ah!" Hails screamed when a new song started on the radio. "It's our song!" She turned up the volume as Beside Me by the Cigarsmoakers came on. She started singing the lyrics at the top of her lungs.

I laughed as she put the windows down and let the breeze flow through her hair as she sang, "We're never getting older." She smiled at me and I swore my heart stopped.

How was I supposed to say goodbye? I didn't want to. It was like my life was a series of events spiraling out of control. If I didn't make stupid, rash decisions, maybe I'd be happy. But maybe I never would have met Hailey. Maybe all those bad choices had allowed me to enjoy this moment. This beautiful girl that was so out of my league had told me she was falling for me. And I was fucking falling for her too. Hell, I had never felt this strong of a connection before. Not even with Penny.

"Stay, and blast that Wink-183 song, that we played to death in Tucson, alright!" She lightly hit my shoulder as she sang the lyrics. "We're so close to Tucson! It's like it was meant to be." She smiled again.

Hailey made me feel better than I had in years. I felt young and carefree and hopeful. I felt alive again. It was greedy, but I didn't want to let go of that feeling. I didn't want to let go of her.

"What?" she said with a smile on her face.

"I was just thinking about how beautiful you are."

She laughed. "Yeah right. Hey, I think we're almost there."

I could see some cars parked up ahead, but I couldn't really see anything. I thought driving up to the Grand Canyon would be this breathtaking experience. But I guess you had to be right on it to even see it. I glanced back at Hailey. Her eyes were glued to the window. It broke my heart a little that she didn't know she was beautiful, that she didn't know how much she affected me. I wanted to give her everything. Yet at the same time, I wanted to give her nothing so it wouldn't hurt so damn much when we went our separate ways.

CHAPTER 33

Hailey

Wednesday

"Oh my God." I opened up the car door as soon as it stopped. I walked out to the edge of the Grand Canyon and stared at the expanse, completely transfixed. There were no words. I swallowed hard as tears came to my eyes.

"It's like standing by the ocean. It makes you feel so small," Tyler said as he joined me.

I shook my head. "I wouldn't know."

"You've really never been to the beach?"

"I visited Lake Michigan a few times. But I can't imagine it's the same. From pictures I've seen of the ocean, I mean." I didn't really think the ocean could be this beautiful, though. Nothing could be.

"Maybe we could add one last stop to our trip?" he said. "I've actually never seen the Pacific Ocean."

I slipped my hand into his. "I'd like that," I whispered as I stared out at the crater in front of me. Breathtaking. It was breathtaking.

He squeezed my hand back in response.

Tyler was right. Looking at it made me feel so small. There must be something more out there. Something that made all this. And something after this. I wasn't really sure why, but I started to cry silent tears.

We both stood there in silence as we stared out at the abyss.

"Hails."

I looked up at him.

With his hand that wasn't holding mine, he reached up and wiped my tears away with his thumbs. He didn't ask me why I was crying. He didn't really need to. It just felt like Tyler got me. And the look on his face said it all. He looked concerned. He looked worried about me. With him, it didn't feel like my biggest fear could come true. I could never be alone if he was with me. But he wasn't going to be with me. I turned my head to look back out at the scenery.

I was crying because my dad might never get to see it. He might never touch the ocean. It wasn't fair. Life was so cruel. Tyler had opened up to me. He had let me see a vulnerable side of him. But I couldn't do it. I couldn't tell him my worries and fears if he was going to cut me out in a couple days. It was already going to hurt too much. Telling him about my dad would make it more painful when we had to say goodbye. Why the hell did we have to say goodbye?

Instead of pressing the issue, he stepped behind me and wrapped his arms around me. We both stared out in front of us. I didn't want to be crying. What I wanted was to scream and throw things into the canyon. I wanted to not give up on Tyler before we had even had a chance to try. I took a deep breath. There was no reason to dwell on it. If he didn't want whatever this was to continue after Friday, there wasn't anything I could do about it. All I could do was have fun the next couple days and see if he still felt the same way. I wasn't pathetic. I wasn't going to beg him.

"It's going to be okay, Hails."

I closed my eyes. The moment was too perfect. For some reason, I couldn't have Tyler's arms around me and see something so beautiful at the same time. It was sensory overload. And I'd rather focus on Tyler's arms. Who was I kidding? I was pathetic. I wanted to cling to him because I loved the feeling he gave me. That anything was possible. It was childish and naive. And fleeting. It's not like I was actually in love with him or anything. That would be crazy. Besides, he was in love with someone else.

It'll be okay? No, it fucking wouldn't. I shrugged out of his arms and stepped to the edge until my toes were actually sticking off the side. And I screamed. I screamed at the top of my lungs. I screamed because I was frustrated with Tyler. Because I was worried I was going to lose my dad. And because I was terrified of actually getting to Pasadena and facing my fears. I knew people were staring at me. But I didn't care. God, this felt good. I balled my hands into fists and screamed again.

I thought Tyler might say something. That he might be embarrassed of me. It would be a normal reaction to some girl you just met screaming at nothing. But I didn't care about the onlookers. Let them judge me. Let them see me scream.

What I didn't expect was for Tyler to step up right beside me and scream too.

"Wow, that feels good," he said. And then he screamed again even louder.

People started stepping away from us.

I laughed and grabbed his hand again. Together we both screamed as loud as we could, letting our pain and fears echo off the dips and valleys of the canyon.

"Feel better?" he asked.

I smiled up at him. "So much better. Come on." I pulled him back toward the car. "I think I want to go to Vegas after all."

"Yeah?"

If it delayed getting to Pasadena by one day, then absolutely. I didn't look back at the Grand Canyon. I felt like I had thrown my worries, fears, frustrations, and insecurities into it. It was now a pit of everything I wanted to offload. And now I needed to move on. No more looking back. I was only looking forward.

CHAPTER 34

Tyler

Wednesday

"There is no way in hell that I'm wearing that," Hailey said as she stared at the red dress I was holding up.

I laughed. "If we're going to Vegas, we should do it right." I tossed it at her.

"Why does doing Vegas right mean I have to dress like a hooker and you get to wear that."

I pulled on the lapels of the $20 suit I had just picked out from the thrift store. "I can't help it that I look good in everything." I winked at her.

She rolled her eyes.

"Plus...I'm paying," I said.

"You're not my pimp, Tyler Stevens. I can pay for my own clothes. And I like this one." She gestured to the frou-frou skirt she was wearing. It covered way too much of her perfect legs. It was almost sinful.

I leaned against the doorjamb of the changing room. "At least try on the red one."

"Fine. But I'm not going to like it."

I laughed and stepped away from the door as she slammed it in my face. I wasn't exactly sure how we had ended up in a thrift store just minutes away from the Las Vegas strip. Hailey had insisted she wanted to do the Las Vegas scene right, and now she was suddenly being shy.

Why she felt uncomfortable showing off her perfect body, I had no idea.

The door to the changing room opened a crack. "Seriously, Tyler, it shouldn't even count as a dress. There's not enough fabric for it to garner that definition."

I pushed the door open. She was breathtaking. The tight red fabric plunged low in the front and tied around her neck, leaving her back completely bare as well. And the hem of the skirt landed right below her ass.

She shifted, trying to pull the fabric down her thighs.

"You look sexy as hell."

Her face turned red. "Stop it."

"Hails, seriously, you have to wear that."

"Wear what? This isn't a dress!"

I laughed and pulled her into my arms. "You're perfect, you do realize that, right?"

She blinked up at me. Her eyes were such a warm shade of brown. Almost caramel colored. Every time they landed on me, I got completely lost in them.

"So you want me to walk around...in public...in this dress?"

"Absolutely." I let my hands slide to her ass. "And in those shoes." I nodded to a pair of stilettos I had placed by the dressing room door.

She laughed. "Fine. But only if I get to pick you out a bowtie to wear."

"Done. I can rock a bowtie."

She reached around me and grabbed the most ridiculous red and black polka dot bowtie I had ever seen. She pulled one of my hands off her ass and placed the bowtie in it.

"It matches your dress. Couldn't get any better than this." I looped it around the collar of my shirt and tied it in place.

Hailey put her hands on her hips. "I'm impressed. I didn't think you'd have any idea how to tie it."

"Being in a frat had its perks. I know how to dress to the nines." I watched her strap on the matching red heels. Her legs looked even longer, if that was possible.

She laughed. "Right. Well, we better get going." She grabbed the clothes she had been wearing and walked toward the checkout. "The night is young," she said over her shoulder with a seductive flip of her hair and a sway of her hips.

I smiled as I followed her. I ignored her protests as I paid for our outfits. And I looped my arm around her waist as we walked back to the car.

"You look so pleased with yourself," she said with smile. "Just for the record, I'm going to make you work for it tonight. I don't just put out for a nice dress."

"I never imagined that you would. That's not the type of girl you are at all."

"And what type of girl am I?"

"Oh, you're definitely a ball buster."

She laughed. "I am not. Although with these shoes, I'm sure I could bust a few."

"Remind me not to upset you tonight." I opened up the passenger side door for her.

"Well aren't you quite the gentleman?" She straightened my bowtie and then climbed into the car.

I wasn't sure what changed her mind about stopping in Las Vegas. She had completely thrown the fact that she was in a hurry out the window. Maybe she screamed away whatever was bothering her at the Grand Canyon. I know that I did. God, it felt so good to scream at the top of my lungs. I don't think I had done that since I was a kid. Maybe everyone needed to throw a temper tantrum every now and then, even as an adult.

Either way, tonight was going to be so much fun. Hailey was in a great mood and it was definitely contagious. I couldn't not smile when she was smiling. One last night with her before she went back to Indiana. I ignored the sinking feeling in my stomach as I climbed into the car. I just needed tonight to count for something. Even though I wasn't going to ask her to wait for me, I wanted her to remember me. Maybe when she was old and gray she'd look back and think this was one of the best summers of her life. I knew I didn't need to wait that long to feel that way about this summer. What had started out as one of the worst summers of my life had been completely transformed by her.

"What are you looking at?" she said.

I shook my head. "Nothing."

"I'm pretty sure you were looking at my breasts." She folded her arms across her chest.

Maybe with some other girl I would have been. But it was more than just physical attraction with Hailey. I was attracted to who she was as a person. Everything she was just made her that much more beautiful.

"It's too low, right?" She adjusted the straps.

"Hails, you look gorgeous."

"It's really unnerving when you call me gorgeous."

"Why?"

"Because no one ever has before."

How could her ex boyfriend not have told her how beautiful she was on a daily basis? Did he really not see how lucky he was? "What about your ex boyfriend?"

"No. He'd call me sexy sometimes. Or hot. But never gorgeous."

"Well, he sounds like an asshole. I hate to break it to you, but you're the most beautiful girl I've ever met." I swallowed hard when she didn't respond. It had just kind of spilled out. But it was true. The only reason I wanted to unsay it was because of how she was staring at me.

She leaned her head back on the headrest. "What about Penny?"

What about Penny? The question seemed to echo around in my head. I used to think about her all the time. But I hadn't thought about her once since Hailey and my conversation this morning. She hadn't even crossed my mind. For a second I let myself feel guilty. I should have been worried about her. I should have been wondering how she was. But I didn't feel guilty. I felt...free. I exhaled slowly.

"Sorry," she said with a laugh. "That was a dumb question." She turned her head to stare out the window.

"Hails?"

"Really, Tyler, it's okay." She tucked a loose strand of hair behind her ear. "I've seen her on TV and in magazines and...everywhere. She's stunning."

Apparently Hailey was as blind as her ex boyfriend. "I meant what I said. You're the most beautiful girl I've ever met."

She laughed.

"I mean it, Hails. It's hard driving because all I want to do is stare at you."

Her cheeks flushed. "You're not so bad yourself."

I laughed. "It's probably the bowtie."

"For sure."

CHAPTER 35

Hailey

Wednesday

Gorgeous. Did he really think I was gorgeous? I had always considered myself lanky. But the way he stared at my legs made it seem like he admired them. What was I supposed to do with that compliment? I tried to keep my eyes glued to the window instead of on him. Was he purposely making it hard for me to say goodbye to him tomorrow?

I bit my lip. Or maybe my plan was working. Maybe he was reconsidering. I understood his concerns. Three years was a really long time. But I was pretty sure he'd get a few days away from the marines every now and then. It's not like I wouldn't see him for three years. Unless he got shipped off. I suddenly realized why he had said his greatest fear was death a few days ago. A chill ran down my spine.

But I didn't get a chance to ask him, because he interrupted my train of thought. "Geez, look," he said.

I turned my attention to the windshield. There were lights everywhere. We must have just turned onto the Las Vegas strip. The sun was setting, but instead of the buildings looking dull, they popped in a million different colors with lights blazing.

"It's...bright," I said.

Tyler laughed. "That's exactly how I was going to describe it."

We slowed down from the volume of traffic on the strip. My eyes stayed glued to the window. It was like we had just driven into a whole other world.

We suddenly stopped. I hadn't even realized that Tyler had pulled over.

He turned off the ignition. "Do you want to just walk around and explore?"

I smiled. "That sounds perfect." I stepped out of the car. There was an electricity in the air. "Is this how New York is?" I asked when he came to my side of the car.

"It's different. I don't really know how to explain it."

A group of women passed by us, laughing. One was wearing a sash that said "bride to be."

"Actually, I know what it is." Tyler slipped his hand around my waist. "The energy is different. People seem happy here."

"And they don't in New York?" I looked up at him. Maybe it was because he wasn't happy in New York. But he was happy here with me.

He smiled down at me. "No, everyone's always kind of in a rush and unfriendly in the city. I grew up in a pretty small town like you. I'm used to people being nice."

We started walking down the street.

"Do you prefer a small town? Would you want to end up in one whenever you settle down?"

"Yeah, I think that would be nice."

My heart seemed to warm. I'd wait for three years for him. Couldn't he see that? I'd wait my whole life for him. This feeling that I had right now didn't even compare to anything I had ever felt before. I couldn't even look around at Vegas because my eyes were glued to him.

"Do you want to check anything out? It would be pretty cool to see a casino."

I reluctantly peeled my eyes away from him and looked around. We were passing by an immense building. There was a huge pond and fountains in different colors out front. "Now that has to be the fanciest building I've ever seen," I said. "It looks like something out of a movie."

"That's because it's been in a lot of movies. It's the Bellagio."

"I've never heard of it."

"It was in Ocean's Eleven."

I shrugged.

Tyler laughed.

I leaned toward the sound. It didn't matter where we were as long as I was with him. But I could feel it in my bones. Tonight was going to be a night to remember. "Is it a casino?"

"I think it's a casino and hotel." He took a step back from me and held out his hand. "Shall we, m'lady?"

I laughed and grabbed his hand. "After you, kind sir."

He held my hand as we walked up to the front of the Bellagio. Valets were rushing around opening car doors. I took a second to turn in a circle, studying everything, taking it all in. For a moment, I felt like a movie star. I'd probably never be standing in front of a building like this again. This was the closest to royal treatment I'd ever get.

Tyler's hand slid around my waist and my eyes landed on his as he pulled me close. My eyes always gravitated back to him. He was all I really wanted to look at.

He leaned down and kissed me right in the middle of the bustle of people. Normally I'd be self-conscious about something like that. But we'd never see any of these people again. And if I felt like kissing the man I was falling for, I was going to kiss him. It was like I was in a dream. If it was a movie, the camera would be spinning around us, taking in the perfect scene. Taste. Touch. Sound. This moment was everything. He made me forget about my worries and fears. He made me feel whole again. And I wasn't ready to let go. I just had to make him see that we could make it work. That we could be more than just this moment.

I straightened his bowtie after he pulled back. Tonight I'd make him realize just how great we could be. "So...it's a hotel too?"

He smiled. "I think you promised me that I'd have to work for it tonight."

You can have me whenever you want. "I guess you better beat me in a game of poker then."

"Are you good at poker?" He raised his eyebrow.

"Tyler Stevens, I'm an ace at poker." I poked him in the middle of the chest and smiled seductively.

"I guess it's time to put your money where your mouth is."

I stood up on my tiptoes and put my lips to his ear. "I'd rather put my mouth on you." I smiled as I watched his Adam's apple rise and fall. I immediately took a step back. "But you'll have to earn it first," I said over my shoulder as I walked up the steps of the casino.

Again I was overwhelmed with sensations. It was all gold and bright lights and noise everywhere. Tyler was right, everyone seemed happy. People came here to party and let loose. And that was exactly what I was going to do.

"This way," I said and grabbed Tyler's hand. I pulled him over to a table with some empty seats. It was time to show him just what kind of girl he'd be walking away from.

CHAPTER 36

Tyler
Wednesday

Hailey wasn't kidding when she said she was good at poker. She was completely annihilating everyone at the table, including me. And it was probably the sexiest thing I had ever witnessed. I was almost convinced that she was counting cards.

I studied her face as she looked at her hand. She bit her lip as she mulled over what to do and then immediately smiled as she switched out a card. I honestly had no idea what I was doing. I knew how to play poker, but she was so distracting. Especially in that dress. Her skin was begging to be touched. Her lips were begging to be on mine. And I wanted it all. I just needed her to finish this game and then I was pulling her away.

"Read 'em and weep," she said as she slammed her cards down on the table. A royal flush.

Fuck, how is she doing this? I put my cards down on the table and sighed. "I'm calling it quits before I lose all my money."

She laughed and her eyes twinkled. "Okay, I'm done too."

The rest of the people looked relieved as we made our way to the bar.

"Seriously, Hails, how are you so good at poker?"

"I'm not actually good at poker. I'm just really good at reading people's tells."

I laughed. "And what's my tell?"

"When you bluff, you scratch the back of your neck."

"I don't do that."

"Actually you do." She reached up and touched the base of my neck. "Right here." She slowly ran her fingertips up my neck and into my hair. "Tyler, I'm not thirsty."

I glanced at the bar behind us and then back at her. "Then what do you want to do?" I had already bought a hotel room for the night after one of the many times she beat me in poker. I had said I was going to the bathroom, but I was growing antsy. This was the last night we had together. This was it. And it was exhilarating and heart breaking at the same time. I pulled one of the key cards to our room out of my pocket and slid it into her hand.

She looked deep into my eyes as a smile spread across her face. "I have a better idea. Let's go for a swim."

"What?"

But she had already grabbed my hand and was pulling me out of the casino. All I could do was laugh and run outside beside her. She really did make me feel like a kid again. I felt alive for the first time in years. She made me happy. She made me live in the moment, and I really needed that.

We came to a stop alongside the biggest pool I had ever seen. The biggest, emptiest pool. There was caution tape around the pool, but it still looked like it was functioning. A fountain in the center of it was lit up majestically. It was beautiful.

She lifted up the caution tape and ducked beneath it.

"Hails, I don't think we're supposed to go under that."

"I'm sure we're not." She kicked off her shoes and smiled at me.

I laughed. "I don't think this is a good idea."

"What? Are you chicken?" She stepped toward the edge of the pool. "What's the worst that could happen? You're already on the run from the cops."

I laughed as I ducked under the caution tape. "So we're in the heart of Vegas and all you want to do is go for a swim?"

She nodded. She looked so pretty in the glow emanating off the pool lights. It almost felt like I was dreaming. The most beautiful girl I had ever laid my eyes on wanted me. This had to be a dream.

"What are you so scared of?" she asked with a seductive smile.

Falling for you. But in my head I knew it was too late. I didn't want to say goodbye to this girl tomorrow. I couldn't even imagine it. No one would ever make me feel this whole again. I'm pretty sure I had already fallen. I swallowed down the lump in my throat. *Fuck.*

"I dare you," she said with smile.

"Oh, well in that case." I walked over to the edge of the pool beside her. "And since you lied during truth or dare..." I grabbed her hand and jumped into the water, pulling her in with me.

Her laughter was drowned out by the sound of us splashing into the water. I had never swam in shoes before and definitely not a suit and bowtie. When I emerged from the water, I was greeted by her smiling face.

"I was actually going to say we should skinny dip," she said as she wrapped her arms around the back of my neck and hitched her legs around my hips. "But this is way better."

"Especially since your dress is virtually see-through when it's wet."

"What?" she said with a laugh as she looked down at the front of her dress. "Oh my God."

I hadn't been lying. You could clearly see her nipples through the tight red fabric.

She pressed herself more firmly against my torso to help hide herself. "I have a confession to make."

I slid my hands to her ass. "And what is that?"

"I don't think Vegas is really for me. I like wearing jeans and tank tops. And watching a movie or reading a book at night. This place is insane. And I really just wanted to come out here because it's way too bright inside."

God this girl was perfect for me. "I agree with all of that. Except I'd probably be wearing sweatpants and no shirt."

She smiled. "I think I could get used to that."

And her words broke my heart a little. Because I could get used to it too. I wanted to come home to her every day.

"Tyler?" she said, batting her wet eyelashes.

"Hailey?"

She smiled. "You do realize that whenever we both get wet we end up in each other's arms?"

"I've noticed."

"I don't want tonight to end." She pressed her forehead against mine. "I just want to stay in this moment forever. I want to stop time."

I took a deep breath. "Me too." *God, me too.*

"Then let me change your mind." She pulled her face away from mine. Her eyes had suddenly grown teary. And it killed me. Because I wanted her to be able to. I wanted to be able to hold on to her. But I couldn't be that selfish. I would never do that to her.

"I can only give you tonight, Hails. That's all I have left."

CHAPTER 37

Hailey

Wednesday

I searched his face. That wasn't true. He had more than just tonight. He had his whole life. Three years wasn't that long. "I'll wait for you."

He tucked a loose strand of hair behind my ear. "I don't want you to."

I knew he was being kind, in his own way. But the words sounded harsh to my ears. Maybe if I was someone else he'd want me to wait. Maybe it was me. I unwound my legs from his waist and unclasped my hands from his neck.

"Hails." His face looked pained. "That came out wrong. I just...I couldn't live with myself if I made you wait."

"You wouldn't be making me wait. I'd be choosing to. And it's not like I wouldn't get to see you for three years. You get leave. We could talk on the phone."

"I can't, Hailey."

"Some girls are married to men who are enlisted. You're blowing this out of proportion. People do this all the time."

"Exactly, Hails. People that are married. They've known each other for a long time. We haven't."

"I know the way you make me feel."

He didn't say anything in response. Which in its own way was the only response I needed. I didn't make him feel the way he made me feel. Or else he'd want to see what we had. It felt like my world was crashing down around me. I swam over to the edge of the pool and hoisted myself out.

I grabbed my shoes and started walking back toward the hotel.

"Hails, wait."

But I was already closing the door behind me. I was so embarrassed. I ran over to the elevator and hit the button with my fist, trying to ignore the people staring at me and the puddle of water that I was leaving on the ornate marble flooring. All day had been fun and lighthearted and I had just ruined it. As soon as the elevator doors opened, I stepped inside.

That had been my last chance to change his mind. I looked down at the keycard in my hand. I had no idea why I was running to our hotel room. It wasn't like that was escaping from him. He was just going to follow me and I was just going to tell him everything was fine. But it wasn't. His constant rejection was slowly unraveling me. Or maybe I was already unraveled. The doors dinged open when the elevator reached my floor.

As soon as I was in my room, I let my back slide down the wall until my butt hit the floor. And I let myself cry. Really cry. For the first time since I had found out about my dad and the bar. For the first time since my life as I knew it was over. I cried because I was terrified. And not just terrified of losing my dad, but terrified of seeing Elena tomorrow. I was upset with myself for feeling weak. I was crying because I had fallen in love with a boy who loved someone else. The thought just made me cry harder. *I loved him.* How could I love him after only knowing him for several days? I shouldn't have felt like this. How had I let myself be this vulnerable?

I heard the door click open, but I didn't look up.

"Hailey?" His voice was gentle as he put his hand on my shoulder.

"Tyler, I get it, okay?" I wiped away my tears without looking at him. "You don't have to say anything."

"I don't think you do."

"No, I definitely do. I'm not worth waiting for. It's pretty simple, really." I pushed his hands off of me and stood up.

"That's not what I said."

"Okay, fine. I'm not as good as her, then."

"Who? Penny? Hails, this has nothing to do with Penny."

"Doesn't it?"

He put his hand under my chin and made me look at him. "It's me, okay? It's nothing you did."

"Just stop. You don't have to feed me some bullshit line, Tyler. If you felt the same way I feel, it wouldn't matter. You make me feel like I can breathe again. You make me laugh. You make me feel like everything is going to be okay. You make me feel safe." *God, I'm pathetic.*

Again he didn't say anything. And again it made my blood boil.

"God, I'm such an idiot," I said.

"No. No, Hails. I feel it too."

I shook my head.

"You make me feel whole again." He stepped forward, effectively sandwiching me between him and the wall. "You make me feel like there's something worth living for."

I watched his Adam's apple rise and fall.

"You make me feel like I'm not broken. I'm so sick of feeling broken."

"You're not broken, Tyler." I touched the side of his face. "Not to me."

He leaned forward and placed a gentle kiss against my lips. I leaned into him. But this was different than our other kisses. There was no haste. It was slow and passionate. And if it was possible, I loved it even more.

"You deserve more than what I can give you," he whispered against my lips. "You deserve so much more."

"I just want you. I only want what you can give me."

He lifted me in his arms and placed me gently on the bed. His face looked pained. Maybe he didn't feel like he could say how he felt. But that was okay, because he didn't have to say it. He wanted to give me the world. I could see it in his eyes. And I just hoped that I was enough for him. That I could fill that hole in his heart.

I held my breath as he knelt down in front of me on the bed. He locked eyes with me as he spread my thighs apart and leaned down between them. He kissed the inside of my thigh and made a slow ascent up.

Jesus.

Every other time we had been intimate I had asked him to fuck me. But that wasn't what I wanted in this moment. I wanted all of him. His body, his soul, his heart. He already had mine.

***

My chest felt tight because we hadn't come to any understanding. He made love to me like it was his last chance. Not like it was the start of something great, but like it was the end. I didn't want to face reality. I wanted to live in this dream world that we created. Where we traveled all over the US and stayed in fancy hotels. I wasn't ready to say goodbye. I wasn't ready to face whatever came next.

Tyler's arms were wrapped tightly around me and his breathing was deep. I knew he was asleep. I turned toward him and stared at his perfect face in the darkness. "I love you," I whispered to him. And I knew he couldn't hear me. It was probably better that way. But I also knew I'd regret it my whole life if I never told him. "I love you, Tyler Stevens."

My eyes prickled with tears. Today was going to be hard. First I had to get down on my hands and knees and beg Elena for money that I feared she wouldn't give me. And then I had to say goodbye to Tyler. Even though my heart was filled with fear at the idea of seeing Elena, I knew the latter would be harder. Saying goodbye to Tyler was going to break me. Especially since I didn't understand why I had to. I didn't understand why his heart wasn't big enough for me, why no one's ever was.

The sun was starting to stream through the windows, casting shadows across Tyler's face. Maybe I was crazy. I didn't really know Tyler. I didn't know his dreams and goals. I didn't even know his middle name. All I knew was his pain. But in my heart, I knew that if this side of him was so wonderful, if he gave me all of him, it would be amazing. I was in love with this pained version of him because it was a reflection of myself. And for a brief moment, we had both been so much better, so much happier.

I studied the scruff along his strong jaw line and the slope of his nose. I tried to memorize every detail. I wanted something to hold on to when I went home. Something good. Something more hopeful than the fear that resided in my own heart. And even as I thought it, I felt myself putting my walls back up. I just hoped it wasn't too late to protect myself from shattering into a million pieces.

CHAPTER 38

Tyler

Thursday

I woke up to the sound of the TV. I slowly opened my eyes. Hailey was sitting on the edge of the bed in a tank top and cutoff jean shorts, completely engrossed in the TV. I glanced at the screen.

The news reporter was standing outside the hospital talking about how tech mogul, James Hunter, had just woken up from his coma. I quickly sat up in bed. "He's awake?"

Hailey turned toward me and smiled. "Yeah."

"Thank God." I sighed. I hadn't realized how worried I had actually been until it was finally over. He was awake. Penny was going to be okay. I didn't have to worry anymore. *I don't have to think about her anymore.* Maybe I could finally let go. Maybe we really could just be friends. I stared at the back of Hailey's head. The truth was, I didn't have feelings for Penny anymore. Josh was probably right. When I had met her, I needed something good to hold on to. What if I was doing the same thing with Hailey? If I was being honest, I was scared shitless of joining the marines. Maybe I was focusing on her so much because it made me feel better. I needed to stop making the same mistakes. I needed to stick to my gut and focus on the decisions I had already made. In three years, if I really did feel the same way, I'd find her. But I couldn't think about that right now. For once in my life, I had to focus on myself.

"Are you going to call her?" Hailey asked. "To see if she's okay?"

I shook my head. "No. I know she's okay." Now that James was awake, she was good. She'd be okay.

Hailey nodded and switched off the TV. "Could we maybe get going? I brought your stuff in from the car." She gestured to the bags on the floor as she stood up.

I wasn't in a hurry to get going. We hadn't really talked about it, but the original plan was to drop her off in Pasadena. To say goodbye. The thought made me feel slightly nauseous. But it was inevitable. Today had to be goodbye. Maybe she'd still want to see the Pacific Ocean though. I just needed a little more time.

"Yeah." I climbed out of bed and stretched. "Do you know where in Pasadena you're going exactly?"

"I have it all mapped out." She pulled the map out of the back pocket of her jeans. "It takes about three and a half hours to get there from here."

I pulled on a t-shirt. "Do you want breakfast before we get going? I'm starving."

"Sure." She didn't look at me. Her fingers were pulling on the strands of fabric on her jean shorts.

I could tell she was nervous, but I didn't really know what to say. Instead, I wrapped my arms around her. "It's going to be okay."

"You don't know that."

I ran my fingers through her hair. "If worse comes to worst and the business fails, you can start over, Hails. I know it seems bad right now, but it won't break you."

She stepped back from me and pulled her sunglasses down over her eyes. "Yeah, of course. What doesn't kill you makes you stronger right?" She didn't try to hide the sarcasm in her voice. "Let's just get this over with okay?" She pulled her duffel bag over her shoulder and walked out of the room.

***

Hailey barely spoke during breakfast. And now I had been watching her knee bounce up and down nonstop for three hours in the car.

This morning I had thought she was worried about going to Pasadena and applying for the loan she needed. But now it seemed like she was just mad at me. And as the minutes ticked by and I got closer to saying goodbye, it was starting to feel like I couldn't breathe. I didn't want to walk away on a bad note. I didn't want to remember our time together like this.

I cleared my throat. "Do you want to talk about it?" I asked.

"No. Not really." Her eyes stayed glued to the map in her lap.

"I need you to know how much this past week has meant to me. How much you..."

"Not everything is about you, Tyler." She was gripping the map so tightly that it was starting to tear under her hands.

"Okay." Neither one of us said anything for a few minutes. I cleared my throat again. "There's plenty of places to get loans."

She shook her head. "Not when you owe as much money as we do." Her knee continued to bounce up and down.

I placed my hand on it. "It's going to be okay."

"Why do you keep saying that?" She pulled her knee away from my hand. "Take a right up here."

I followed her directions.

"How about I come in with you? I'm good at negotiating..."

"Tyler, please stop. Take a left here."

"Well, how about I wait for you outside then?" I turned left. "We talked about seeing the Pacific Ocean for the first time together. We can walk around the beach and get lunch. I don't have to report to basic training until tomorrow."

"Why are you making this harder than it needs to be?"

"I don't want to just leave you in Pasadena alone. We can hang out for the rest of the day and I can drop you off at LAX on my way to San Diego."

"Turn right, into that neighborhood."

Why the hell are we going into a neighborhood? But I turned right and started driving past the fanciest houses. They reminded me of Josh's, only even bigger. The only word I could think of to describe them was ostentatious. No one needed a house this big unless they had ten children and their in-laws living with them.

"Stop right here." She pointed to a house on the right.

I pulled up out front of the long driveway that led to what I would classify as a mansion. But all I could focus on was her knee bouncing up and down. We sat there for a moment in silence, the engine still running. I felt like I was going to be sick.

Hailey sighed. "I don't really know what to say, Tyler. You know how I feel about you. And I understand where you're coming from with your decision." She shrugged her shoulders. "So, I guess this is it. I really appreciate the ride." She stuck out her hand to me.

"Hails..."

"Tyler, please don't make this harder than it has to be." She lowered her hand.

"I'll just wait right here and when you're done we..."

"I don't want you to wait," she said, throwing back the words I had said to her last night.

I swallowed hard.

"Can you respect that or not?"

"Yeah, Hails. Of course."

She opened the car door and grabbed her duffel bag out of the back seat. "You know where to find me after you get out," she said as her fingers wrapped around the passenger's side door. "If you want to."

"I know where to find you."

We locked eyes for a second and she nodded.

"Good luck, Tyler. I hope you find what you're looking for."

"Good luck to you too."

And with that, she closed the door. When she was halfway up the driveway she turned around to look at me.

And then she pointed with her finger to the exit of the neighborhood.

I had asked her not to wait for me. The least I could do was not wait for her either. I waved.

She waved.

And then I drove away, without looking back, even though it felt like I was suffocating.

CHAPTER 39

Hailey

Thursday

I watched Tyler's car disappear down the street. I felt like sitting down in the middle of Elena's driveway and crying. But I had completely shut down this morning. I felt the pain, but I didn't truly feel it. The only way to deal with today was to try and not feel anything. Tyler was gone. And I was still standing. I was still breathing. I knew I had been defensive with him this morning. But what other choice did I have? I had to do enough begging today as it was. I wasn't going to beg him to be with me if he didn't want to be.

I stowed my duffel bag behind a bush. As soon as I was done talking to Elena, I'd call an Uber and get the fuck out of Pasadena and go home. I missed my dad. I missed my home. This adventure had been fun, but this was the reason I was here. Not to fall in love. Not to have fun. But to save my dad. Nothing else mattered.

With a deep breath, I looked up at the disgustingly immense house in front of me. My dad and I lived in a ranch house with two bedrooms. It was cozy and wonderful and perfect. I clenched my hand into a fist. But it still bothered me that Elena lived in something like this. She had so much and I had so little. I took another deep breath. But I didn't want any of this. I didn't need any of this. I just wanted my dad to be healthy again. He was all I needed.

I walked up the rest of their ridiculously long driveway and along their front walkway. But my feet froze at the steps up to their front door. I stared at the perfect family through the window. They were all sitting around a table laughing and passing food around. It looked like something you'd see in a Christmas movie. Only it was lunchtime. In the summer. Who eats lunches like this in the middle of the summer? Elena leaned over and kissed her husband on the cheek. It looked like the little girl squealed and covered her eyes. The little boy took a piece of food from his plate and fed it to the dog underneath the table.

A chill ran down my spine. Maybe I didn't want a big house and fancy things. But I had always wanted this. A family. I loved my dad with all my heart. He gave me the world. But of course I always wanted this. I couldn't help it. I watched the family around the table laugh again. Elena looked so happy. Why couldn't I make her happy? Why did she choose them over me? Why was I never good enough?

Stop. I took a deep breath. I told myself I wouldn't feel any of this. So what if Elena had a new family and was happy? I didn't give a shit about her. I came here for her help because I was desperate. That was it. I walked confidently up the front steps and knocked on the door.

Luckily it was Elena who opened the door.

For some reason, I lost my voice. The woman in front of me made me feel small, cast aside, forgotten. She may have forgotten about me, but I had never forgotten her. How could I? I tried to speak, but no words came out.

"Can I help you?" she said impatiently. Hearing her voice brought back even more painful memories.

I swallowed hard.

"There's no solicitors in this neighborhood. Sorry." She slammed the door in my face.

Did she really not even recognize me? I bit my lip. I'd never forget her face. It looked too much like mine. I knocked on the door again.

Elena opened it. Her mouth was in a set, thin line. "Look, I said we don't have solicitors. Do you not speak English? I won't warn you again." She went to close the door, but I put my hand out to stop it.

"Elena, it's me."

She drew her eyebrows together as she regarded me and my outfit. I had never felt so instantly judged in my life.

"Hailey." I clenched my jaw. "Your daughter."

Her eyes grew big. She stepped outside and closed the door behind her. "What are you doing here?" she asked in a hushed voice.

No hello. No, how are you? No, look how big you've grown. I hadn't seen my mother in 15 years. And now she was staring at me like an intruder. An intruder she wished would disappear. And I couldn't help myself. I wanted answers. I wanted to know why she left. Because I had been wondering why my whole life. Why was I not good enough? Why was this new family so much better?

"I wrote you letters every day for weeks." I kept my voice even. "And then every month for years. I was just a kid. How could..."

"A kid that I never asked for," she snapped.

And there it was. The reason why my dad didn't want me to see her. Because she had said all this to me before. That I was unwanted. That I was a mistake. That she hated me and my father for ruining her life. I blinked away my tears. *Stop feeling.* I had watched her pack her bags on a summer day like this 15 years ago. And I had begged her not to leave. I had begged my mother to not abandon me. And she had told me she didn't love me. She had told me she never wanted me. She had told me I meant nothing to her.

But that wasn't why I was here. The past needed to stay in the past or else it might break me again. "I'm sorry, I'm not here to talk about what happened."

"Good. Because I'm in the middle of something and I really don't have time for this." She turned around and reached for the front door handle.

"Dad's dying. He has lung cancer."

"Well he has no one to blame but himself. Maybe he shouldn't have started smoking."

"He didn't. But you did." *He's dying because of you.* "That's one of the only things I remember about you actually. You sitting on the back porch with a cigarette in your hand."

She smiled. "Is that what this is about? You think your poor father is dying because I smoked a few cigarettes around him? Grow up, Hailey. Lung cancer is caused by things besides cigarette smoke. Jeff isn't my problem anymore. I think I've made that very clear."

"By returning every letter a seven year old wrote to you? Yeah, I got that, Elena. And I'm not asking you to help Jeff. I'm asking you to help me. Because he's the only family I have. Because you abandoned me. I'm asking for your help because I'm about to lose my whole world."

"Then you should have surrounded yourself with better people. I made a decision that made my life better. And look at me now. So don't blame me for knowing I could do better."

Better than me? Stop feeling. "I'm not. I'm just asking for your help. He needs experimental treatments. I need to borrow some money. I'll pay you back every cent with interest. I'm not asking for a handout. I'm asking for a loan. Please." I hated how desperate I sounded. I hated how small she made me feel.

She eyed me coolly. "How much money do you need?"

The amount terrified me. Because Elena hadn't given me anything in years. And now I was asking for so much. "Treatments cost anywhere from 20 to 70 thousand dollars."

She laughed. "Get off my property."

Her words made my whole body feel cold. "I'll pay you back. Please, Elena. I've never asked you for anything."

She laughed. "Never asked me for anything? When you were born you ruined my life. Don't be ungrateful for my sacrifices. And as far as I'm concerned, you have no right to ask me for anything else."

"Of course I do. You're my mom."

Elena frowned. "I'm not your mother anymore, Hailey."

"You don't just get to choose whether you are or not. We have the same blood in our veins. We have the same eyes. And nose. You're my mom. Whether you like it or not. And I need your help. Just this once. I'm begging you."

"I'm asking you one last time to get off my property."

"Please. I'm just asking for a loan."

"And I'm not giving you a cent. Because you and your deadbeat father will sink the money in that stupid bar and I'll never get it back."

"I'll pay you interest. I'll..."

"Hailey, that's enough. This conversation is over. We may share some genes, but you are nothing like me. You and your father will always be broke because you'd rather ask for handouts than work hard. Me giving you money will only hinder your future. Now get the fuck off my property before I call the cops."

I was blinking hard, trying to hold back my impending tears.

The front door suddenly opened. "Is everything okay, honey?" The man she had kissed on the cheek wrapped his arm around her waist. He smiled at me. He looked kind. How could someone like that love such a monster?

But as soon as he had stepped outside, Elena's smile had returned. "Yes. It's just a solicitor, sweetie. And she was just leaving."

I'm your daughter. You're supposed to love me. I hadn't asked Elena for anything in 15 years. Not since I had begged her to stay. She owed me this. "One favor. And you'll never see me again. I'll never ask you for anything else the rest of my life. It'll be like I never existed. Isn't that what you want? Please, Elena."

Her new husband looked back and forth between us. Maybe he was seeing the similarities in our features. Or maybe he was just wondering why a solicitor was asking his wife for a favor. "Maria, what's going on?"

Maria? Who the hell is Maria?

"Richard," Elena said and looked up at her husband. "I've been trying to explain to her that there are no solicitors allowed in this neighborhood. I asked her to get off our property. And she's refusing to leave until we buy whatever she's selling. Do you think we should call the cops?"

"I don't think that's necessary," he said. "You were just leaving, right? If you'll excuse us. Have a nice day." He pulled his wife inside the house with him and closed the door in my face.

I didn't travel halfway across the country for nothing. I wasn't leaving until my stupid excuse for a mother wrote me a check. It wasn't like she didn't have the money. I pounded my fist on the door.

"Maria, it's fine," I heard him say from the other side of the door. "I'll handle it. You call the cops." The door opened. Richard stood there, with his wife nowhere in sight. His expression had turned cold. "My wife has already warned you. She's calling the police right now."

"You don't understand."

"I understand that I've already warned you once and..."

"I'm her daughter." I didn't want to intentionally throw Elena under the bus. I hadn't come here to ruin her life. I had come here to save my dad's.

"I'm sorry?" He shook his head and stared at me again. "That's impossible. You're too old to be Maria's daughter. My wife is only 32."

So she lied to her new husband about more than just her name. That wasn't surprising at all. "She's 38. And her name is Elena."

"You must have the wrong house." He looked confused.

"I don't have the wrong house." I was getting exasperated. " She had me when she was 16. You must see the similarities. You must see how much I look like her."

He shook his head.

"Your name is Richard, right?"

His lips parted, but then he closed them again and nodded.

"Richard, my whole life I've felt unwanted. She left me and my dad and started a family with you. She chose you over us. And I always wondered what I did wrong. Why I wasn't good enough. I wouldn't be here if I didn't need to be. It kills me to beg her for money. But my father is dying. And I know she has money to spare. I haven't asked her for anything in 15 years. And I'll never ask her for anything again. Of either of you. And I'll pay you back. Every dime."

He seemed to be staring at me, studying my facial expressions.

I felt like I was winning him over. "You're a father. You understand a bond between a father and daughter. Please help me so I don't lose my dad. Please."

"I'm sorry, I don't..." his words died away.

"She's not who she says she is. She's been lying to you."

He looked over his shoulder and then back at me. "How old did you say you were?"

"I'm 22."

He lowered his eyebrows and shook his head. "I'm sorry...it's just...it's not possible."

"Please believe me."

"I will not stand here and listen to this slander." He nodded his head as if he was trying to convince himself.

"Please, Richard, I just..."

This time he slammed the door in my face.

I pounded my fist against the door again. *No.* I hadn't faced my fears of seeing her just to leave feeling like this. She wasn't allowed to abandon me when I needed her again. She wasn't allowed to make me feel second best anymore, with her new family and her fancy house. My whole life it felt like there wasn't enough room in her heart for me in addition to her new family. News flash, Elena. There was room for me. I pounded my fist on the door again.

My whole life I had convinced myself that if she didn't need me, I didn't need her either. And I thought I'd be able to hold on to that notion. So why was I falling apart? I truly didn't need her. I didn't need my mom. I wrapped my arms around myself and let myself start to cry. Because the truth was, no matter how many times I told myself otherwise, I did need her. I wanted to be first in her life. I wanted me and my dad to be the family she chose. I wanted there to be room for me in her heart. My whole life I had felt rejected. Abandoned. And now my dad was going to die. I was going to be left all alone. Didn't she see that? Didn't she see how much she was hurting me? I needed her. I needed her help and I hated that I needed it. I hated myself for believing that she might actually help me.

I heard sirens wailing in the distance. I didn't have money to post bail. I didn't even have enough money to fly back home. My knees tried to give out as I ran down their front steps. But I kept running. I needed to get home to my dad. I couldn't end up in some prison in Pasadena. I grabbed my duffel bag from behind the bush and froze.

Tyler's car was sitting at the end of the driveway. *He waited for me.* And my heart broke into a million tiny pieces. *He waited for me.*

CHAPTER 40

Tyler

Thursday

I watched as the guy slammed the door in Hailey's face. It took every ounce of restraint to not run to her. She had asked me to leave. It was bad enough that I had come back. And it felt like I was spying, because I was. She didn't want me here. I couldn't really explain it, but I felt in my gut that she needed me here, though. I wanted to be there for her.

She put her arms around her torso, hugging herself. I watched the girl I was falling in love with fall apart. And I watched her be strong as she pounded on the door again.

Maybe she didn't need me. But I was going to be there for her anyway. I'd be right here waiting for her if she wanted me.

Sirens wailed in the distance. I glanced in my rear-view mirror but didn't see anything. When I looked back out the side window, Hailey was standing at the end of the driveway staring at me.

I couldn't tell if she was furious or happy to see me. I opened up the car door and stepped out.

"You came back." She wiped her eyes with the heel of her palm.

"I came back."

She nodded as more tears slid down her cheeks.

The sirens were starting to sound closer.

"Does the offer still stand to go see the Pacific Ocean?"

I smiled. "Get in."

She looked down at the ground as she climbed back into my car.

"Do you want to talk about..."

"Can you just drive?" She didn't say it defensively. It came out as more of a plea.

I glanced once more at the large house and pulled off the curb. There were a million questions I wanted to ask her. But first I needed to get her as far away from this place as possible.

It was hard to focus on the road. Her eyes were squeezed shut and tears were still streaming down her cheeks. Her hands were balled into fists.

"Hails," I said as gently as possible.

She shook her head.

Talk to me. Let me in. I drove on in silence. I wanted to say something that would make her feel better, but I didn't know what to say.

"We're almost there," I said. *Really, that's what I came up with?*

Hailey didn't say anything.

There were so many things I wanted to say, so many things that would have been better. *I couldn't leave because I'm in love with you. It physically hurts me to see you cry because I care so much about you. I want to be with you. I want you to wait for me. I'm scared that you'll hurt me like Penny did.*

But maybe Hailey had pegged me right at the very beginning. Maybe I was a coward. Because instead of saying anything, I pulled into a parking lot alongside of Venice Beach. *Tell her.*

I didn't get a chance to find the courage though. She opened up the door and starting sprinting toward the sand before I had even cut the engine.

"Hailey!" I yelled as I chased after her.

CHAPTER 41

Hailey
Thursday

There was no room in my mother's heart for me. There was no room in Tyler's heart for me. In four months I'd be alone. It was my worst fear coming true. My dad would be dead. And it was my fault. Because I couldn't save him. I couldn't fix it. It felt like I was drowning.

I dropped to my knees in the sand and wrapped my arms around myself. I couldn't breathe. My lungs ached as I gasped for air.

Tyler's arms wrapping around me felt like an anchor. Suddenly I felt like I could breathe again. Suddenly I didn't feel so alone. The smell of freshly cut grass was all I could smell. It was the most comforting scent in the world.

He pulled my face onto his shoulder and let me cry. And maybe it was weak, but I clung to him. Because he was the only thing in the world that seemed to know how to calm me. He was the light to my darkness. He was the missing piece to my puzzle. He was it. And it made me cry even harder because I wasn't his missing piece. And I never would be.

"Tell me who those people were so I know who to beat up," Tyler said.

I laughed. It came out as more of a choking noise. I swallowed hard and pulled away from him, but not enough so that our bodies weren't pressed together. Because I needed to know he was beside me. Even if just for a few more moments.

"Tyler..." my voice cracked as I put my face in my hands.

"It's okay, you can tell me. Talk to me, Hailey."

I looked up. He looked so concerned. And I needed to talk to someone about this before the pain swallowed me whole.

Tyler leaned forward and tucked a loose strand of hair behind my ear. The gesture was so comforting.

"I know that when you asked about my mom, I said I didn't have one anymore. I made it seem like she was dead. Because...well, I don't know. It's easier that way when people ask, I guess. But, she's alive." *And better off without me, I guess.* "She left my dad and me when I was a kid. And I still remember it like it was yesterday, you know? All the things she said." I looked down at my lap. "That I was a mistake. That I ruined her life. That it was my fault that she was unhappy. That she never loved me."

Tyler slipped his hand into mine. "How old were you?"

"Seven."

"Jesus." He squeezed my hand. "Please tell me you didn't believe her? Hailey, you're remarkable. You're everything good this world has to offer. You're perfect."

Perfect? I laughed. "Of course I believed her. I was seven. And I've felt abandoned my whole life. I've always felt like I wasn't good enough." It was hard to look at him, so I looked past him at the ocean instead. It really was beautiful. So why was I focused on this pain instead of its beauty? Why were some things so all consuming? "I used to write her letters every day, begging her to come home, asking her what I could do for her to love me again. She never wrote me back. Hundreds of unanswered letters. Eventually my dad told me that she had gotten remarried to some hotshot lawyer and that she had asked for me to stop trying to contact her. She started a new family. She replaced us so easily. And I don't know why I can't move on like she did. I don't know why it hurts so damn much."

"So that was her? Back at that house?"

I nodded. "She didn't even recognize me. Which is so hurtful because I can't ever forget her. I see her every time I look in the mirror. I have her eyes and her nose and I hate it so much. And I hate how much it hurts my dad that I look like her." *God, my dad.* I had failed.

"You're your own person, Hails. You're beautiful in spite of her."

I wiped away my tears and laughed. "I don't even know why I'm talking about that. It doesn't even matter. What's important is the fact that I haven't asked her for a damn thing in 15 years. And when I asked her for a loan, she just laughed at me and told me she was going to call the cops. She looked at me like I was trash that she had thrown out."

"How much money do you need? I can give you some money for the bar for a few months. I'm not going to be using it anyway."

"It's not even about the bar."

"Just tell me what you need. Let me help, Hails. I want to."

"You can't help. It's not that simple." I felt myself closing off again.

"Please, just let me in. Let me..."

"Why, so you can break my heart? So you can make me feel second best like my mom has my whole life? I don't even know why you came back. Why are you even here?"

"Because I care about you." He said it so earnestly that it made me start to cry again. "Please, Hails, let me help." He wiped away my tears with his thumb. "It seems pretty simple to me. I have some money saved up. I can give you a loan. I want to give you a loan."

"It's not just a small loan to pay the rent." I sniffed and wiped my eyes again. There was no reason not to tell him. It was a reality now. It was going to happen and I couldn't stop it. I had failed. "My dad's dying, Tyler." I hated saying it out loud. I hated that it was true. I hated that there was nothing I could do to save him.

Tyler lowered his eyebrows like it physically pained him to hear that.

"He has cancer. All that's left to try are these expensive experimental treatments." I tried to swallow down the lump in my throat. "But insurance won't pay for them. He took out a loan against the bar and the house already." I shook my head. "And now we have my college loans on top of everything else. I wouldn't have done all this unless we were truly out of options."

"How much do you need?"

"The cheapest treatment is $20,000."

He nodded his head. "Okay. Well, let's go to a bank. I can get..."

"No. I'm not taking your money, Tyler."

"You wouldn't be taking it. I want to give it to you."

"I can't." I stood up.

He immediately stood up next to me. "Let me help you."

"I don't need your help!" I didn't mean to snap at him. But I didn't need his pity. "I don't need anyone's help." I turned to look out at the ocean.

"It's okay to rely on other people. You're not alone, Hails."

I shook my head. "Aren't I, though? My mother despises me. My father is dying. In a few months I'll be alone. My whole life I was too scared to let anyone in. And when I finally did let my guard down and dated my asshole of an ex, he cheated on me. With my best friend. So yes, actually, I will be alone. I have no one but my dad. That's it, Tyler." *And I wanted you. You told me no. And it hurts so damn much.*

"You have me."

"I don't have you. You've made that clear." It felt like I couldn't breathe again. "God, none of that even matters. I didn't get into your car to fall in love with you." The laugh that escaped my lips sounded strangled. "I did it to save my dad. I did it to face my fears and talk to my mom. And I failed on both accounts. She still made me feel like trash. And I didn't get the money. I failed." My lip trembled as I said the words. "He's going to die. It's my fault that he's going to die. It's my fault."

He pulled my face into his chest and let me cry again.

"It's all my fault," I mumbled into his chest.

"Hails, I'm sorry that you're in pain. I'm sorry that your dad is sick. If there is anything I can do..." his voice trailed off. "But it's not your fault. Don't put that blame on yourself. Don't make the situation darker than it needs to be. You've done everything you could."

His words just made me cry harder. "Stop saying nice things to me."

"Hailey..."

"You're not allowed to be sweet when you're kicking me to the curb." I couldn't seem to stop sobbing.

His hands seemed to tense on my back. "That's not what I'm doing. And I don't want to say goodbye. I don't want to. I'm doing this for you."

"For me?" I shoved him off of me. "Maybe I blame myself for things I shouldn't, but own up to your own problems, Tyler. You're doing this for you."

He shook his head. "I'm trying to protect you..."

"Well don't!" I turned to face the ocean. I tried to concentrate on the sounds of the waves, but all I could focus on was my anger pulsing through me.

His hand on my shoulder made me flinch.

"Okay," he said slowly. "You're right."

I laughed. "Yeah, right. It's fine, Tyler. I'm used to being pushed away. So just go, okay? Please just go." I dug my heels into the sand. I needed something to ground me, because it felt like I was a million miles away. It felt like I was already grieving for my father, even though he was still alive. I couldn't do this. And I certainly didn't want to fall apart anymore in front of Tyler.

"No, Hails. I mean you're right about me. About everything. Maybe I was just trying to protect myself."

I tilted my head toward him. There was so much pain in his eyes. I could feel it wafting off of him. We were both drowning. We were both barely holding on. How could two people so broken possibly fix one another? What had I been thinking? But at the same time, I felt like clinging to him again. For some reason he was my lifeline. I wasn't sure I could keep going without him. My bottom lip started trembling again. "Tyler..."

"I think we should try this."

"What?"

"I don't want to say goodbye. No matter how many times I tell myself it's best if I walk away, I can't. I want to try to make this work."

I swallowed hard. I couldn't even comprehend what he was saying. *He wants me? He's choosing me?* "If you're doing this because you feel sorry for me..."

He grabbed both sides of my face. "I'm doing it because I'm selfish. I'm worried that if I walk away I'll lose myself. I need you. I'm falling in love with you, Hailey. I can't let you go. I'm done living my life with regret. You're what I want. And I know that I'm asking the world from you. Because I know how it feels to put your life on hold..."

I shook my head. "This is different." I placed my palm on the left side of his chest. "I would never break your heart, Tyler. I promise."

He grabbed my waist and pulled me against him. I'm pretty sure my heart stopped beating as his lips crashed down onto mine. He kissed me hard. But it wasn't filled with urgency. For the first time, it didn't feel like the end. It felt like the beginning.

CHAPTER 42

Tyler

Thursday

No one deserved to be dealt the hand Hailey was given. My blood was still boiling at the thought of her mother treating her that way. A part of me wanted to drive back there right now and tell her just what kind of girl she had given up. I wanted to defend Hailey. I wanted Hailey to know how wonderful she was. And I wanted to throw it in her mother's face. No kid should grow up thinking that they're second best. Especially not Hailey. She deserved the best. She deserved the whole world.

And, somehow, despite everything, Hailey was the kindest person I knew. She had such a big heart. She was able to look past all my flaws and see the best in me. I wasn't sure I deserved it, but I wanted to deserve her.

Hailey was right. About all of it. This whole time I had been telling myself I was protecting her. But that wasn't entirely true. I was scared of getting hurt again. I was scared of putting myself out there because rejection hurt so fucking much.

But Hailey wasn't Penny. Hailey was choosing me. Despite everything, the amazing girl in front of me was choosing me. And I wanted to be better for her. I needed to be better for her.

I wasn't sure how long we stood there. I loved the feeling of her in my arms. If it was up to me, I'd stand in the middle of Venice Beach for the rest of my life. I'd stop time for her if I could. She sighed against my chest, pulling me out of my thoughts.

"Hailey..."

She looked up at me. "Tyler."

I let myself get lost in her brown eyes. I let myself see a future. I let myself dive so deep that I would never break the surface again. My whole life I had been blind. Hailey Shaw was everything I had been missing. *Everything.* And I was done fighting it. I was done trying to protect myself from pain. Because what was the point? Bad things happened. And if you didn't embrace the good moments, the painful ones would swallow you whole. I was done drowning. I wanted anything she'd give me.

The ocean breeze made her hair dance across her face. I tucked the loose strands behind her ear as she smiled up at me. I wanted to tell her everything was going to be okay, but I couldn't force the words out of my mouth. Because I knew how hard it was to lose my dad. I knew how much it hurt. And I wasn't going to lie to her. But I also wasn't going to just do nothing. She needed to get back home to her father. She needed money. I'd help her with both, whether she wanted me to or not.

"What now?" she said as she stared up at me.

"Now you go home. And I..."

She put her finger against my lips. "No, not yet. Just for this one moment, let's be us. Uncomplicated, easy. I need something to hold on to." She shook her head. "For some reason you're the only person that makes me feel strong enough to deal with everything."

I pressed my lips together. I was already holding on to every moment of this trip. Her face was imprinted in my mind. And she was giving me strength to face my fears tomorrow. As much as I wanted to spend one more day together, though, I couldn't ask her to stay. I couldn't let her live with as much regret as I did. "I'm going to take you to the airport. You have to go home."

She lowered her eyebrows slightly. "I'm not ready."

"Hailey, you can't put it off. You need to be there when..."

"He dies?" Her voice wavered slightly. "You think I don't know that? I'm just asking for one day. Just one more day." She glanced toward the ocean. "He has four months to live. And I'm not giving up hope yet. This is a setback, but I'll find another way. I always find another way. I'll do whatever it takes. He's not going to die. I just need...one more day." She looked back up at me. "And we haven't even touched the Pacific Ocean yet."

Despite all that she was going through, there was still a twinkle in her eye. That playfulness made me follow her down to the water. I loved her optimism. I loved everything about her. But most of all, I loved that she made me feel like I wasn't missing any pieces anymore.

Her laughter made me smile as we stepped into the water.

"Jesus, it's freezing!" she squealed. She tried to run back toward the hot sand, but I wrapped my arms around her, keeping her in place.

"Is it everything you hoped it would be?"

"No! It's so cold!"

I laughed and released her from my grip.

"And, actually, it smells kinda weird." She retreated to the sand.

I shook my head. "That's how the ocean smells. Like salt."

Hailey scrunched up her nose. "It smells more like fish to me."

I laughed. "You know what? I have an idea. Come with me." I grabbed her hand and pulled her back toward the parking lot.

"Where are we going?" she asked as we walked past the car.

"I was hoping we'd wind up at Venice Beach. I was doing some research the other day about things to see here."

"And..." her voice trailed off as we sidestepped a skateboarder.

"And you'll see in a minute." We walked down the street and I pulled her off the sidewalk behind a building.

"Are you finally going to live up to the hitchhiking stereotypes and murder me?" Her fingers tightened around me, contradicting her words.

"Eh, not today. Wait," I said and turned her around to face me. "Close your eyes."

"Tyler, I don't think..."

"Just do it, Hails."

She pressed her lips together and shook her head at me. But after a brief stare-down she slowly closed her eyes.

"No peeking," I said as I grabbed her hand and led her past the building.

"Now I really am worried..."

I would have been in awe of what was in front of me if I wasn't completely in awe of Hailey. I stopped, grabbed her shoulders, and turned her toward the canals. "Okay...open your eyes."

"Oh my God." She seemed completely transfixed as she walked onto the small bridge. "What is this place?"

"The Venice canals. They made them to look like Venice, Italy." I joined her on the little bridge. She was looking out at the water, where more little bridges could be seen in the distance. Colorful houses were on either side of the canal. It was almost like we had stepped into a different world. And maybe time did stop for a minute, because the smile on Hailey's face would last a lifetime in my mind.

"This is the coolest thing I've ever seen." Her smile grew even wider.

I wrapped my arms around her. "Better than the Grand Canyon?"

"Absolutely."

"Better than the ocean?"

She nodded.

"Better than that speck you thought was a buffalo?"

She lightly slapped my arm. "I did see a buffalo. I swear. But yeah...this is better." She smiled up at me. "Seriously, I could stay here. In one of these houses."

"What about the fishy smell?"

"You can't smell it over here. Besides, I'm already used to it. Really, this is amazing." She leaned forward on the railing of the bridge. "There's even little fish in the water!"

I looked down at the orange fish swimming.

"I want to stop time," she said softly as she placed her hand on top of mine on the railing.

I looked down at her. She looked wistful. And beautiful. God, she was so damn beautiful. But time couldn't stop. She needed to go home. Maybe she did have four months, but now there was this sense of urgency. I had this awful feeling in the pit of my stomach. "Hails, let me drive you to the airport."

She laughed as she looked up at me. "You're really trying to get rid of me, aren't you?"

"It's not that, I..." I let my voice trail off. Why was I holding back? I had already confessed my feelings to her. She was still standing here. And she hadn't run off when she found out about Penny or the investigation. She was invested in us too. This wouldn't scare her off either. But I hated talking about it. I hated reliving it.

CHAPTER 43

Hailey

Thursday

"Tyler, what's wrong?" His face had suddenly changed. I wanted him to be in this moment with me. But I could tell his mind was somewhere else completely. And the look on his face worried me. Was he upset about tomorrow? He didn't have anything to worry about. He was brave and so much stronger than he realized.

"I just, I don't want you to regret spending one more day with me."

I laughed. "I couldn't possibly."

"You know what I mean." He put his hand on my hip and pulled me close enough to feel his body heat. His words and his actions always seemed to contradict each other. He was trying to push me away, yet pulling me closer.

"My dad is going to be okay. He's going to fight this just like he has everything else. He's going to be fine. Why are you pushing this?"

He scratched the back of his neck. He slowly looked back down at me. "I'm sorry." He leaned his back against the railing and folded his arms across his chest.

I wasn't sure if it was intentional, but it felt like he was shutting me out. For the first time in a long time, he had made me feel like I could rely on someone. I wanted him to feel that way about me too. "You're not alone either, Tyler."

A small smile crossed his face. "I know. I have you."

"Which means you can talk to me." I felt like I was on the cusp of finally getting to know him better. I didn't want him to hold back. I wanted him to trust me. I had finally put all my worries and fears out there. If he could do the same with me...maybe we really would have a shot here. Distance wasn't an issue as long as we were completely open with one another.

"I miss him. My dad, I mean."

So that's why he was being weird. He missed his dad. He didn't want me to experience his pain. "I'm so sorry, Tyler." I stepped forward and put my hand on his chest. I didn't really have any other words to express what I felt. But I wanted him to know that I understood. That he was living my biggest fear. "If you want to talk about what happened..." I let my voice trail off.

Something flashed across his eyes. It was only for a moment though. And it was too fast for me to be able to tell what it was. "I have a better idea." He grabbed my wrist and pulled me into his arms.

I laughed as I steadied myself by putting my hands on his biceps. He was really good at distracting me. If his piercing blue eyes weren't doing it, his muscles certainly were. "And what is your great idea?"

"Crepes." The smile was back on his face.

"Crepes?"

"Yeah. There's a great place like a block from here."

I laughed. "When in the world did you do all this research about Venice Beach?"

"I thought it was going to be my last day to have fun for a while. I wanted to make it count."

He had planned a send off party for himself. I didn't care if he had originally pictured me here or not. I knew he wanted me here now. And I was going to give him the best send off ever. "What else is on your list?"

"I want to check out the Santa Monica pier. Apparently the views from the Ferris wheel are amazing."

"Honestly, I'm a little scared of heights."

"Last time I checked, you were damn good at facing your fears, Hails. Besides, I'll be right there with you."

Just that thought alone warmed my heart. I slipped my hand into his. I truly felt like together we could face anything. "Come on then, we don't have much time to waste."

***

"I'm not drunk enough yet."

Tyler laughed.

God, I was going to miss his laugh. I put my chin in my hand as I took another sip of the ridiculously huge drink I had ordered.

"I'm pretty sure it'll be even scarier if you're drunk."

"How would you know? You're not scared of heights. And stop making me talk about it behind it's back. You're going to jinx everything."

Tyler turned around and glanced at the Ferris wheel. "Hails, you can't talk about an inanimate object behind it's back. It can't hear you." He raised his eyebrow as he stared down at my drink and then back up at me.

I took another sip. "Maybe I've had enough to drink," I said with a laugh. But I continued to take another sip.

"Delay it all you want, I'm still making you do it."

"Right, right." I smiled to myself. "I guess we might as well get this over with then." I slowly stood up as he pulled out his wallet. "If you can catch me first."

"Hailey!" he shouted after me.

But I was already running down the pier. The sound of my flip flops on the wooden boards, the seagulls calling, and the waves crashing in the distance were my new favorite sounds in the world. I felt alive. I looked over my shoulder. Tyler was quickly gaining on me. Right before he caught up to me, I jumped off the pier and into the sand. I may not have loved the smell of the ocean, but I absolutely loved the feeling of sand between my toes.

I laughed as Tyler wrapped his arms around me, pulling us both down into the sand. In a matter of seconds he had me pinned beneath him. I thought I had felt alive a moment ago. But now all my senses seemed heightened.

"Gotcha," he whispered against my lips.

All I wanted was his lips on mine. "How about instead of going on the Ferris wheel, I just seduce you in the sand?"

He leaned forward and gently brushed his lips against mine.

The teasing gesture sent shivers down my spine.

"Are you trying to get me arrested so I can't join the marines?"

"If that's an option...then yes." I squirmed beneath him as he laughed. *God that laugh.* That would be one of the things I missed the most. "I'm going to miss you so much."

"Then we better make tonight memorable." He smiled seductively.

"By getting arrested for public indecency? Deal."

He laughed again. "No, by facing your fears and seeing this amazing view before the sun sets completely." He gave me a chaste kiss and pulled me to my feet.

I could feel the buzz of the alcohol coursing through me. I felt brave and safe and whole. Because of him. I really would miss him. The feeling of his hand in mine and his arms around me. The intensity of his blue eyes. The way he looked so surprised by some of the things that came out of my mouth. Like I was embarrassing, but he loved me anyway. *Love.* I stole a glance at him as we made our way back onto the pier. Was this really love? Was that crazy? It felt real to me.

"Hey, look," I said and pointed to a sign in the middle of the boardwalk. "Santa Monica. 66. End of the Trail." I pulled him toward it. "We have to get a picture!"

"You're just procrastinating."

"No, I just realized I didn't take a single picture this whole time. My dad's never going to believe I was here," I said with a laugh.

Tyler pulled out his phone. "Okay, I'll ask someone to take one for us."

"Don't bother strangers, we can take a selfie."

"Don't bother strangers? Since when did that become your motto? I'm pretty sure you jumping into my car last week was bothering a stranger."

I lightly hit his arm and tried to resist wrapping my fingers around his bicep. "I don't think I was a bother at all. Look how far we've both come." I pointed to the sign again.

Tyler laughed. "Fine." He held out his phone in front of us.

"Wait, I have a better idea." I stepped up onto the bench next to the sign and climbed onto Tyler's back.

He started laughing again. I really did love his laugh. It instantly made me smile. He snapped a picture with our cheeks pressed together cheesing for the camera.

"It's perfect," I said. I couldn't remember the last time I had looked so happy.

"Now it's time for the Ferris wheel."

"If you insist." Before I could slide down his back, he started walking back toward the pier. I tightened my hold on his shoulders and nestled my face into his neck. I don't think anyone had ever carried me piggyback style in public. Besides for when I was a kid with my dad. There was something so comforting about it. I loved how carefree Tyler was. He didn't care about what anyone else thought. He just wanted to make me happy. I closed my eyes. I wanted to remember this moment. I couldn't think of a better way to sear it into my memory than by focusing on how whole I felt.

When we came to a stop in the line next to the Ferris wheel, I slid down his back. I didn't even bother to look up. No matter what, I knew I was safe when I was with Tyler. There wasn't anything to be scared of.

"You don't seem hesitant at all anymore," he said as he smiled down at me.

I shrugged my shoulders. "Maybe you're rubbing off on me."

He laughed as he scratched the back of his neck. "Well, I don't know about that."

"What? You're probably the bravest person I know."

"You do remember that a few days ago you called me a coward, right?"

"Which I didn't mean. Obviously. Really you were just being an asshole and I was mad at you."

He raised both his eyebrows. "I don't know which one is more offensive...being an ass or being a coward."

"It doesn't really matter. You're neither of those things." I cleared my throat. "Speaking of being brave, you're going to be careful right?" It had suddenly hit me just how dangerous his new career was. I'd be worried about him.

"We're up," he said.

I didn't have time to focus on the fact that he hadn't answered my question. Because as soon as I stepped up to the ride, my stomach seemed to drop. How was the flimsy looking bar supposed to protect me from falling to my death? I gripped Tyler's hand even tighter as we sat down.

"Trust me, you're going to love this, Hails."

Him calling me by my nickname soothed me slightly. But I felt like I was going to be sick when the cart swayed forward and we started rising into the air.

CHAPTER 44

Tyler

Thursday

Hailey squeezed my hand so tightly that it almost hurt.

"I'm right here, nothing bad is going to happen to you."

She gave me an uneasy smile.

I wasn't sure if it was because at this time tomorrow I wouldn't be here with her, or because she was so nervous about being this high up, but it made me feel like shit either way. Was I doing the right thing? I couldn't be there for her. I'd be on the other side of the country. If her dad didn't get better, she needed someone that could be there for her.

"Oh my God," she said and leaned her head against my shoulder.

It took me a second to realize she was actually admiring the view instead of being terrified of it.

"It's breathtaking."

I wrapped my arm behind her back as we stared out at the horizon. The sun was setting, casting a beautiful spectrum of colors across the water. If I listened closely I could even hear the waves splashing over the laughter of the people on the pier. It really was amazing. And not just because of the view. But because of the beautiful girl beside me that trusted me enough to face her fear of heights. "This is the best sunset I've ever seen."

"Mhm."

I glanced down at her and laughed. Her eyes were shut tight. "Open your eyes, Hails. You're missing it."

She shook her head.

I put my hand on the side of her face. "Open your eyes."

She shook her head again and squeezed her eyes shut even harder. "The most beautiful things in life aren't seen. They're felt by the heart."

Just like that, all my reservations were gone. I was never letting go of this girl. It was like I was blind my whole life and suddenly I could see. Hailey Shaw was it for me. Because she was right, and not just about this moment but about us. This was more than just physical attraction or a crazy summer fling. She healed my heart. She healed my soul. She had touched my life in such a meaningful way. She saved me.

"I love you." The words tumbled out of my mouth before I even realized what I was saying.

Her eyes flew open.

It was too fast. It was too crazy. So why the hell did I not regret saying it?

She pressed her lips together as she looked up at me. It looked like she was about to cry.

"It's okay if you don't feel the same way. It doesn't change how I feel. And I wanted you to know." I meant it, but I could feel myself closing off.

"No, Tyler, that's not it. I just..." her voice trailed off.

She doesn't love me back. Of course she doesn't. What the hell is wrong with me? It was just like it was with Penny. I wasn't enough. Why the hell would Hailey want me? I was going to be gone for three years. If there was one thing I had learned from Penny, it was to not be so transparent and optimistic about something I couldn't control. I was repeating my mistakes. That was something I couldn't afford to do. It felt like I couldn't breathe. I was such an idiot.

"I'm sorry, Tyler, but I'm scared to say it. I'm so scared of losing you."

I swallowed hard.

"A few hours ago I didn't think you wanted me back. But now that you do, it's suddenly hit me how dangerous what you're about to do is. And I'm terrified. I'm so worried that I'm never going to see you again."

"Nothing's going to happen to me." She had given me something to live for, something to fight for. I wasn't giving up anymore. I tightened my grip around her waist. "I'm going to do whatever it takes to come back to you."

She nodded.

"And it's okay if you're not ready to say it back. I don't want to pressure you into saying something you don't mean."

"I fell in love with you in Kansas, Tyler."

Kansas. I smiled. "Singing karaoke to our song?"

"And when you didn't kiss me back. I was a little surprised by how much it hurt. That's kind of when I realized it was more than just a little crush."

"I never meant to hurt you." I slid my hand to the back of her neck. "Hailey, I promise I'll never hurt you again. We can make this work. I know we can."

A smile spread across her face. "I'm pretty sure this is where you're supposed to kiss me."

She didn't have to tell me twice. My lips crashed down on hers and I kissed her like I'd never get a chance to kiss her again. Everything about her was sweet. I was addicted to her taste. And suddenly I needed more than this. This was the last night we had together for I didn't even know how long. My hand slid into the back pocket of her jean shorts and she moaned into my mouth. I leaned into her. I wanted her to know how badly I wanted her all the time. How I could barely think straight when we were together.

If it wasn't for the Ferris wheel technician clearing his throat, I'm pretty sure I would have gone down on her in the middle of the ride.

She pushed my shoulder so I'd stop kissing her neck. Her cheeks were rosy when I pulled away.

I slowly slid my hand out of her pocket. I tried to hide my smile as I grabbed her hand and helped her out of the cart. "Sorry," I said to the technician as I tried to discretely shift my pants so that everyone on the boardwalk wouldn't see how hard I was. Not that I really cared.

"Can we maybe go somewhere that we can be alone?" she said breathlessly.

"It's still early," I teased. "Are you sure you don't want to do anything else first?"

"Actually," she said as she pulled me in the opposite direction of a hotel with a glowing vacancy sign. "Now that you mention it, I saw some people dancing earlier. That could be fun."

"I was kind of joking, Hails. I think being alone sounds perfect."

She briefly glanced down at the front of my shorts. "I'm pretty sure you're going to enjoy dancing too."

"It depends on the dancing." Fuck, I just wanted to be inside of her.

"Oh trust me. You're going to like this." She started to shake her hips as we got closer to the music.

She was probably right. I loved grabbing her hips. I just preferred it with our clothes off. She lifted my arm in the air and spun underneath of it as we entered the crowded open-air bar.

"This place is so packed!" she yelled over the music. "Maybe I can learn a few things for my dad's place."

"We're not here for work," I said and pulled her against my chest.

She laughed as she looked up at me. The music was fast paced, but we clung to each other like it was a slow song at a high school dance. She had completely consumed all my senses. I couldn't take my eyes off her. I could smell the faint scent of cinnamon as I nibbled the side of her neck. I could feel the softness of her skin on her lower back where my fingers had pushed up her tank top.

"Give me one second," she said and lightly tapped my chest.

I reached out for her but she was already disappearing through the crowd of people. Without her, I felt unsteady, like I needed to hold on to something. She grounded me. I needed her to hold on to me too. It's partially what had fixed me, knowing that someone needed me. I could be her anchor too.

After a few minutes passed, I began to get antsy. I pulled out my phone, but I remembered that I didn't even have her number. I started pushing through the people dancing as I searched for her. It didn't take me long to find her. She was standing next to the D.J. I was surprised by how instantly jealous I was that she was whispering in his ear and had her hand on his arm. It was silly. I knew it was just a habit from working at a bar for years. It still made me want to punch the guy in the face, though.

But then she glanced over to me with a huge smile on her face. Our song immediately started pumping through the sound system. *Our song.* I smiled to myself.

She pointed at me. "Babe, I thought I was good before I met you." It looked like she was mouthing the words as she ran over to me. But when she got closer I realized she was singing at the top her lungs.

I laughed as she jumped into my arms. I held on to her thighs and kept her legs wrapped around me as she laughed too. She leaned forward wrapping her arms tightly behind my neck, as my hands slid to her ass.

"We're never getting older," she whispered in my ear. She pulled back and stared down into my eyes.

We stayed like that for the whole song. Silently staring into each others' eyes as the lyrics blared around us. She was good at stopping time. I didn't want to move. I didn't want tonight to end.

"I wasn't actually good before I met you," she said.

"Neither was I."

"I think we were meant to run into each other."

"I know that we were."

The smile she gave me made my knees feel weak.

"I love you, Tyler Stevens," she whispered as she pressed her forehead against mine.

I breathed in her exhales. "I love you. And I need you, Hails."

"You can have me whenever you want me. I'm yours."

God I loved the sound of that.

CHAPTER 45

Hailey

Thursday

He kicked the door closed with his foot and slammed my back against it. Our lips hadn't parted since the elevator. It was like I didn't need to breathe. I just needed him.

His palms slid up my thighs as I tightened my legs around his waist. God, I was soaked. As soon as he had caught me mid leap in that bar I couldn't stop thinking about being alone with him. This was the last time we could be together for a long time. I was going to make it count.

His breathing was labored when he pulled away from me. "There were nicer hotels a little farther down the..."

"This is perfect, Tyler." I intertwined my fingers in his hair and kissed him again.

He pulled us away from the door and set me down on the edge of the bed.

I grabbed the hem of his shirt and pushed it up his abs. I wanted to see him. I needed to memorize every inch of his hard body. But when he didn't take it off, I grabbed the fabric and pulled him closer to me instead. He had no idea what he was doing to me. I needed him right this second or I was going to internally combust.

"Lean back," he whispered seductively in my ear.

I ignored him as I spread my thighs even more for him. If he wanted me to beg, I'd beg. "Tyler, I need you."

"Trust me, Hails, you're going to enjoy this." He slowly pushed my tank top up the sides of my torso, trailing his fingers against my skin. His touch sent shivers down my spine.

I put my hands in the air so he could take my shirt off more easily. But that didn't make him go any faster. He kissed up the length of my arm as he slowly pulled my tank top off over my head.

I was practically panting as he unhooked my bra.

The groan that escaped his lips as my breasts spilled out just made me even wetter. What the hell was he trying to do to me?

He slowly pulled the straps down my arms. "You are the most beautiful girl I have ever met."

I swallowed hard. I hoped he meant that. I knew he had been hung up on Penny...

"Inside and out, Hails," he said as he put his hand on the side of my face. He slowly trailed his fingers down my neck to the center of my chest and lightly pushed, so that I'd lay down on the bed like he wanted. He leaned over me so that his arms were on either side of my head. "You're gorgeous. And I'm going to keep telling you that until you believe it." He kissed the side of my neck and I immediately moaned.

I felt him smile against my skin. "And I love what I can do to your perfect body." He left a trail of kisses down my neck and between my breasts.

"Tyler," I panted. "I need you."

"I need you too, Hails." His breath was hot against my skin as he took one of my nipples into his mouth and lightly tugged.

Oh God. It was like my nipple had a direct line to my groin. I was practically dripping with desire.

"Fuck me, Tyler," I moaned.

He sucked on my nipple even harder, ignoring my plea.

I reached down and unbuttoned my shorts. I couldn't wait another second. I needed him inside of me.

He grabbed my hands to stop me, as he left a trail of kisses down my stomach. He tugged on the waistband of my shorts and slowly pulled them and my thong down my thighs. I was so aroused that just the feeling of the fabric trailing across my skin turned me on even more.

"Tyler, please, I need you." I kicked my shorts off as soon as he pulled them past my knees.

"I know." He lightly kissed the inside of my knee.

God, kill me now. I was going to die from horniness. "No, I need you to fuck me." I could hear the desperation in my voice.

"Not tonight." He kissed the inside of my thigh.

What?

He continued his torturously slow ascent of kisses up my leg.

"Please, Tyler." I swore I felt him smile against my skin again. He kissed high up my thigh and then I felt his breath against where I needed him most. *Please.* "I'm losing my mind."

"If I don't taste you I'm going to lose my fucking mind."

Jesus, that mouth.

He thrust his tongue deep inside of me.

Oh, God yes that mouth! He was finally answering my pleas. And it was even better than I could imagine. I gripped the sheets as he slowly swirled his tongue inside of me.

I would have grabbed his head so he wouldn't stop, but I didn't think I needed to. He was completely devouring mc. It was like I was the only sustenance he needed.

My hips arched toward him. It was like they had a mind of their own. I loved his tongue but I needed more.

He pressed down firmly on my thighs, spreading them even farther apart, as he swirled his tongue, hitting all my walls.

"Tyler, please."

He thrust his tongue even deeper.

Jesus. What was he trying to do to me?

He rubbed his nose against my clit and I completely shattered.

"Tyler!" My hands clenched the sheets even tighter. I hadn't been expecting that at all. How had he done that with just his tongue? I tried to catch my breath as the bliss started to subside. And I tried not to think about the fact that I was lying naked on the bed, completely spent, and he was still fully clothed. "That was amazing," I said breathlessly.

He didn't say a word as he grabbed his t-shirt by the nape of its collar and pulled it off over his head.

I swallowed hard as I stared at his perfect abs. When my eyes met his, I realized he was staring down at me with a smile on his face. I pressed my thighs together. I didn't want to feel self-conscious around him, but when he looked at me like that I couldn't help it.

He put his hand between my knees and spread them apart again. "I don't think I've ever seen you more beautiful."

I closed my eyes and shook my head.

"Hails?"

I felt the bed sag.

"I love the freckles on your nose." He kissed the bridge of my nose. "And the line you get in your forehead when you're overthinking everything." He kissed my forehead. "And the way you live your life with so much hope despite how easy it would be to hold on to all the darkness." He kissed my clavicle. "And I love that you let me in even though you were scared." He kissed between my breasts. "And I love when you tell me that I'm being an idiot."

I laughed as I shook my head.

"And I love your laugh. Your smile makes me smile." He placed a soft kiss against my lips and I opened my eyes as he pulled away.

"You don't have to sweet talk me, Tyler. You're already getting lucky."

He shook his head. "You deserve the world, Hailey. And I know you don't see that for some reason." He put his hand under my chin. "But I'm going to spend my life giving you everything I can."

I felt a tear run down my cheek. Because it had just hit me. We had a future. He could be my forever. I touched the side of his face. He was right. Tonight wasn't about fucking in some cheap motel. Tonight was about loving each other. I might not get to see him for months. Tonight was about making memories that we could hold on to. I wanted him to know that I understood. I wanted him to know how real my feelings were. "Then maybe you should start by making love to me."

"I thought you'd never ask." He kissed me again, slower this time. Our tongues swirled together as his hand slid down my back. I'd remember this kiss for my whole life. It was thc kind of kiss that makes your head spin. Nothing in the world could beat that.

But when I heard the zipper of his jeans, I knew he was about to. He entered me slowly, inch by inch. "I was made for loving you," he whispered as I buried my hands in his hair.

Never in my life had I felt so full. I moaned as he slowly started moving in and out of me. "Tyler." My fingertips dug into the muscles of his back. Every inch of him was hard. I felt so safe in his arms. Something happened to me as we held each other. I think I realized that without him I'd break again. He was the glue that held me together. He was everything good that was left of me.

"Hailey," he said softly and kissed away the tears I hadn't realized I had shed. "I love you."

"I love you too."

"Promise that you'll remember that you're mine." He pinned the back of my hands to the mattress as he thrust a little faster.

Yes! "I promise." I'd love him for the rest of my life. I wrapped my legs around his waist.

He groaned in response.

The intensity was too much. Sex for me had always been quick and pretty anticlimactic, except with Tyler. Every time we had been together was somehow more amazing than the last. And this was a whole different level. I felt so close to him. I felt like we were one.

My fingers tightened around his as he made me come. "Tyler!" I'm pretty sure people down the hall could hear me scream his name.

I immediately felt his warmth spread inside of me. I was complete. Perfectly and utterly complete.

He collapsed beside me and pulled me against him.

I breathed in the smell of him as my hand rose and fell on his chest. The ocean breeze made the curtains flutter. I wanted moments like this for the rest of my life. I wanted him for the rest of my life. But in a few short hours I'd be saying goodbye. Just the thought made my chest feel tight.

CHAPTER 46

Tyler

Thursday

"Promise you won't forget all about me?" she said, breaking the spell of silence.

I pulled her closer against my side. "Whenever you think of me, I can assure you that I'll be thinking of you too."

She nestled her head into my chest. "I did some research about your training."

"Yeah? To see when I can come visit you?"

"And to see how dangerous it all is."

I tried not to hold my breath. I hadn't looked up anything about it on purpose. I didn't want to know. Before it was because I didn't care what happened to me. But now it was because I did.

"Training lasts for four months. It doesn't seem like it's going to be that bad for you. You're already in great shape." She ran her fingers along the lines of my six pack.

"Four months. That doesn't seem like that long." I instantly regretted what I said. Four months was exactly how long the doctors had given her dad to live. *Shit.*

"I know," she said softly.

Before I could think of something to fix what I had said, she continued talking.

"You get ten days leave after that. Before you have to report to your first assignment."

I could feel my heart start to race. I didn't want to think about where I'd have to go. I just wanted to focus on the ten days I'd get with Hails. But it might not be the best circumstances. If the doctors were right about her dad...

"I know that you'll probably want to visit your mom and your friends for part of it. And I don't know what's going to be going on with my dad. I mean, he'll be recovering I'm sure. I know I'll be busy helping him. But I hope you'll come visit for a few days no matter what's going on."

"I'm spending all ten days with you and your dad." I hoped I would get to meet her father. I wanted to tell him how amazing his daughter was. I wanted the chance to shake his hand.

She lifted her head slightly so she could look up at me. Her long hair splayed against my chest. "He's going to like you, I know it."

I ran my fingers down the arch of her back. "I can't wait to meet him."

"Hmm." She smiled and put her head back down on my chest.

I breathed in the smell of her hair and let my fingers dance across her bare skin. It was like something happened to me as I held her. My heart didn't hurt anymore. I felt at peace. With everything.

I felt her fingers trace the scar on my hip.

For a second I held my breath. She had asked about it before, but I had deflected. She didn't need to ask me again. I wanted to tell her. I needed to get it off my chest.

"When you asked me why I was pushing you to go home earlier, it wasn't because I wanted you to go."

She lifted her head and looked up at me. "I know."

I thought she might say something else, but she stayed silent. I ran my fingers through her hair. It wasn't like I had done the motion a million times, but it still felt comforting. "I didn't get a chance to say goodbye to my dad, Hails. I just didn't want you to miss out on that too."

She bit her lower lip. "Why won't you tell me about the accident?"

I pushed my hair back with my hand and dropped my gaze. I didn't want to hold back anymore, but that didn't mean it was easy to talk about. It felt like my throat was constricting. I swallowed hard, trying to remove the lump. But it didn't go away. "My dad's dead because of me. And my grandfather is dead because of me." I immediately felt her hand on the side of my face, making my eyes meet hers again.

She shook her head. "I'm sure that's not true."

"I was driving, Hails."

She pressed her lips together.

I knew she wasn't expecting me to say that. I knew she thought it was just the pain of rejection that I was holding on to. That I was a mess because Penny didn't like me back. But it was way more than that. I felt guilty.

"It was an accident." She put her hand on my forearm.

"That doesn't mean it wasn't my fault."

"Of course it does. I'm sure whatever happened could have happened to anyone. You can't..."

"Blame myself? Yes, I can. We were driving back late after a camping trip and my dad kept saying he was tired.

He wanted to stop at a motel, but I had to be back for an exam. My grandfather was already asleep in the back seat. On a whim he had decided to come back with us too. A fucking whim." It felt like my throat was constricting. "So I offered to drive. And...I don't know..." I let my voice trail off. "I must have fallen asleep too."

Sympathy was written all over her face.

I didn't want her sympathy. It was almost like I wanted her forgiveness. She was losing her father. I had let her believe my situation was the same as hers. Like I had lost my dad in some tragedy too. But I didn't just lose him. It was my fault that he was dead.

"Tyler..."

"My father died instantly. My grandfather died in surgery. And I walked away with a scratch."

She put her hand on the center of my chest. "It was an accident."

"He trusted me. He trusted me to get him home safe and I..." I balled my hand into a fist and put it up to my mouth. I couldn't remember the last time I cried. I hurt all the time. But it was a constant struggle to not give into my grief. I knew if I gave in, I would drown in it again.

"Tyler." She put her hand on the side of my face again but I shook it off.

"My dad and grandfather died because I didn't want to miss an exam. Who the fuck cares about a stupid exam? And when I think about it, I can't breathe. Because I feel like it should have been me. I should have been the one that died. It should have been me, Hails."

She sat up, straddled me on the bed, and threw her arms around me. "My heart is broken for you," she whispered against my neck.

And somehow that was so much better than an "I'm sorry" or an "it's okay." It was like she could feel my pain. And that her heart was breaking into a million pieces just like mine. "I failed them." I let myself give into my grief because I knew she was there to hold on to. I knew that I wouldn't drown as long as she was in my arms.

"You didn't fail them." She tightened her grip around me. "It was an accident. It could've happened to anyone."

"But it happened to me. And I don't know how to move past it." I could feel my tears making her hair wet. I squeezed my eyes shut as tightly as I could. "I'm broken, Hails. What are you doing with me?"

"You're the missing piece to my puzzle." She wiped the tears away from underneath my eyes. "And I love you."

I wanted to believe her. But we barely knew each other. I was rash. I clung to her because I needed to. She didn't need to cling to me. She was whole. She was perfect.

"I love the sound of your laugh." She kissed the side of my mouth. "And the feeling of your skin on mine." She kissed the side of my neck. "The goodness of your heart." She kissed the left side of my chest. "I love the way you look at me when you think I'm saying something insane." She smiled as she kissed the tip of my nose. "You're so strong, but you don't need to do everything alone. You have me."

"Hailey..."

"And I even love how hard you are on yourself, even though I don't understand why. But it's part of what makes you you. And I love the person that you are. I love you. All of you."

I grabbed the back of her neck and brought her lips down to mine. And I made love to her again. I made love to her like it was the last time I'd ever see her. Because I feared that it would be. Despite what she thought, there was probably a puzzle piece that fit her a lot better than I did. Someone full of life and energy and optimism. Someone worthy of her. Because Hailey Shaw was perfect. Way too perfect for me.

***

It took all my strength not to look back at her. If I did, I wouldn't be able to walk out the door. I placed the envelope down on the dresser and walked out into the hallway, closing the door as quietly as I could.

The decision was in her hands. I wasn't good enough for her. She deserved so much more than I could give her. But I still hoped she'd choose me. Because I was selfish. I wanted the world even though I deserved none of it.

I exhaled loudly as I walked out the front door of the motel. The seagulls called in the early morning. The sun was just rising over the mountains in the distance.

I stole a glance at the window that I knew Hailey was sleeping behind. And then I drove away. Leaving my heart behind in a crappy motel in Santa Monica. A motel room that in my head was even grander than a room at the Bellagio.

CHAPTER 47

Hailey

Friday

I reached out expecting to find Tyler, but I only felt empty sheets. I slowly opened my eyes. "Tyler?" I sat up and looked around the room. He wasn't there. He was gone.

I had a sinking feeling in my stomach as I threw the sheets off of me. He left without saying goodbye? *No.* I quickly pulled on a tank top and shorts. He couldn't leave without saying goodbye. I needed to tell him that I loved him again. I needed him to know that I truly meant it. That I'd wait for him. That I wouldn't hurt him.

Before I grabbed the doorknob of the hotel room, I noticed an envelope with my name on it on the dresser.

I quickly tore it open. There was a plane ticket back to Indiana, a picture, and a note. I swallowed hard. *He left without saying goodbye.* Why would he do that? I sat down on the edge of the bed and looked down at the picture. It was of us in front of the Santa Monica Route 66 sign. He looked so happy. The sun was setting in the picture, casting a glow around us. It made the picture look like it was from an old scrap book that my dad had from when I was a baby. I wasn't sure how something could look so faded yet vibrant at the same time. I stared down at Tyler's handsome features. Why did it already feel like he was so far away? I slid the photo of Tyler into my pocket. Maybe that would make him feel closer.

I slowly unfolded the letter. Part of me didn't want to read it. I had this awful feeling that yesterday had been a lie. That he pitied me. That maybe he would be telling me the truth in this letter. I took a deep breath and stared down at the words.

Hails,

When we first met, I was broken. I wasn't looking for someone to put the pieces of my life back together, but you did. I don't know how I can ever thank you for that. All I really have to give you in return is my heart. And that's what I'm giving you. I love you, Hailey Shaw. I love you with everything that I am.

Before I met you, I thought I knew what love was, but I was wrong. I promise I have never felt the way I feel about you with anyone else. Because I love the warmth of your brown eyes and the freckles on your nose. And I love your laugh. Your real one, the one that bubbles up from your stomach and makes your eyes twinkle. I love how stubborn and determined you are. I love how you always tell it like it is. I love how strong you are, not just for yourself but for the ones you love. And most of all, I love that you see goodness in the world in spite of everything. That you see goodness in me.

Unlike in our song, I wasn't doing just fine before I met you. Because before I met you, I had given up. I signed up for the marines with the intention of starting over. But really, I think deep down, maybe I thought it might be the end. As much as I wish that wasn't true, that thought was there. The idea that I could at least go out in a way I could be proud of. That maybe people would remember me better than I was. But I don't want to die. Not now. Not now that I've found you. You saved me.

But I need you to think about what being together would mean. I love that you make rash decisions like climbing into strangers' cars. But I don't want you to make a rash decision about being with me. This is going to be hard. You'd be making an incredible sacrifice, one I can't ask you to make. But it's your choice. I hope that you make the right one for you. I'm all in though, Hails. I need you to know that if you choose me, that's it for me. You're it for me.

My new address is on the back of this letter. Write to me if that's what your heart truly wants. I promise I'll always write back. I promise that you can always count on me. No matter how many miles apart we are, you're not alone. Ever.

I know you're probably fuming right now because I didn't stay to say goodbye. But I didn't stay because this isn't goodbye. It's only just the beginning. If you'll have me. I'm going to come home. And I mean to Indiana, not New York. You're home to me, Hails.

Love,
Tyler

P.S. When you board the plane check the front pocket of your duffel bag.

He didn't know me as well as he thought. I wasn't mad. I was bawling my eyes out like a baby. Being with him wasn't a sacrifice. It wasn't rash. It was just how it was supposed to be. We were supposed to meet. I knew that. He needed to know that too.

I grabbed my phone to call him. But I realized that I never even got his number. The thought just made me cry even more.

When I finally composed myself, I took a deep breath. He wanted letters. I could respect that. He'd be adjusting to his new life. Hopefully he'd change his mind soon. I wanted to be able to hear his voice. I thought maybe we could even Skype so I could see his face.

I wiped away the remaining tears in my eyes. I'd write to him right away. He'd probably get it tomorrow if I mailed it before I got on the plane. I didn't need to wait to think about anything. I loved him. That was all that mattered.

***

As soon as I stepped onto the plane, I opened up the front pouch of my duffel bag. It was another envelope with my name on it. I found my seat and shoved my bag in the overhead compartment. I was already tearing open the envelope before my butt hit the seat. There was another letter inside.

Hails,

This is every cent I have to my name. I know you said you didn't want it, but I'm giving it to you anyway. You faced your fears of visiting your mom. You didn't let pride get in the way of what truly matters. So don't let it get in the way now either. Maybe I was the answer the whole time. I think we were meant to find each other.

You don't get to say goodbye to me, and you don't have to say goodbye to your dad either. No goodbyes. Do whatever it takes. And stay strong. I can't wait to meet him.

Love,
Tyler

I looked back in the envelope. There were two credit cards with Tyler's name on them. And there was also a check for $24,000.

I closed the envelope and held it to my chest. Tyler was the answer to my prayers. He was the miracle I had been looking for. I was going to be able to save my dad.

CHAPTER 48

Tyler
Friday

I watched the sun set, casting yellow, orange, and purple shadows across the water and turning the sky into a masterpiece. This was it. My last few minutes of freedom. I took a deep breath.

All I wanted to do was hear Hailey's voice. I had purposely not left her my phone number. It was better that way. Because I was scared. I didn't want her to be able to hear it in my voice because I didn't want her to worry about me. She had enough on her plate. If she could be strong, so could I. Letters would be better. At least at first, until I settled in.

But for some reason, I found myself pulling out my phone anyway. I stopped when I found the picture of Hailey and me in front of the end of Route 66 sign. She had already told me she wanted to be with me. But I hoped she was really thinking about what that would mean. Three years apart was a long time. I wanted her to be happy. As happy as she was in this picture. I smiled down at her smile. The sun was setting behind us, creating almost a halo around her face. No matter what happened, I'd always have this summer. I'd always have the memories of her. That could be enough if I knew she was happy.

Like with Penny. The thought of her crashed through my mind like an unwelcome guest. If I really was going to treat this as a new beginning, I needed to make sure everything was wrapped up in my past. I needed to know that the dust had settled. Because even though I didn't love Penny, she was still my friend. And I'd always care about her. But it was time to put thoughts about her to rest once and for all. It was time to say goodbye.

I found Penny's name in my contacts list, clicked on it, and stared back out at the water. I was a little surprised to hear her answer immediately. It was pretty late on the east coast.

"Hey, Tyler."

"Hey. I heard he woke up."

"Yeah."

It was strange. Her voice used to make me smile. Now it just made me miss Hails even more. I tried to clear my thoughts. "How is he doing?" I asked.

"Good. He's a lot better today than he was yesterday. And I think they're going to discharge him for his birthday."

"And how are you holding up?" *Be good. Let me be able to let go.*

"Better now that he's awake."

I let a breath I didn't realize I was holding escape. *She's good.* "The cops stopped calling me. I saw what happened on the news. How Isabella broke into your house. Are you okay?"

"I'm good. And yeah, they arrested her. They shouldn't be bothering you anymore."

"Thanks, Penny."

"How are you?"

"Better. Actually, I met someone." I wasn't sure why I said that. Penny didn't need to know about my life anymore. But maybe a part of me didn't want her to be thinking about me anymore either. We were better off without each other in our lives. I could feel the distance between us, and it was actually comforting.

"Really?"

I laughed. "Don't sound so surprised."

"I'm not. Any girl would be lucky to be with you." She sounded sincere but there was something sad in her voice.

This wasn't the time to throw my happiness in her face. Her husband was lying in a hospital bed. She was probably staring at him as we spoke. "Oh, no, we're not dating or anything. She actually just needed a ride to the west coast. We're just friends." I was pretty sure my lie wasn't convincing at all. Because just thinking about Hailey made me smile. Besides, Penny and I were too good of friends. She could tell when I wasn't telling the truth.

"What's her name?"

Yup, she didn't believe me. "Hailey."

"So you're on a road trip with a relative stranger. Are you trying to get yourself killed?"

I laughed again. *Not anymore.* "No, just learning how to live again."

"You're having fun then?" She sounded hopeful.

"Yeah. I'm having lots of fun." There was no reason to tell her what I was about to do. There was really no reason why she would care anyway.

"Good," Penny said.

"This was exactly what I needed." Hailey was exactly what I needed. I closed my eyes and pictured Hailey. Hailey was right. The best things in life weren't seen, they were felt by the heart. And if I really concentrated, it almost felt like she was beside me.

"Hailey or the trip?"

I smiled to myself. "Both, maybe. I should go, Penny." My time was running out.

"When do you think you're coming back?"

"I don't know. I'll stay in touch, though. Tell James I said I hope he makes a speedy recovery."

"I will. And don't pick up any scary hitchhikers."

"I think I'm good with just the one." Hailey was all I ever needed. "Bye, Penny."

"Bye."

I hung up the phone and opened my eyes. I wasn't going to stay in touch. And I was never going back to New York. It was time to start over. The marines. Hailey. This was my life now. Sometimes it's best to keep the past in the past.

I glanced once more at the waves crashing against the rocks. I had this peaceful feeling that wherever Hailey was right now, she was thinking about me too. I didn't need to wait for a letter from her. She was the air I needed to breathe. And for some crazy reason, I was that for her too. We were going to figure this out together.

CHAPTER 49

Hailey
Friday

Even though it felt like I left a part of myself in California, it was good to almost be home. Just seeing normal trees again from the plane window instead of palm trees was relaxing.

I squeezed my eyes shut as the plane touched down. Flying had been a relatively terrifying experience. But take-off and landing were definitely now my two least favorite things in the world. For some reason I just feared that we had been lucky the whole flight and the plane would just explode as soon as it all came back in contact with the ground. I exhaled when the plane slowed. *Disaster averted.* Everything was going to be okay. For the first time in a long time, it really felt that way.

For a moment I let myself think about what Tyler was doing. I had seen a few movies about people joining the army. He was probably standing in a line right now getting yelled at by his commanding officer or something. I just hoped he was okay. I hoped he knew that he could count on me too. I pulled the picture of us out of my pocket. Before I turned it over, I noticed something written on the back. I smiled at the words. "We're never getting older," I whispered to myself as I ran my fingers across the inscription. To me it meant that we could stop time. That in three years we'd still be the same. That we could really make this work.

The pilot came on and said it would be a minute before we pulled up to a terminal. I smiled and slid the picture back into my pocket. I needed to schedule an Uber to pick me up. I hit the button to turn my phone back on. I couldn't wait to see my dad and tell him the good news. He'd be thrilled about me being home. But the money? He'd be ecstatic. I couldn't wait to tell him about the Grand Canyon and the Pacific Ocean. And one day he'd be able to see those things now. Thanks to Tyler.

As soon as my phone turned on, it started buzzing. I had dozens of missed calls, voicemails, and texts. At first I thought Tyler had changed his mind and decided he wanted to hear my voice. But then I saw that everything was from Anna, the assistant manager from my dad's bar.

I could almost hear my heart thumping as I hit play on one of the voicemails and pulled the phone to my ear.

"Hails, it's Anna. Where are you, hon? I really need to speak to you. No one knows where you are. Please call me back as soon as you get this. It's urgent." The voicemail clicked off.

I wanted this to be about her raise. But I knew it wasn't. Anna wouldn't call me about that. She would have just talked to my dad. Something must have happened to him. I clicked on another of the voicemails.

"Hon, you need to come home. I was trying not to startle you in my other messages, but your father has taken a turn for the worse. It's not looking...good. He's asking for you. Please call me back."

I pressed on her name in my phone but there wasn't any service in the plane. *Damn it.*

I pressed on another voicemail. "Hon, your father..." Anna tried to stifle a sob. "You need to come home as soon as you get this message. Where are you?" The voicemail clicked off.

My father what? My father what?! I wrapped my arms around myself. *Please don't let me be too late.* He was supposed to have four months. It had only been a week. I was only gone for a week! But it didn't matter what I told myself. The guilt was already swallowing me whole.

As soon as the plane pulled into the terminal I pushed my way past the other passengers. I clicked on Anna's name.

"Oh, Hailey, thank heavens!"

"Anna what happened? How is he?"

"We're at the hospital." There was a long pause. "He's not good, hon."

"But he's awake? He's alive?" I started running through the airport.

"He's been holding on, waiting for you."

Waiting for me for what? This wasn't the end. He had four months. "I'm going to be right there, okay? I'm coming now." I didn't have time to wait for my Uber. I waved down a taxi instead. "Tell him I'm coming. Tell him I got the money."

"Hails it's too..."

"Just tell him, okay?" I hung up the phone as I climbed in the cab. I couldn't hear the rest of what she was going to say. Because I already knew what it was. I was too late.

***

I threw some cash at the cab driver and ran into the hospital. "I'm looking for Jeffrey Shaw," I said to the receptionist.

Her eyebrows lowered slightly. *Sympathy.* I was so fucking tired of getting people's sympathy. The whole car ride over here I thought about the extra time I spent in California with Tyler. I should have just come home. He was right. *God, please don't let me be too late.*

"He's in room 237."

"Thank you." I took the stairs two at a time. I didn't even need to find the room. I saw the employees from the bar and friends from town all clustered together at the end of the hall.

I ran over to Anna and shoved the envelope that contained the check and credit cards into her hands.

"Hailey..." There was the sympathy again. All over Anna's face.

"Please just find the doctor and give that to him."

"Hailey..." but I was already pushing the door open to my dad's room.

She caught my arm before I could enter. I never would have guessed how strong Anna was.

"Hailey you need to be prepared for what you're walking into."

"I got the money. He's going to be fine."

"Hon, he's not going to be fine." She grabbed my shoulders so that I would face her. Her eyes were filled with tears. "He's dying. You're lucky he held on this long. He doesn't have much time left."

"He has at least four months."

Anna shook her head.

I didn't have time to listen to Anna fill me on what I had missed. I knew what I had missed. I had missed my last few days with my dad. I shook away from her grip. *No.* No, he was going to be okay.

I turned away from her and pushed through the door. But I immediately froze when I saw him. He looked ten years older. He looked...he looked like he was dying. I bit the inside of my lip, trying to hold back the tears. I needed to be strong for him. "Dad?" I whispered. It looked like he was sleeping.

He coughed into his hand, which had tubes sticking out of it. "Honey?" He coughed again and slowly opened his eyes.

"Hi, Daddy." I peeled myself from the wall and walked over to him. I grabbed his hand as I sat down next to his hospital bed. His hand felt so cold in mine. *Dad.*

"I missed you, honey." His voice sounded hoarse and his eyelids looked heavy.

I squeezed his hand. "I missed you too."

"Did you see her?"

I nodded my head.

"Promise me you didn't listen to anything she said."

I blinked faster so the tears wouldn't start. "No, of course not."

"Hails, look at me."

I blinked away my tears as he touched the bottom of my chin.

"Hails, you are not your mother. There's goodness in your heart." He coughed again. This time there was blood on his hand.

"I should get a doctor."

"No, wait." He coughed again. "I talked to a financial advisor. You need to sell the house. And the bar. I had a life insurance policy in case anything happened to me when you were a kid. It's still good. It should be enough to settle all my debts. Enough to give you a fresh start."

I shook my head. "Dad, I got the money for the treatments. You're going to be okay. Everything's going to be okay."

"It's too late, Hails.

"It's not too late. You can fight this."

"I don't have any fight left in me."

Please don't give up. "Of course you do. You're the strongest person I know."

He smiled. It looked like it pained him to do it. "Go live your life, Hails. You're bigger than this town. Go make me proud."

"Dad, this town is my life. You're my life. I love it here. This was always enough for me."

He smiled. "You were always enough for me. You were the best thing that ever happened to me. The greatest blessing that this life ever gave me. That's why you need to keep your heart open, Hails. Don't go your whole life being scared to let people in. You need to know that I never regretted what happened with your mother. Because she gave me you."

The tears streamed down my cheeks. It was such a contrast to the things Elena had said. My dad had always made me feel like I was a gift. That I was special. That I was loved. Why had I ever felt like I was missing something? I didn't need a mother. Because I had the best dad a girl could ask for.

"For me, the sun rose and set with your smile. Don't ever stop smiling. Don't ever change, Hails. I love you so much, honey." He touched the bottom of my chin again.

"I love you too. Dad, we can fight this together."

He coughed again. More blood came out on his hand.

"I'm going to go get a doctor." I ran over to the door as the machine he was attached to started to beep.

A doctor was already standing by the door talking to Anna.

"He's coughing up blood and the machine started beeping..."

The doctor rushed into the room.

Anna gently touched my arm. "Is he..." her voice trailed off as she stared at me.

"No, of course not. He's going to be fine." I shook her hand off me and followed the doctor back into my dad's room.

But the doctor wasn't doing anything. He was just writing something in his notebook. The machines had stopped. Everything was eerily quiet.

"Is he okay?"

He turned toward me. His facial expression matched Anna's from earlier. Matched the receptionist. Matched the cab driver's when he saw me bawling in the back seat of his car.

Fuck all of them. "Why aren't you doing anything?"

"I'm so sorry, you must be his daughter. I'm doctor Klein. We didn't realize how fast the cancer was spreading. We did everything we could."

I shook my head. "What? No. I got the money for the treatments."

"I'm so very sorry." He pulled the envelope I had given Anna out of his coat pocket and handed it back to me.

I tried to push it back at him. "Use it to save him."

"I'm sorry, Miss Shaw. He's gone."

What was he talking about? Tears were streaming down my face. "He's right there. Why aren't you doing anything?!" I could hear the hysteria in my voice, but I didn't care.

"Hon..." Anna touched my arm.

I shook her off again.

"Someone do something! He has four months! Do something!"

"Oh, Hailey." Anna tried to embrace me in a hug but I brushed past her.

"Dad." I grabbed his hand again. "Dad, wake up."

"Miss Shaw, the time of death was..."

"No. Please. Dad. You can't leave me." I squeezed his hand. "I need you. Daddy I need you. Please." Someone touched my shoulder and this time I didn't push them off.

There were so many things I hadn't gotten to say. I held his hand even tighter and leaned my forehead against his arm. *I love you. You were all I ever needed. You were enough for me too.* I couldn't seem to stop my sobbing. *I saw the Grand Canyon, Dad. And the Pacific Ocean. I faced my fears. And I fell in love with a boy. I opened my heart just like you wanted me to. But*

I'd take it all back. I'd redo all of it if I could have one more week with you.

CHAPTER 50

Tyler

Friday

My stomach was twisted in knots. I was terrified. But for the first time since I had enlisted, I felt a small amount of excitement too. The reasons I had signed up were real. I wanted my grandfather to be proud of me. I wanted my dad to be proud of the person that I had become. I could do all that here. Even though a piece of me was in Indiana, I needed to do this. I didn't regret my choice to enlist. And I could survive this. I would fight and I would come home. For Hails. For my mom. For myself.

I took a deep breath and pushed through the front doors. There were a few men sitting behind a desk along the far side of the wall. I looked around the room. No one else was in sight. I walked over to them.

"Name?" one of them asked without looking up. He started thumbing through his clipboard.

"Tyler Stevens."

He immediately looked up at me and glanced at the man sitting next to him. He cleared his throat and set the clipboard down on top of the desk. "Right, we've been expecting you." He opened up a drawer in the desk and pulled out a file with my name on it. "Follow me, please." He stood up and started walking down a hallway.

I almost had to jog to keep up with him.

He opened up a door and gestured for me to go inside. "If you don't mind taking a seat, someone will be right with you."

"Of course." I stepped inside.

The man immediately closed the door and I swear I heard it lock. I grabbed the handle and, sure enough, it wouldn't budge. I looked back at the room. There was an empty metal desk in the middle of the room and two chairs, one on either side of it. If I didn't know any better, I would have thought I was in an interrogation room. Maybe I was. Maybe this was their way of intimidating recruits or something. I should have done some research this morning about what to expect. Instead I had spent the day trying to remind myself that I had made the right decision. Or maybe I was just trying to convince myself that I hadn't made the biggest mistake of my life.

After a few minutes of standing by the door, I walked over to one of the chairs and sat down.

***

"Tyler Stevens?"

I lifted my head off the desk. I had completely lost all sense of time. But my neck hurt and my back was stiff. I must have fallen asleep. I cleared my throat. "Yes?" This wasn't what I had been expecting at all. I immediately stood up when he didn't respond. *I'm supposed to do that, right?*

He eyed me coolly. "I'm Lieutenant Colonel John Williams."

I thought he might shake my hand but he continued to size me up. I just stood there awkwardly.

"Please, sit down."

I guess I wasn't supposed to stand. I sat back down in the metal chair under his scrutiny.

He opened up the file with my name on it. "Tyler Stevens." His eyes darted across the page. "Current residence of New York City. You grew up in Delaware. One living parent. No siblings. Not in a relationship. You are the perfect candidate for the Marine Corps."

Why did he sound so angry? "That's good, right?"

"It would be. Except for the fact that we obviously do background checks." He ripped the file with my name on it in half and tossed it into the trash as he sat down across from me at the table.

"What are you talking about?"

"Many people that enlist are trying to escape from their problems. We help people find themselves. We help them discover their full potential. But not criminals."

"I'm not a criminal."

"You have a warrant out for your arrest. For your refusal to appear for your questioning in regards to the ongoing investigation of James Hunter's shooting. With immediate request to be transferred to New York City."

"It's not ongoing. They just arrested Isabella Hunter for that. She was behind everything."

He lowered his eyebrows. "Isabella Hunter is dead. She died at 0200 Eastern Standard Time. The investigation is being reopened. And your original charges are being reinstated."

Isabella was dead? I wasn't sure what time it was, but I had just talked to Penny. Everything was fine. What the hell had happened? "Original charges?"

"You have been officially un-enlisted from the United States Marine Corps effective immediately."

"What original charges?"

Lieutenant Colonel John Williams stood up as a police officer walked into the room.

Shit. What the hell was happening?

The police officer grabbed my shoulder and pulled me to my feet. "Tyler Stevens, you are under arrest for blackmail and conspiracy to commit murder. Anything you say can and will be used against you in a court of law..."

I drowned out the rest of his words. *Blackmail? Conspiracy to commit murder? What the fuck?*

He pushed me against the wall and cuffed my hands behind my back.

CHAPTER 51

Hailey

Saturday

I tried to focus on my breathing. In and out. *Slower.* Inhale, exhale.

I lifted my head off the kitchen table. The house was eerily quiet. All day people had buzzed around me. I just kept nodding my head, not really hearing anything anyone said. By the end of the day there was a for sale sign sticking out of the middle of our yard. It felt like I had signed my life away. But what did it matter? My life here was my dad. Without him, there was nothing left.

But I couldn't listen to anyone say how wonderful my dad was one more time or I was going to scream. I knew that he was wonderful. I knew him better than anyone else in the world. And all I could feel was his loss. This huge hole in my heart. Yet, when I looked around the kitchen I could still feel his presence. I could see him making pancakes for me on Saturday mornings. I could hear him whistling. I could see him reading the paper while I did dishes after dinner.

It hurt. It hurt so fucking much. *Inhale. Exhale.* I just needed to keep breathing.

I closed my eyes tight. What I really needed was to hear Tyler's voice. He should have gotten my letter by now. He should know that I chose him. Could he feel that

I needed him right now? I tried to remember the touch of his skin. The smell of him. Anything. But I just felt alone. I felt myself getting swallowed whole by my grief.

I wiped my tears from my eyes and pulled out my phone. I could find his number online. Everything could be found online. I typed his name into Google but there were thousands of results. Apparently Tyler Stevens was a very common name.

If I linked his name to one that was famous, that would certainly give me the results I wanted. I slowly typed in Penny Taylor after his name. The first thing that came up was a tabloid from earlier this year. The headline read, "Penny Taylor having affair with college sweetheart?" There was a picture of Penny holding Tyler's arm, laughing. He was smiling at her. There was so much adoration on his face. Obviously it wasn't real. Tabloids were meant to provoke people. But Tyler's feelings clearly were real. I thought that seeing something like this might upset me. But I think I was already as low as I could possibly be. I closed out of the internet browser.

Why was I purposely torturing myself anyway? I was already in a dark place, there was no reason to add fuel to the fire. I could have kept searching for Tyler's number, but instead I set my phone down. Tyler had his own things to face right now. Even if I found his number, he probably wouldn't have time to answer. No one could help me feel better right now. I had to face this myself. I looked down at the check Tyler had left me. I could have used it to save my house. I could have used it to save the bar. But that wasn't what it was for. Tyler gave it to me to save my dad. And what was the point of having the house and the bar if my dad wasn't here to share it with me? I tore the check in half.

I needed something to hold on to. But it felt like I had nothing. Despite what Tyler had promised, I did feel alone. My dad was dead. Tyler was halfway across the country. And I was here. Alone in my grief.

The more I stared at the picture Tyler had given me, the less real it seemed. The edges were already worn from me keeping it in my pocket all the time. I thought that looking at it would give me strength, like Tyler so often did in person. But a picture wasn't the same. This picture didn't speak a thousand words. It was just a reminder that I was alone.

I pulled out a sheet of paper and confessed my darkest thoughts. I wrote pages and pages of how much I regretted not staying with my dad. How much I regretted not being there for him during his final days. And then I balled it up and threw it in the trash. Because I couldn't put that on Tyler. I couldn't let him see how much I needed him when he couldn't be here. He told me I was strong. My dad told me I was strong. So I was going to fucking be strong.

I sat back down and wrote a short note to Tyler saying that I needed to speak to him. I left him my number and asked him to call me. That it was important. That I needed to hear his voice. And then I sealed it and put it out in the mailbox. He promised he'd write me back. No matter what, I'd be hearing from him soon. It was hard to have faith in a time like this. But somehow I still had faith in him. We were worlds apart, but I knew he was out there thinking of me too.

CHAPTER 52

Hailey
Monday

A pat on the back. A kiss on the cheek. A squeeze of the shoulder. There were tons of people around me. So why did I feel so alone? It was like I couldn't feel anything but my aching heart.

I dropped the first handful of dirt on top of my father's coffin. It made this horrible thud. That sickening sound was the cue for everyone to leave. But I continued to stand there long after everyone else was gone. Long after the rest of the dirt had been shoveled onto his grave. Long after the last look of pity.

It was the middle of summer but I was freezing cold. I wrapped my arms around myself.

People were heading back to the house, but I couldn't bear to follow them. And I didn't want to leave my dad. I didn't want him to be alone. I knelt down in the dirt by his grave and touched the headstone.

"Dad," I whispered. "I miss you." I let my hand fall from the stone and clutched it around myself again. "I don't know how to keep going without you."

I lay down beside his grave. "It's not the same here without you." I pressed my hand against the dirt and let my tears fall. I closed my eyes and thought about our last conversation. He had told me I was bigger than this town. But this was my home. Where else would I go?

***

"Hon."

I opened my eyes. I hadn't realized that it had grown dark. "Anna."

There were tears in her eyes as she knelt down beside me.

I had been pushing her away ever since I had come home. And I wasn't even sure why. She was the closest thing I had left to family. I had known her since I was a kid.

"Everyone's waiting for you." She put her hand on my shoulder.

"I can't. I don't want to leave him alone."

"He'll never be alone. Your father is in all of our hearts."

I wiped the tears off my cheeks as I slowly sat up. "Anna, I'm so sorry."

"It's okay." She pulled my head to her shoulder as she let me cry.

She didn't mention going to the house again. Instead she just silently lay down beside me and we both stared up at the stars. I used to do this all the time with my dad. He'd point out constellations and I'd usually pretend I saw them too. No matter how hard I tried, I just couldn't see them, though. Maybe it was because I so easily got lost in the vastness of the sky. What had he always said was in the sky in the middle of summer? I searched the stars. Why couldn't I remember? Why couldn't I see it?

"Scorpius is out tonight," Anna said and pointed to the sky.

And for some reason, the realization hit me hard. Anna was a single mom. She came over to our house all the time. I considered her kind of an unofficial Aunt. But it was more than that. I wasn't sure why I didn't see it before. I felt a million years older after the past few days. How long had my dad and her been more than friends? I had been so blind. About my dad being sick. About this. I bit the inside of my cheek. "Did you love him?" I asked.

She sniffled beside me. "With all my heart."

I grabbed Anna's hand in the cold grass. "Thank you for being there for him when I wasn't."

She squeezed my hand. "He wanted you to go out there and live your life. He was happy that you were doing that, even though he did miss you."

The stars blurred in the sky.

"And he certainly didn't want you to stop living your life after his ended. You need to go out there and live."

I don't have anywhere to go.

CHAPTER 53

Hailey

Wednesday

I ran to the bathroom and threw up everything I had left in my stomach. I sat down on the cold tile floor next to the toilet. Even getting sick made me cry. Because when I was little my dad was always there with me. I rested my head against the vanity and closed my eyes.

Adding a stomach bug to the list of ways I was falling apart didn't make a difference. I took a few deep breaths and slowly stood up. I had found out that it was better for my sanity if I didn't sit for too long. Sitting made me cry. Which made me curl up in a ball with a blanket and not move for hours at a time. But I had just slept. And I still had a lot to pack. The realtor wanted to start showing the house. I thought it was best if there wasn't someone crying in a corner with boxes everywhere. In the meantime, I'd sleep in my dad's office at the bar. Apparently that was going to be a harder sell, so I'd have some time to crash there.

I walked down the hall and stopped at the doorway into the kitchen. I ran my hand up the lines marking my height as I grew up. Last night I had gotten lost in photo albums. I remembered everything, but I couldn't stop looking. It was good that I had to get out of here. Because I could lose myself in the house. In the memories.

A knock on the door made me jump. People had been stopping by all week giving me condolences. But I'm pretty sure Anna had just been sending them to check up on me. I knew she was worried about me. No matter what she said, I felt guilty for not being here with him. He had specifically asked me not to go to Elena's. And he was right. Nothing had come from it.

Except Tyler. But I hadn't heard from him since he left without saying goodbye in Santa Monica. That was starting to weigh on me too. Not because I doubted his feelings. But because I was worried about him. I had written him at least a dozen letters now. It was starting to become a nervous tick. Whenever I was struggling the most, I just grabbed a piece of paper and wrote down everything that I was struggling with. Then I would throw that paper out and write something a lot calmer that I actually would send him. So that he wouldn't worry about me. But I always ended the letters the same way. Telling him that I needed to hear his voice. It was probably desperate. But I was desperate. I couldn't hide that fact. Was he not writing me back because I was being too obsessive? Just thinking about it made me want to write to him again.

I slowly walked over to the door, wondering who had been sent to check on me this time. I was more than a little surprised to see my best friend from when I was little standing there with a casserole dish in her hand.

"Hey." I tried to hide the surprise in my voice.

She smiled weakly. "Hails." She moved the dish to her side, revealing her huge pregnant stomach, as she leaned in for a hug. "Hails, I'm so, so sorry about your dad."

I patted her back awkwardly. "Thanks." I thought the next time we spoke that maybe she'd apologize for kissing my boyfriend in high school. She had apologized before, but she never sounded that sincere. Or maybe I just didn't forgive very easily.

She pulled back. The small smile was still on her face. "Can I come in?" She didn't really wait for an answer. Instead, she just stepped beside me into the house. "I spent so much time here when I was little," she said as she made her way to the kitchen.

"That was a long time ago."

"Yeah. It really was." She set the dish down on the table. "I made you tuna casserole. I know how much you used to love your dad's. Do you want me to warm it up?"

I immediately shook my head. "No, I have a stomach bug or something. I'm not going to be eating anything for a while."

"Sure you don't just have morning sickness?" She laughed at her own joke as she touched her stomach. "God, morning sickness was the worst. Luckily I'm past that now."

Shit. Am I pregnant? No. There's no way. "No."

"You hesitated."

"I didn't hesitate."

"Hails."

I shook my head, but didn't say anything for a moment. "Congrats on the baby, by the way. You must be so excited."

She just stared back at me.

"What?"

"Do you still feel sick?"

"I mean, no not really. I feel a lot better now. Because I just threw up whatever it was that was making me sick probably."

"Well, do you have a temperature?"

"I don't know, I don't think so."

"Have you had sex recently?"

"Claire!"

She smiled. "It's just like old times."

Except I had never had sex with Jack. Is that why she was here? She wanted to know about her husband's sexual history? If it was a problem for her, maybe she shouldn't have started dating someone who was currently in a relationship with me.

"I can run to the pharmacy real quick if you want."

"That's not necessary. I'm definitely not pregnant." *Definitely not.*

"Okay." She awkwardly tapped the kitchen table with her fingertips. She always used to do that in class whenever she was called on. When she was nervous.

I exhaled slowly. I didn't want to hold on to this anger anymore. I had enough problems without this. My dad wanted me to live my life. How could I do that if I was harboring all this anger? "I forgive you."

"I'm sorry," she said at the exact same time.

We both smiled.

"Hails, I've missed you so much. You were my best friend. And I don't have an excuse except that love makes you do crazy things. I never meant to hurt you. I just...I loved him so much. But I'm so, so sorry."

"I'm sorry too. There was never a future between Jack and me. You two were clearly meant to be together. And I'm sorry that I made you feel bad about that."

She wiped tears off her cheeks. "God, I'm such a mess. Pregnancy hormones are insane."

But I was crying too. Because it really felt like I had just let something go. And I could breathe a little easier. I wrapped my arms around her.

I couldn't help but think that my dad would be proud of me. He was never able to forgive Elena. But that wasn't for his own pain. He hadn't forgiven her because of how she had hurt me. And I loved him even more for that.

CHAPTER 54

Hailey

Thursday

I threw up again that morning. And now I was standing in the drug store staring at all the different pregnancy test options. Even though I definitely wasn't pregnant.

The things Claire had said last night about love had really resonated with me. People did crazy things for love all the time. If I left this town, maybe I did have somewhere to go. I could live near the Marine Corps training base. I would be able to see Tyler more often. And if I was really pregnant...I immediately shook away the thought. It wasn't possible. It couldn't be.

But I still pulled one of the tests off the hook and placed it in my basket. I had driven out of town to get the test. If I had gone to the local pharmacy, everyone would be talking about it. Word would probably still get back to town, but it would take a while. Maybe I'd be in California by then. I just needed to wait for Tyler's phone call. Or his first letter back to me.

I checked out and climbed back in my car. I turned on the ignition and started driving back to town. Claire had spent all of last night helping me pack up the rest of the house. It was easier to do it with someone else. Especially someone who I hadn't realized how much I missed. It truly felt like we were friends again. She had sent Jack over to help this morning with moving boxes to the bar. Which was the first time in years that it hadn't been awkward to see him.

And Anna had sent her son Billy to help move everything too. I congratulated Billy on getting into college. And he laughed for about five minutes and asked what the hell I was talking about. Apparently he had already been taking classes at a local trade school and had known he wanted to be an electrician for years.

I had told him his mom asked for a raise just a few weeks ago because he had gotten into school. Which made him laugh some more. He said she probably just said the first thing that she could think of so that I wouldn't suspect anything. Apparently my dad and her had pretty much been in a relationship since I had gone off to school. It made me feel better that they had never explicitly told Billy either, though. Billy had just been a much better detective than me.

For the first time since my dad had died, I didn't feel so alone. There were people in this town that still cared about me. It was better to talk to people instead of shutting everyone out to grieve by myself. Because really, this whole town was grieving with me. This town was everything to me. But I was going to take a crazy chance on love. After all, my dad wanted me to start opening up my heart. I could feel him rooting for Tyler and me.

I pulled into the parking lot of the bar and put my car into park. There were cars everywhere. Anna must have decided to open the bar for the night. She had mentioned it earlier, but I told her I wasn't up for it. I glanced down at my phone. That was my other new nervous habit. Checking my phone constantly, hoping Tyler would call me. He'd call me soon. I nodded to myself as I climbed out of the car.

When I walked into the bar, everyone started clapping.

For a brief second, I thought that Claire had told the whole town I was pregnant or something.

But she immediately ran over to me and hugged me. "We raised the money!" she shouted over the music.

"What?"

"To keep the bar open."

I'm pretty sure my jaw actually dropped. "What? How?"

"We all pitched in. I mean, it's just enough for a few months. But if business is good, it'll survive on its own." She was beaming.

"You guys didn't have to do that."

"We wanted to," Anna said as she gave me a hug too.

I was suddenly surrounded by everyone who had come out. And it made my heart feel so full. But at the same time, it broke it too. If my dad had told people he was sick, maybe they would have raised the money for his treatments. Maybe he'd be standing here too. That was the thing about us Shaws. We were too proud for our own good.

***

Eventually, I was able to sneak away to the bathroom. I stared down at the pregnancy test as I paced around the bathroom stall. Slowly two lines appeared. *Two.* I glanced at the instructions on the box one more time. *Two lines. I'm pregnant.*

I'm pregnant?

I glanced at the instructions on the box again. *I can't be pregnant.* I couldn't even tell if I was happy or sad. I was just in shock. I pulled out my phone. *Nothing. Tyler, where are you?*

I needed to talk to him. I needed to see him. I needed to tell him. I opened up the stall door, walked over to the sink, and stared at the reflection staring back at me. My cheeks looked hollow. I barely recognized myself. I hadn't been eating because I was too upset. And then I thought I had a virus or something and wouldn't be able to keep it down anyway. Now I had a reason to keep going though. A reason beyond myself, which I think I needed. I heard people laughing outside in the bar. The reflection staring back at me smiled. *I'm going to keep living, Dad.*

And I was done waiting. I quickly washed my hands and made my way out the back door of the bar. There was a slight breeze. It reminded me of the pier in Santa Monica. The only thing missing was Tyler.

I pulled out my phone and brought up the website for the Marine Corps Recruit Depot in San Diego. I scrolled through the phone directory. *Recruiters School? That might work.*

I clicked on the number and put my phone to my ear. After a few rings a very serious sounding man answered the phone.

"Hi, yes, I was trying to contact one of your recent recruits. He just started training last week."

"Please hold and I'll transfer you."

"Okay..." but there was already light music playing.

A minute later someone with an even deeper voice answered the phone. "How can I help you?"

"I'm trying to get a hold of one of your recent recruits. He just reported for training last week. It's important."

"Name?"

"Hailey Shaw."

There was silence on the other end. "The name of the recruit, ma'am."

"Oh, right, of course. Tyler Stevens."

"One second, ma'am."

I closed my eyes as I waited. I wouldn't tell him over the phone. I'd come see him. He needed to hear it in person. But I needed to hear his voice. If I knew he was okay, it would give me the strength to be okay too.

The man on the other end cleared his throat. "Sorry, there are no records of a Tyler Stevens in our recent trainees."

What? "He just reported last Friday."

"Yes, I'm looking at that list, ma'am. Would you like me to pull up older records?"

"No, he just got there."

"Then maybe he reported to the Parris Island recruit depot in South Carolina then. Would you like me to transfer you?"

I shook my head even though I knew he couldn't see me. "Could you look again? I know he went to the San Diego recruit depot."

He was silent for moment. "There is no one by that name. I'm sorry. I hope you have a good night, ma'am."

The line went dead.

I pulled my phone away from my ear and stared down at it. If Tyler wasn't in training, where the hell was he? For a second it felt like the last few weeks had been a strange dream. Maybe I had made him up. I shook away the thought. My high was quickly turning back into a low.

He lied to me. He lied about joining the marines. I shook my head. That didn't make any sense. There was no reason for him to lie to me about that. There must have just been a problem with their records. *That must be it.* Tyler had no reason to lie to me. Unless he never wanted to see me again.

CHAPTER 55

Hailey

Friday

The makeshift cot in my father's office was not the best place to sleep. Or maybe it was this desperate feeling in my chest that wouldn't go away. I stared up at the ceiling. I should have been happy. The bar could keep functioning for at least two more months now. I had a purpose again. I could keep my father's memory alive right here.

But it wasn't the same without him. I closed my eyes. This office still smelled like him. Like his aftershave. I slowly breathed in and out.

If I stayed here, it felt like time would stop. I so badly wanted to stop time in California, but I didn't want to stop it here. I didn't want to freeze this sad state I was in. That was the exact opposite of what my father wanted.

I had convinced myself last night that I did have a future outside of this town. I put all my eggs in one basket. *A lying basket.* I bit my lip. This whole thing had to be a misunderstanding. Tyler was definitely in San Diego. I put my hand on my stomach and opened my eyes again.

This was definitely a misunderstanding. The more times I tried to convince myself, the more real it seemed. I'd call the recruiters office back today and ask them to look in the older records. Maybe Tyler's name had been filed in the wrong place or something. That had to be it. I slowly sat up and put my hand over my mouth. Claire was right. Morning sickness was the absolute worst.

***

"Hi, Dad." I sat down in the wet grass near his headstone. There were small blades of grass already coming up in the dirt where he had been buried. Time was definitely not standing still.

I placed my hand on the cold tombstone. I had called the recruiters office again, only to receive the same response. Even the recruit depot in South Carolina didn't have Tyler's records. It wasn't a misunderstanding. Tyler wasn't there.

I wasn't sure why I felt so abandoned. We had only shared one week together. To me it had been magical. But who knew what it really was to him.

If my dad was standing in front of me right now, I'd have a hard time telling him. But here in the grass, I wasn't worried about his reaction. I felt like no matter what, he'd be proud of me. Even though I had made a terrible mistake. *No, not terrible.* I placed my hand on my stomach. This baby wasn't terrible. It was exactly what I needed. My dad had me. He was alone most of his life except for me. And somehow the world knew that I needed that too. I needed this baby. The sun would rise and set with his smile. *His.* I smiled to myself. I'd be happy with a boy or a girl. But it felt like it was going to be a boy.

For a brief moment I frowned. What if it looked like Tyler? What if every time I saw him, I'd be reminded of the boy who disappeared? It would be just like how my father saw my mother when he looked at me. I didn't know if I could handle that.

What the fuck am I doing? I wasn't my dad. And Tyler wasn't my mom. I needed to go find him. I needed to go to San Diego and hunt him down. I wouldn't let my baby grow up feeling unwanted. That had put me through hell. Tyler at least needed to be given the chance to decide. And he was a good guy. This whole thing was definitely a misunderstanding. He loved me. And I loved him.

I had been spending too much time alone in my own thoughts. I had damned myself to a life of isolation for no reason.

I placed my hand on the dirt. "Thanks for reminding me, Dad. I'm not going to let you down." I stood up. I was going back to California.

CHAPTER 56

Tyler
Friday

"Stevens?"

I lifted my head. A police officer was walking toward me. Maybe I was finally allowed to have my phone call. I had asked enough times.

I stood up.

"All your charges have been dropped."

"Really?"

"Don't sound so surprised, son. Makes you sound guilty," he said with a laugh as he unlocked my cell. "You're free to go."

Free to go? Just like that? I had been thrown into a cell in California, driven across the country in handcuffs, and then sat in this cell for God knows how long without any-one telling me anything. "What happened? Did they find who did it?"

"Oh, yeah. A while ago. It was Isabella Hunter. But the detective working on the case was crooked. Paperwork was a nightmare. Sorry about the confusion."

Confusion? That's what they were calling it? "What about the marines?"

"You can re-enlist if you want, I guess. There won't be anything on your record about this incident now. You're all clear."

Re-enlist? The first thing that popped into my head was Hailey. Right now she needed me. If I still wanted, I could do this in the future. But not right now. I needed to see her. I needed to know if she read my letter. I needed to know what she was thinking.

I signed some papers, grabbed my things, and stepped out into the sunshine. The light was blinding. I blinked several times before I could see anything. I was standing in the middle of NYC, my least favorite place in the world. My car was still in California. And I didn't even have Hailey's phone number to call her. *Shit.*

I opened up my wallet. I had given Hailey everything. All the money in my bank account. My credit cards so that she could max them out for the money she needed. All I had was $37 in cash. It was at least enough for me to get back to my old apartment. After a shower and a change of clothes, I'd figure something out.

I hailed down a taxi and climbed in the back seat. I had some money hidden in a drawer in my apartment. It might be enough to rent a car. My plan started to form in my head as the taxi slowly drove through the city. I'd pack up some essentials and drive to Hails' Bar where we had met. If I drove non-stop I could make it there by tomorrow morning.

Luckily the taxi only cost $20. I paid the driver and entered my apartment building. I made a silent prayer that Melissa wouldn't be there. Hopefully she had moved out by now. I didn't want to see anyone, because I knew I couldn't explain my thoughts. Maybe I was out of my mind. But I just needed to see Hailey. It's the only thing I could focus on. It's like I knew she needed me. I knew I needed her. *Please need me back.*

I put the key into my door and opened it.

Penny was sitting on the living room floor, taping up a box.

"Oh, finally, I'm starving," she said without looking back at me.

She looked different somehow. Maybe it was the fact that she was married. Maybe it was the fact that I didn't have feelings for her anymore. But she did look different. Everything was different.

"Hi, Penny."

She immediately looked over her shoulder. "Tyler?" She looked surprised to see me. "Tyler!" She ran over to me and threw her arms around my neck.

And I felt nothing. No spark. No rush. Nothing. Usually a moment like this would have killed me a bit inside. But not anymore. I was glad to know she was okay, though. She had a smile on her face as she stepped back from me.

"What are you doing here?"

"I live here. What are you doing here?"

She laughed. "I'm helping Melissa pack. What I meant was why didn't you call me to say you were back?"

"I'm not really back. I just need to grab a few things. I have to go somewhere." I couldn't explain myself to her. I didn't want to. I walked past her into my bedroom and opened up my sock drawer. I pulled out the small stack of money. There was only $112. Shit was that enough to rent a car? I sat down on the edge of my bed and typed in car rentals in my phone.

"Tyler, are you okay?" She hesitated by the door of my room.

"I'm fine." I recounted the money. It wasn't enough. Did car rental places negotiate? I stared at the information on my phone. *Shit.* They required a credit card just in case there were any damages.

"Tyler?"

"What?!" I didn't mean to snap at her. I instantly felt terrible when I saw her face.

She pressed her lips together. "Melissa and James will be back any minute with some pizza if you want to eat with us. Or, just in case you want to leave before they get back. I'll leave you alone." She walked away from my bedroom.

Damn it. I quickly changed and then stuffed the money into my pocket. I grabbed a few changes of clothes and shoved them into an old backpack. When I walked out of my room, Penny was sitting on the floor again, taping up another box.

"I'm sorry, Penny. I'm just in a hurry."

"It's okay," she said without looking at me. "I'm actually just going to get going. I'll tell them I'd rather do this another day." She stood up and grabbed her purse off the couch.

"You don't have to go."

"Actually I do. I'm so tired of always being in your way. For the last few years it's seemed like I was holding you back. And I don't know how to fix it. I don't know what you want me to do." She wiped the tears away from underneath of her eyes. "So I'm just going to stop bothering you."

I walked over to her and hugged her hard. "You were never in my way."

She wrapped her arms around my back. "I never meant to hurt you. I just want you to be happy. That's all I ever wanted, Tyler."

"I know." I had known that all along. For the past three years I had made myself unhappy by pining over her. That wasn't her fault. It was mine. Penny wasn't a cure to all my problems. I had learned more about myself in the past few weeks than I had in those three years that I was being an idiot. I'm pretty sure I needed the pain of her rejection to cover up the pain of missing my dad. The pain of feeling guilty. And I would always be grateful for her distraction. I needed her because of that. But I didn't need to mask my feelings anymore. I found someone who understood me.

"Are you happy? Does Hailey make you happy?" She kept her arms wrapped around me.

"Yes."

"Then what are you doing here? Go get her." She leaned back slightly so she could smile up at me.

"Great, you set her off again," Melissa said.

I released Penny from my hug and turned to see Melissa and James standing by the door. Neither one of them looked excited to see me.

Penny laughed as she wiped away the rest of her tears.

"And before you say anything, don't flatter yourself, Tyler. She wasn't crying over you," Melissa said.

"I didn't..."

"We brought the pizza you requested, hot momma," Melissa continued, cutting me off.

"And the watermelon," James said and placed it on the counter. He put his hand down on the counter beside the watermelon. It almost looked like he needed to do it to steady himself. He looked paler than I remembered. And skinnier. Penny had looked so healthy that I had completely forgotten about what they had just been through. He was recovering from three gunshot wounds. Since I had been trying so hard to ignore the news, that was the extent of what I knew. But it was pretty clear that he shouldn't have been carrying a huge watermelon through the city. The smile he gave Penny hid his grimace.

"And the pickles," Melissa said and placed a bag on the counter beside the rest of the food.

I wanted to ask James how he was feeling. But I knew James was trying to hide his pain. I wasn't going to hurt his pride by asking. If there was one thing I knew about him, it was that he didn't like to look weak. Instead I said, "Weird lunch combination," as I looked back at Penny.

She shrugged. "That's because..." she glanced at James and smiled. "...I'm pregnant."

"What?"

Now she was beaming. "I'm pregnant!"

"Congratulations, Penny." I hugged her again. Maybe at one point in time, I thought that might be us one day. It seemed like a long time ago. "Congratulations, James." I stuck my hand out to him.

He hesitated, but only for a second, before grabbing my hand in a death grip. "I heard you tried to get Penny to run away with you the morning of our wedding," he whispered.

I tightened my grip back on his hand. "I heard you broke up with her the night before."

He leaned forward slightly. "Just so that we're clear, Tyler..."

For a second I thought he was going to kill me. I hadn't expected there to be any strength in his grip when he was so clearly struggling. But if anything, he squeezed my hand even harder after my comment.

"...that was the biggest mistake of my life. I won't be making it again." He immediately released my hand.

"You better not."

He smiled and nodded at me. "Should I cut up the watermelon?" he asked, turning his attention back to Penny.

She looked back and forth between me and James. "Yeah. Can you stay for lunch, Tyler?"

I needed to get to Hailey. "I don't think I can."

"Certainly don't leave on my account," Melissa said. "I have a new boyfriend and everything already."

"I'm happy for you," I said.

She smiled. For the first time since she had seen me, she actually looked happy. "Thanks, Tyler. I hope you find what you're looking for too."

I have. But I didn't want to talk to them about Hailey. That would just delay me getting back to her and I just wanted to get to her as soon as possible. "I should actually get going."

"Please stay," Penny said. She gave me one of her pleading smiles. The kind that always drew me back in.

But it didn't this time. I knew that this was it. These were my friends. This was my life. But it was all before Hailey. And none of it seemed good without her. "I'm really sorry, but I'm kind of in a rush. I have to get going." I didn't tell them about the fact that their case had kept me locked up for a week. I didn't tell them that it had ruined my new career. I didn't tell them how much their relationship had fucked me up for years. Because I forgave them. I finally had some perspective in my life. I just needed to see Hailey. That was all that mattered.

"Go get her," Penny whispered in my ear as she hugged me goodbye. "I will always have a special place in my heart for you, Tyler Stevens." She kissed my cheek. "Go get your happily ever after."

I smiled as she released me from her hug. "You're going to make a great mom, Penny." I squeezed her arm.

I gave Melissa a quick hug goodbye. James and I just nodded at each other.

And I walked away from the life I knew without looking back.

"Wait," James said before I stepped onto the elevator. He slowly walked over to me. "Here." He pulled his car keys out of his pocket and tossed them at me.

How did he know I needed a car? "Are you serious?"

"Don't get too excited. It's not the Lamborghini or anything."

"Thanks, man."

He shrugged. "Penny told me about the girl you met. It's about time you found who you were supposed to be with. Instead of trying to constantly mess up my life." He smiled.

"Look, I owe you all an apology..."

"It's okay. Really. I'm actually trying to do this thing where I try to let things go." He folded his arms across his chest and leaned against the wall beside the elevator. "I know you just wanted what was best for her. And I respect you for that. I try to be better for her. Better than what I was before we met. Maybe one day you'll see that."

I didn't really know what to say to that. "How are you feeling?" I said instead. I couldn't help asking. He didn't seem okay.

"Honestly?" He sighed. "I'm in fucking pain all the time. It hurts to breathe. It hurts to walk. It even hurts to sit down. Don't tell Penny." He gave me a small smile.

That was probably the first time that James had ever opened up to me. Near death experiences did change people. I respected him for coming out to talk to me. And I respected him even more for being strong for Penny. He was a good guy. I had judged him ever since we met. I had never really given him a chance. But now that I wasn't so jaded, it was like I was seeing him for the first time. He was good for Penny. And she was good for him. "My lips are sealed."

James nodded.

"Thanks for this," I said and lifted up the keys. "I don't know how I can ever repay you for this."

"Don't. That's what friends are for."

I smiled. I never thought I'd hear the day when James Hunter called me a friend. "Just for the record, I do see it. I just didn't want to see it. That was the problem. But you're good for her. She needs you."

He nodded.

I hit the elevator button again. "Get better, man."

"Good luck with Hailey."

I stepped onto the elevator. Maybe I needed to clear the air between me and James even more than I did with Penny. It felt like a weight had been lifted off my chest. Without realizing it, I had been torturing James ever since we met. Trying to steal the only thing he loved in this world. I had been an asshole ever since I stepped into his classroom. And he forgave me.

The dust had settled. Now I could really start over. I was un-enlisted. I wasn't holding on to anything in NYC. All that I had was the fact that I had fallen in love with a girl from Indiana. So that was where I was going. As Penny put it, it was time for my happily ever after.

CHAPTER 57

Hailey

Friday

I threw a few things into my duffel bag and zipped it shut. For the first time since my father had passed, I felt hopeful. There was no doubt in my mind that this was all just a terrible misunderstanding. I'd go to him. He needed to know about the baby. This couldn't wait. And I knew he'd be as excited as I was. This baby would have a mother and a father who loved him. We'd be a family.

My heart was open. I was going out into the world. I would be doing everything my father wanted. I pulled the duffel bag over my shoulder. He'd be proud of me. I was proud of myself.

The mailman was placing down a huge stack of mail on the bar counter when I walked out of my dad's office.

"Morning, Hailey. You have quite a bit of mail there." He tapped the side of the counter. "How are you holding up?"

"I'm good, Chuck." For the first time, it wasn't a lie. I was taking a step forward. I was living my life again.

"That's good to hear." He tipped his hat. "Keep your head up." He whistled on the way out the door.

I lifted up the stack of mail and it felt like my heart crashed to the floor. I dropped my duffel bag and let myself sink into one of the bar stools. All the letters I had written to Tyler were sitting on the bar counter. They were all stamped with different things. *Undeliverable as addressed. Return to sender. Insufficient address. Rejected.*

Every single letter I had sent. They looked just like the letters I used to write to my mom. The ones I'd always get back.

He promised he'd write back. I swallowed hard. This was a bigger offense than the lie. Who the hell cared if he was really in the marines? I'd rather he wasn't. But this? He knew about the letters I wrote to my mom. He knew and he still gave me a fake address? I bit my lip.

This past week had been a living hell for me. But I saw a light at the end of the tunnel. I thought...*fuck, I don't know what I thought.*

I turned over each envelope. They had all been opened and then taped shut again. *He read them?* I swallowed hard. My pleas for him to call me. My desperation. He hadn't given me a fake address. He had seen all of it. He just didn't care enough to reach out to me. He didn't care about me.

I would have driven to the end of the earth for Tyler. But I didn't even know him. I didn't know where he was. I didn't know if the week we had spent together was even real.

Time hadn't stopped. Time had sped up, chewed me up, and spit me back out. I felt ten years older. And ten years wiser. Love did make people do stupid shit. It had given me hope about something that never would be. But I was done being stupid. *Fuck him.*

I didn't need Tyler Stevens. Which was good, because I was probably never going to see him again.

I grabbed all the letters and went back into my dad's office. I was embarrassed that I had thought that it was more than what it was. My grief had made me grasp on to straws. But I was stronger than this pain. I was. I slammed the letters down on the desk.

I didn't need anyone. I could pick up my own damn pieces. It suddenly felt like I couldn't breathe. *God, I'm such an idiot.* I collapsed into the desk chair in a fit of tears.

Just like with every guy in the history of men, it had been about sex. That's all it ever was. I should have never climbed in his car. I should have been with my dad.

I put my face in my hands as I let my grief swallow me whole.

CHAPTER 58

Tyler

Saturday

I turned on my blinker and exited the highway when the annoying voice on my GPS instructed me to. Even though I hated it, I didn't want to miss the exit. For some reason it felt like I was running out of time. It had been over a week since I had left her in that motel in Santa Monica.

She had probably been writing to me, wondering why I wasn't writing back. I never wanted to make her feel like I didn't want to respond. I knew how much that hurt her because of her mom. *Please don't let me be too late.* I wanted her to jump into my arms, not slap me.

I drove by the sign promising a gas station and smiled. It was like I had turned back time. Except this time I wasn't heartbroken and lost. I had fallen in love with a girl from Indiana. And she loved me back. I hadn't signed my life away. I was free. Free to stay, free to love her. I'd get to hold her in my arms again. I'd get to shake her dad's hand.

As soon as I saw the bar, I sighed with relief. There were a few cars parked outside, but I didn't doubt that it was packed inside. I put the car in park and grabbed the bouquet of flowers.

When I walked into the bar I thought Hailey would be standing behind the counter and that our eyes would instantly meet. And that I'd see her beautiful smile as she ran toward me. It would be the perfect reunion. In reality, Hailey was nowhere in sight. I glanced around the bar. The only person that seemed to be working was an older woman. She was wiping down the counter.

I walked over to her. "Hi, is Hailey here?"

She gave me a small smile. "May I ask who's asking? I don't really think she's expecting anyone today."

"I'm Tyler."

She gave me a blank stare.

For some reason I thought Hailey would have told everyone about me. That she'd be excited about us. I shook away the thought. We hadn't discussed labels or anything. Yes, I viewed Hailey as my girlfriend, but I never actually asked her to be. I'd make sure I asked her that tonight. I wanted to tell the world. I wanted her to officially be mine. "I'm a friend," I clarified. I was definitely tired of referring to her as that. Hailey was everything to me. "I was actually trying to surprise her."

"Oh, it's nice that you came by. Did you want me to take those?" She reached out for the flowers.

For the first time I realized that there were flowers all around the bar. On the tables, on the bar counter, in the corners of the room. I didn't remember it looking like that. "No, that's okay. I'd like to give her them in person."

She smiled. "Okay, hon. She's in her dad's office down the hall to the right. But," she grabbed my arm. "She's not feeling very well today. Hopefully seeing an old friend will cheer her up. Maybe you're just what she needs." She looked hopeful.

"Yeah." *I hope I'm still what she needs.* "Why isn't she feeling well?"

The woman winked at me. "That's the spirit. With that attitude, you'll have her back out here in no time."

What? "Mhm," I said awkwardly. "So, down the hall to the right?"

She nodded.

I walked around the bar and toward the back hall. There was a door marked with "Jeffrey Shaw," on the right side. I knocked on it.

There was no answer.

I knocked again and slowly opened it. Hailey was sitting at the computer typing furiously. She didn't look up from the computer.

"Anna, I told you I was fine, you don't have to keep checking on me. I'm not good at coding, it's going to take me a while to get the website up. But I have to get this done." She nodded to herself. "I just need to get this done," she said under her breath as she continued typing.

She looked skinnier. Her cheeks almost looked hollow. She was still breathtakingly beautiful, but she did look like she wasn't feeling well. That's what the woman behind the bar had said. Was she sick?

"Hails, it's me."

She stood up, causing the chair to squeak against the floor. She ran her fingers through her hair and then immediately shook her head and wrapped her arms around herself. It was almost like she looked scared of me.

"God, it's so good to see you." I took a step toward her, but she immediately took a step back, even though the desk was already separating us.

"What are you doing here, Tyler?"

"I came to see you." I held the flowers out for her. When she didn't take them, I set them down on the desk. I thought she might look excited to see me. I hadn't spoken to her in over a week. I missed her like crazy.

But she didn't look happy to see me at all. She glanced back down at the computer screen. "I'm a little busy right now. I have a whole bunch of stuff I need to finish. I can't do this right now."

Do what? I laughed. "What are you talking about? I just drove twelve hours straight to come see you."

"Twelve hours?" She wrapped her arms a little tighter around herself. "Were you in New York?"

I remembered our discussion about NYC being twelve hours away from here. This wasn't how I wanted to tell her my news, but it seemed like now was as good a time as any. "Yeah, it's been a crazy week. I..."

"Did you see her? Is that why you were there?"

"That's not why I was there." This conversation was not going how I planned it. "But yes, I saw Penny."

She nodded and then immediately shook her head. "Look, Tyler, I had a lot of fun on our little road trip. But I think we both know what that really was. And I really am busy right now."

"It was the best week of my life."

She laughed. But it wasn't her real laugh. Not the one I loved so much.

"Well, I highly doubt that. We both needed a little escape from our real lives. Which was great, but that's all it was. Now I need to get back to my real life. And you need to get back to yours. Whatever the hell that is. Because it certainly has nothing to do with the marines."

"Not now. I..."

"Not ever, Tyler. You lied to me."

"I never lied to you. It's a long story..."

"And I don't have time to hear it!" She bit her bottom lip, but it didn't hide the fact that it was trembling. "I called the recruit depot. They didn't have any record of you even enlisting. You left me for no reason without saying good-bye. And went to New York? To see someone else? I'm not an idiot, Tyler. I can connect the dots."

"That's not what happened."

"It doesn't matter what you say. I'm not going to believe it. I can't believe anything you ever said to me. God, I don't even know why we're having this conversation." She pulled open a drawer in the desk and held out two credit cards to me. "These are yours. I didn't use them. And I tore up the check, so you don't have to worry about that. You can go now. I don't owe you anything else. We're done here."

"We're not done."

"Yes, we are. We were done as soon as I got all the letters that I sent you back. And you read them! You knew I was hurting and you ignored me. So yes, we're done. You never gave a shit about me. I was just too naive to see it."

"I never got those letters."

She shook her head as she opened up another drawer and pulled out a handful of envelopes. "Not only did you get them, you read them, you asshole. And then returned all of them to me. You're heartless."

"Hailey, I swear to God I never got those letters. I..."

"I don't care about your excuses. I needed you and you weren't there. You promised me you'd write back. You promised." Her voice cracked. "I told you about my mom. You knew how much that would hurt me and you did it anyway. So I'm not going to let you lie to me anymore. I need you to leave. Now."

Shit. "Hails, I didn't lie..."

"Don't call me that." She put her hand on her chest, like it physically pained her to hear me call her by her nickname. "You need to go."

"But I..."

"I don't need you."

"Hailey."

"What did you expect, Tyler? Time doesn't stop just because you want it to. Time doesn't stop." She was shaking. She put her hands on the desk to steady herself.

"You wanted to know why I'm here. I'm here to start my life with you. I'm here because I love you."

"Well I don't love you. I just got caught up in the moment. And now the moment's over." She set her mouth in a straight line.

"Nothing's changed. My feelings for you, if anything, have gotten stronger."

"Please stop."

"Can't we just pretend that the last week never happened? Can't we go back to Santa Monica and just continue where we left off?"

"My dad died."

Fuck. She needed me. I wasn't there for her. *Damn it!* "Hails, I'm so sorry." I wanted to reach out for her. I wanted to comfort her. But it seemed like she was in pain looking at me. I had hurt her and I had no idea how to fix it.

She shook her head. "You said I wouldn't be alone. I have never felt so alone in my entire life, Tyler. If anything, meeting you made all of this way more painful because I let myself hope. I'm done. I'm tired. So I'm going to focus on saving the one thing that's left of him. And I can't have any distractions. I think it's best if you leave."

"But I can help you."

She shook her head again. "I don't need your help."

"Hailey." I could hear the desperation in my voice. "Remember what we have."

"A summer fling. That's it." She put her arms in front of her stomach, closing herself off from me. "That's all it ever will be. I don't love you."

"It's more than that, and you know it.

"You abandoned me. You went to New York to be with your ex instead of me. I needed you, Tyler. I needed you and you weren't there."

"I didn't choose to go to New York."

"Great. I don't really care. Because I realized that I don't need anyone. I'm just fine on my own." She seemed to wince at her own words.

"Hailey..."

"And you know the worst part? My dad was always there for me, and I wasn't there for him when he needed me the most." She walked around the desk and shoved me hard in the chest. "Because I lost sight of what was important in my life." She shoved me again and I stepped backwards into the hall. "I'm never going to do that again." She shoved me even harder.

The bar had suddenly grown quiet. I could feel everyone's eyes on us. All I could focus on was that even when she was mad at me, I still felt the spark of her touch. But I didn't know what to say. Because deep down I knew I had already lost her. "I love you." I meant it as a declaration, but it came out as more of a plea.

"I'm done giving people second chances." She threw all the letters she had written to me at my face and slammed the door.

CHAPTER 59

Hailey
Saturday

My back slid down the door until my butt hit the floor. I hugged my knees to my chest and let myself cry.

I wanted to be able to hear him out and forgive him. But I couldn't even stand to look at him. He put me through hell. Never in a million years would I have thought he was in New York. He said he hated New York. He said he had moved on from Penny. He had told me he loved me. But nothing he said was true.

He looked thin. Had he been struggling through something too? Was he in as much pain as me? I shouldn't care. He was an asshole. So why the hell did I care?

I put my forehead on my knees. I wanted to throw my arms around him. I wanted to breathe in his scent. I wanted to feel his arms around me. I shook my head. I guess the only thing I actually wanted was for him to be the man I thought he was.

And the worst part was, I would never move on from him. Because that one week we had was the best of my life too. I loved him so much that it made my chest ache. I loved him, but I couldn't be in love with him.

I placed my hand on my stomach. But it wasn't really about us. No matter what, this baby deserved to know his father. I could put aside my own pain for that. Couldn't I?

Yes, Tyler and I were both a mess. Somehow our lives were a little less messy when we were together, though. That's how I knew this baby was going to be so good. He'd be the best of both of us. I wiped away my tears as I slowly stood up. We were complicated. But I would not put my own problems in front of my child's. He would always come first.

That's what gave me the strength to open the door and go after him. But he wasn't in the bar and his car wasn't outside.

"Did you see a guy in his mid twenties with shaggy blonde hair, Anna?"

"Yes, he left you this." She shrugged as she handed me a few napkins. There were words written hastily on both sides of three napkins. It almost felt like I was in a trance as I walked back to my dad's office. I closed the door with my foot and sat down at the desk as I started to read what Tyler had left.

Hailey,

I know that you probably won't believe me, but I needed you to know the truth. When I showed up at the San Diego Recruit Depot, they immediately detained me. They threw out my file and un-enlisted me because the case of James' shooting was still open. That's why there was no record of me when you called. They arrested me and sent me back to New York. I didn't choose to go. They held me in a cell until yesterday morning. I thought of you the whole time. I was worried that you might be sending me letters. I was worried that not hearing back from me would hurt you. I swear I never meant to cause you pain.

When they released me, all I wanted to do was come see you. I had to go back to my apartment to grab some cash because my car is still in San Diego and I had given you my credit cards and everything in my bank account. When I got to my apartment, Penny was there helping Melissa pack. I didn't seek her out. And I want you to know that I felt nothing. All I was focused on was how much I missed you. I didn't stay. I left as soon as I could to come to you. I don't know how to explain it, but it felt like you needed me. And I needed you.

I understand why you're upset. I'd be upset with me too. But I need you to know that the week we had together was real for me. My feelings were real. I do love you. And that's why I'm respecting your wishes. You won't see me again. But I just needed you to know the truth.

I'm so sorry about your dad. It breaks my heart that you lost him. I just hope you got a chance to say goodbye. If I kept you away from him for that, I'll never forgive myself. I can't say that I'm sorry enough. But I know you'll save the bar. I know you'll find someone better to share your life with. You deserve the world. Don't ever settle for less.

Thank you for giving me that week. Thank you for helping me feel whole again. I'll never forget you.
-Tyler

It's what I wanted. So why did I feel abandoned all over again? There was no phone number. There was no address. That was the only chance I'd get to tell him about the baby. I closed my eyes. To tell him how I really felt. I shook my head and opened my eyes again. I could add it to everything else I regretted.

I switched the computer back on and stared at the website I was trying to make. That was what I needed to focus on. This bar was my future. It always had been. I always wanted it to be. But I wasn't excited about it anymore.

CHAPTER 60

Tyler
Saturday

She was better off without me. I already knew that. It didn't make it any easier to drive away, though. I couldn't seem to focus on the road. I felt lost. Maybe it was because I had nowhere to go. I pulled over to the side of the road and put my forehead against the steering wheel. All I wanted was Hailey. So now what?

I needed someone to tell me I was doing the right thing by driving away. I just wanted her to be happy. But all I really wanted to do was turn around and burst into her office again. She was hurting. She was in so much pain. And I had caused some of it. It killed me.

My phone started ringing. For a second I let myself think it was Hailey. But I hadn't left her my number. The caller ID said that it was my mom. Maybe a familiar voice would make me feel better. I swiped my finger across the screen. "Hey, Mom."

"Hi, sweetie. It's so good to hear your voice. How is training going?"

I had been so preoccupied by getting to Hailey as quickly as possible that I completely forgot to tell my mom the news. "Actually, I'm not joining after all."

She exhaled loudly. "Thank heavens."

I laughed. "I thought you might be excited."

"I'm ecstatic! How did you get out of it? I thought you said you couldn't change your mind?"

"It's kind of a long story."

"I have time."

I looked out the windshield. "Actually, Mom, I'm coming home for a visit." It had been far too long since I had seen her.

"When will you get here? Your bed is already made up."

I smiled. Some things never changed. "I can be there by tomorrow night."

"Perfect. That'll give me some time to go grocery shopping. Will you be here in time for dinner?"

"Probably later than that."

"Dessert then. I'll make you those brownies with pecans you love so much. I should go start getting everything ready. I'll see you soon, sweetheart. I love you."

"I love you too, Mom."

That did make me feel better. I still had people I could rely on. I didn't have to go back to my old life. I couldn't. Either way, this was going to be a fresh start. I pressed on Josh's name in my phone and put it to my ear.

After a few rings he picked up.

"Does that job offer still stand?"

"Yeah. But I thought..."

"Change of plans."

He laughed. "How the hell did you get out of the marines? Are you on the run from the government now?"

"No, nothing like that. I just got incredibly lucky." The marines weren't for me. I wasn't my grandfather. I wasn't my dad. I was me. And maybe that was enough. "It was a mistake to sign up in the first place."

"You're telling me. You're not exactly combat ready."

"What is that supposed to mean?"

"You're too soft."

I laughed. "Thanks, asshole."

"Do you talk to your new boss with that mouth?"

"Apparently I do."

"Good enough for me. You're hired."

I laughed.

"Can you come back to Texas for a few days so I can get you all set up? Then you can work from wherever you want."

"You know what, I'm thinking I'd like to move there."

"Yeah?"

Why the hell not? "Yeah. Like you said, it'll be like we're in college again."

"Yes! This is going to be awesome. Did you want to crash here for a bit?"

"Just until I find my own place."

"Are you bringing that chick with you again? She was a firecracker. I liked her for you."

Me too. "No, Hailey and I didn't work out."

"Sorry, man. But that's even better. Now it'll really be like we're in college again. You can be my wingman."

"Sounds great." It didn't really, but it was better than the alternative: sitting alone in a motel room analyzing where everything went wrong. Because I already knew I had fucked it all up. And I already knew she'd never forgive me. She had made that perfectly clear. The best thing

I could do now was respect her wishes and try my best to not lose myself again.

"When can you get here?"

"I'll be there in a few days. I was going to go visit my mom first."

"Tell Mrs. Stevens I said hi. Oh, you should get her to make those awesome brownies and then bring me some."

I laughed. "She already mentioned she was making them."

"Sweet. Okay, I gotta run. Don't you dare eat all those brownies yourself."

"I can't make any promises."

"I'll make you sleep on the floor when you get here if you do."

"Later, man."

"See ya."

A new job. A new state. I'd be okay. *Right?* I was trying to convince myself as I pulled back onto the highway. But the farther I drove away from Hailey, the more I felt myself unraveling.

CHAPTER 61

Hailey

Saturday

"He wasn't writing back because he was in jail. He didn't lie."

I stared up at the starry sky. I had given up on coding hours ago. I didn't even know the first thing about creating a website. The only place I ever felt comfort now was when I was lying beside my dad's grave. So that's what I was doing again. The groundskeeper thought I was insane. Every now and then he'd walk over and ask if he should call someone.

The answer was always no. If there was anyone I'd rather be talking to, clearly I'd be talking to them instead of a gravestone. Besides, it was therapeutic being able to talk to my dad. Even though he couldn't respond, it still made me feel close to him.

Yup, I'm losing my mind.

But that didn't seem to stop me. "If everything he said on those napkins was true, then he didn't do anything wrong. He came back to me as soon as he could. But how do I know if he's telling the truth? Why is it so hard to believe him?"

Because you're in pain.

"I love him. I love him even though he hurt me. Does that make me weak?" I bit my lip. "But it takes strength to forgive someone. I know it does. Because I'm not strong enough to forgive Elena. I want to be able to. I know you wanted me to be able to."

I stared at the sky, trying to find Scorpius, trying to ignore my own thoughts. But it just looked like millions of stars to me. "I lied, Dad. I never could see it."

"Me either."

I turned my head to see Anna standing above me. "Hey."

"Hon, we're all worried about you. Come back to the bar. Let me fix you a drink."

A drink would be nice. But I couldn't exactly do that anymore. "That's okay."

"I'm not saying you should drink away your sadness. I'm saying let's have a girls' night. It'll be fun."

Fun. I don't like having fun anymore. "I'm pregnant." It was like I didn't even have a filter anymore. I was so used to just confessing all my thoughts to the dead. I pressed my lips together. I hadn't meant to say it out loud.

"I see." She sat down next to me in the grass. "Who's the father?"

"You met him last night."

"The gentleman in his mid twenties with shaggy blonde hair who looked dejected after talking to you?"

"That would be him."

She was quiet for a moment. "He doesn't want the baby?"

"No. No, it's not that. I didn't even get a chance to tell him."

"Hon, you have to tell him."

"I know. But I don't even know his phone number. I don't know how to find him. All I know is that he lives in New York." I continued to stare up at the stars.

"You know, when I said I couldn't actually see Scorpius, I meant that you have to really search for it. You have to believe it's there."

I guess I could find Penny and James' address. That would be easier. They were famous. And they'd know where Tyler's apartment was. I needed to go. It wasn't just the fact that his baby was growing in my stomach, either. I still loved him. And I felt horrible.

But at the same time, I couldn't just leave. I had responsibilities. "I need to stay and take care of the bar. I can't let anything happen to it. It's his baby."

"Your father isn't the bar, hon."

"It's all that's left."

"Then you're not looking hard enough. He's in the stars."

The sky blurred above me. *Of course he's in the stars.*

"And he's in your heart. You're what's left of him, Hails. You're his baby. Not the bar. The bar never mattered. He just did that to support you."

"He loved it, though." *And he loved you.*

"He wanted you to go out and live your life. He didn't even want you to stay here when he was living. He wanted more for you. You know that. He was trying to give you everything he never got."

She was right. My dad would be horrified that I had been spending every night lying by his grave, shutting myself off. I had to stop this. I had to have faith for once.

Just like he had enough faith to give love one last shot. "Will you take it?"

"What, the bar?" She seemed shocked.

I sat up and brushed the dirt off my back. "Yes. Will you take it?"

"I can't do that. I can watch it while you're gone, though."

"He'd want you to have it. If he wanted me to go out in the world, he'd want you to have the bar."

"Hails, I can't. You just said it was all you had left of him."

"And you showed me that wasn't true. Just promise you'll keep the name. Don't make it unrecognizable or anything."

"I won't change a thing. And if you decide to come back, it'll be waiting for you."

I shook my head. "It's yours. Take care of it for him." I nodded to myself, convincing myself I was doing the right thing as I stood up. "I have to go."

"Hailey." She slowly got to her feet too. "Stay in touch, okay? I'm going to want to meet that beautiful baby." She gave me a hug. "Your father would be so proud of you."

I hope so.

CHAPTER 62

Tyler
Sunday

I knocked on the door even though I had a key. My mom had moved after my dad died. She said it was too painful to live in the house they shared together. So even though this was technically my home now, it had never really felt like it. I had only ever spent summers during college here.

It only took a few seconds before my mom opened the door with a huge smile on her face. She threw her arms around me before I could even say hello. "I'm so glad you got here safely. I always worry about you when you drive long distances." She kissed my cheek but kept me in her embrace. "How are you? Are you hungry? I have leftovers from dinner if you're hungry..."

"I'm okay, Mom. It's just really good to see you."

She slowly released me from her hug.

"You don't look good." She put her hands on my shoulders.

I laughed. "Thanks."

She waved my comment away. "You know what I mean. Have you been eating okay? I guess you've been mostly eating at restaurants and such. You need a home cooked meal. Come in, come in."

I dropped my backpack in the hall and followed her into the kitchen. Even if I had just eaten a Thanksgiving feast, if my mom believed I was hungry, I'd have to eat. So I might as well have some food. Besides, a home cooked meal actually sounded perfect.

I tried to ignore the fact that she was staring at me while I ate. It was clear that she could tell something was bothering me. But I didn't feel like talking about it. Just thinking about Hailey put a lump in my throat.

"Is this about Penny getting married?"

I choked on my food. "Is what about Penny getting married?"

"This." She waved her arm in front of me.

"I don't know what you're talking about, Mom."

"You've been in love with that girl ever since you met her. And if I've told you once, I've told you a thousand times, that girl is not the one for you. You know I love her to death. She's a sweetheart. But you need someone with a little more oomph if you know what I mean. To deal with all this." She waved her arm in front of me again.

I laughed. "Am I so hard to deal with?"

"Yes. You get it from your father."

I shook my head. "So basically you want me to be with someone a little more like you? Is that it?"

"Exactly. Someone who can take care of you. And remind you to eat."

"I've been eating."

"If you say so. Really, it should be a sweet girl who pushes your buttons enough to get you to tell her what's really bothering you."

I put my fork down.

"One that will tell you that you're being an idiot when you try to do something like sign up for the marines on a whim." She raised her eyebrow at me.

"It wasn't a whim. I was trying to make Dad and Granddad proud."

"And you think you would have asked me if joining the marines would have done that. I would have told you that it wouldn't. Just because your grandfather did it doesn't mean it was the right fit for you. They both wanted something better for you than they had. That's what all parents want. But no, you didn't ask me."

"I'm sorry. You're right. I should have asked you."

"Exactly. Now that's enough food for you." She stood up and pulled my plate away. "You can eat again when you tell me what's wrong with you."

"There's nothing wrong."

"If there wasn't anything wrong you wouldn't have driven across the country. If nothing was wrong you wouldn't have somehow miraculously un-enlisted from the marines. And don't tell me you're on the run because I don't want to be any part of that."

"I'm not..."

"Hush."

My mom hadn't hushed me since I was a kid. Geez, she really was mad at me.

"And you certainly wouldn't be here if there wasn't something wrong. You have a perfectly good apartment in New York. So tell me what's wrong or you can go to your room."

I laughed. But it didn't look like she was joking. "It has nothing to do with Penny."

"Then tell me what it does have to do with."

Fuck. She really did know how to push my buttons. "I messed everything up."

She sat down next to me and squeezed my hand.

"I met this girl on the way to basic training. She's sweet but she tells me when I'm being an idiot. She's real. And she's way too good for me."

"Sounds like a keeper."

"Yeah, well...she hates me now."

"So fix it."

"It's not that simple."

"Of course it is."

"Not everything can be fixed. I can't be with someone who cries when she sees me." I suddenly felt like I was breaking. "I can't...I can't..."

"Bring dad back?"

"What?"

"Tyler, sweetie, you have to forgive yourself. It was an accident."

"It's not about that."

"Everything has been about that ever since the accident. You were a happy, carefree boy. And you've been nothing but trouble since then."

"Trouble?"

"Yes, trouble. All I do is worry about you. You go around pretending everything is okay, when I can see that you're suffering. Your father was so proud of you. Your grandfather was so proud of you. They both loved you more than life itself. They wouldn't want you to be living like this."

"Living like what?"

"Like you don't deserve happiness!"

I wanted to say I wasn't doing that. But I was. I convinced myself I was in love with Penny for three years. Probably just to torture myself. And I sure as hell told myself enough times that I didn't deserve her. That I was meant to be alone.

"You need to do what makes you happy. Isn't that really the only thing that matters? We don't have enough time on this earth to spend sad and regretful. It's too much work, sweetie."

"I miss him."

"Then look in the mirror. You're a spitting image of your father when he was your age." She patted my cheek and stood up. "You can have brownies now."

"I'm really not hungry."

"Nonsense. You're too thin." She put the pan down in front of me. "These were your dad's favorite too."

CHAPTER 63

Hailey
Monday

Elena,

I forgive you. I forgive you for the things you said to me before you left when I was a kid. I forgive you for abandoning me. I forgive you for not responding to my hundreds of letters. I forgive you for asking my dad to make me stop writing. I forgive you for pretending I was a stranger after ignoring me for 15 years. I forgive you for not giving me the money to save my dad. I forgive you.

Life is too short to hold on to all this anger. My wonderful father taught me that. He was all I ever needed. He shaped me into the person I am and he was proud of me. That's enough for me. I sincerely hope you find whatever it is you're looking for in life. Because I've found what I've been looking for.

-Hailey

I folded the letter and put it in an envelope as the taxi sped through the city. I no longer hated her. And I'd never love her. I don't even remember a time when I did. Now she was nothing to me at all. Now I could let go.

The taxi pulled up in front of a tall building adjacent to Central Park. I couldn't help but think how amazing the view would be from inside. That was, if I was allowed to see it. I stepped out onto the city street after paying the cab driver. As soon as I did, the cabbie pulled away from the curb, leaving me alone in the middle of the city.

But there were people everywhere. I spun around in a circle. It was like I had stepped into a movie. The whole city felt alive. It was exhilarating. *And intimidating.* Someone bumped into me, almost knocking me over.

Luckily there was a big blue mailbox right outside the building. I dropped the letter I had written to Elena into it and sighed when I closed it. One thing down, one to go. My hands shook slightly as I opened up the door to the apartment building that I'd never in a million years be able to afford. As soon as I stepped inside, I realized how underdressed I was in my tank top and jean shorts. The man behind the front desk was in a suit. But none of that really matter. I just hoped this was the right place. And I prayed that they'd be willing to speak to me.

"Hi," I said. "I'm here to see Penny Hunter."

He looked down at a clipboard. "I'm sorry, the Hunters don't have any scheduled visitors today. Can I please get your name?"

"Oh, yes, I didn't call ahead. I'm a friend of a friend. My name is Hailey Shaw."

He opened up another binder. "You're not on their list of approved guests." He looked me up and down.

"I know. I'm a friend of Tyler Stevens. I'm sure he's been here before."

"Mr. Stevens is on the list. You, unfortunately, are not." He just stared at me.

Was he expecting me to go? I wasn't going to go. I wasn't going to give up that easily. "It's really important that I speak to her. Can't you call her and tell her that it's me?" Would she know me? She had seen Tyler a few days ago. Would he have told her about me?

"I'm sorry, Ms. Shaw. There isn't anything I can do."

"You can just tell her that it's Tyler's friend. She'll understand. Please can't you just ask if she's willing to speak with me?"

His eyes bulged slightly. "Excuse me for one second." He grabbed a stack of mail and walked around the desk and toward the door.

James Hunter had just walked into the building. I swallowed hard. It was like seeing a celebrity. He grabbed the mail from the concierge and thanked him. The concierge tried to hurry him along to the elevator. He was trying to make it so that I couldn't speak to James.

Finally my feet started working and I walked up to them. "Are you James Hunter?" I don't know why I said it like that. I knew it was him. He looked just like his pictures.

He glanced at the concierge and then me. "Yes?"

"Oh, don't mind her," the concierge said. "Ms. Shaw was just leaving. Right?"

"James, I'm a friend of Tyler Stevens. We met a few weeks ago. And I need to speak with him. I don't have his number or his address and I was hoping you could help me find him."

"I'll call security, sir," the concierge said. "She's probably just paparazzi. I'll take care of her."

"No, it's okay, Rodgers," James said slowly. "What did you say your name was?"

"Hailey. Hailey Shaw. Tyler and I were on this crazy spur of the moment road trip and I just really, really need to speak to him."

"We've actually heard all about you. But my wife is having really bad morning sickness. Let me see if she's up for a visitor." He pulled out his phone and put it to his ear.

Penny's pregnant? I couldn't believe I didn't know that. But I had been pretty isolated the past week. It had been a while since I had last turned on the TV.

"You'll never guess who's standing in our lobby right now." Pause. "Hailey Shaw. Tyler's Hailey." He smiled at me. "I thought that would be your answer. We'll be right up." Pause. He looked in the grocery bag he was holding. "Yup. And one extra thing I hope you'll like." Pause. "I love you too."

That had to have been the cutest conversation I had ever witnessed.

"Thanks for checking, Rodgers. But you can add Miss Shaw to our list."

"Very well."

James nodded toward the elevators and I followed him. "I'm sorry about all that," he said as we both stepped on. "After everything that happened, I just wanted to make sure we wouldn't be getting any unexpected visitors."

"No, I completely understand. And I'm glad you're okay."

He smiled. "You don't even know me."

"I've read about your story. About you and Penny specifically. I was always rooting for you two."

"Thank you." He looked a little surprised to hear that.

I knew they had gotten a lot of bad publicity for their relationship. A professor falling in love with his student probably wasn't usually front page news. But a professor as famous as James Hunter? Their relationship had been smeared in front of the whole country. I had read that they couldn't leave their apartment for months because the paparazzi were harassing them. They had been through so much already. And then they were finally getting their happy ending and he was shot.

I tried not to blatantly stare at him. He was classically tall, dark, and handsome. But he looked a little paler than he did in pictures I had seen. I watched him put his hand out on the railing of the elevator, as if he was steadying himself. He was clearly still in pain. And rightfully so. He had been shot three times, all just barely missing his heart. He probably should have still been resting.

"Did you want me to carry that?"

He smiled. "I'm okay. But thank you for offering."

"Are you sure? I know you're still recovering. Shouldn't you be resting?"

He laughed. "My wife nags me enough about that, trust me." He let go of the handrail and stood up a little straighter.

I wish he didn't feel like he needed to do that for my benefit. But I also understood. I was a proud person too.

The elevator dinged open. James pulled out his key and unlocked the door.

The first thing I noticed when I stepped inside was the breathtaking view. All I could see was miles and miles of Central Park and tall buildings in the distance. The apartment was immaculate. It was all marble and glass and stainless steel. I turned in a circle. Penny was sitting at the kitchen island drinking a cup of tea. She was every bit as beautiful as she was in pictures and on TV. She slowly got up out of her chair with a big smile.

"You feeling better?" James asked and kissed her forehead.

"Yes, you were right, the tea helped." She peeped into the grocery bag James was holding and pulled out a bag of potato chips. "You're the best." She smiled up at him.

James cleared his throat. "This is Hailey Shaw," James said and gestured to me.

"Hi, Hailey." She walked over to me and stuck out her hand. "I'm Penny."

I shook her hand. "I know. I mean, I've seen you guys. Well, like, I've heard of you." *Stop being awkward.* I couldn't help myself. This was the closest I had ever really been to celebrities. Even if they didn't consider themselves as such, I sure did.

Penny smiled. "It's okay. I guess we've been on the news a lot recently with everything that's been going on. It's really nice to meet you. But I am surprised that you're here. The last time we saw Tyler, he was heading to you. Did you two miss each other?"

"No, not exactly."

She opened the bag of potato chips. "I promise I'm more excited to see you than a bag of chips. I'm just hungry. Did you want some?" She held it out for me.

"No, I'm okay."

"I'm sorry, I'm being rude. Come in and have a seat. Did you want something to drink?"

"I'm fine. I'm not trying to inconvenience you at all."

"It's no inconvenience."

Penny was probably the sweetest person I had ever met. She wasn't feeling well. James wasn't feeling well. Yet here they both were, being nice to a complete stranger.

"No, no, I'm really okay," I said. "Tyler and I had this fight. He might not even want you to give me his number, but I had to try. I thought he lied to me. When I called the San Diego Recruit Depot they said they had no record of him enlisting. I freaked out. It's hard to explain, but I was writing these letters and they all got returned and I just thought he had abandoned me."

"The San Diego Recruit Depot? Isn't that where the Marine Corps trains?" Penny asked.

"Yeah. He was reporting to basic training last Friday."

"Why would he do that?" She looked upset. Like she knew maybe her decisions had pushed him there.

"He had a lot of reasons." I didn't want her to feel bad. "He said he needed to start over."

She pressed her lips together and nodded. "So what happened? You said he's not there now, right?"

"They immediately un-enlisted him. They held him in a jail cell for a week while they closed your investigation. Something about him being a part of it."

"What? The case was closed last week. James, I thought..." her voice trailed off when she looked at him.

I turned toward him too. He hadn't said a word. He was just looking down at his hands.

"James, what did you do?" Penny asked.

"Nothing you wouldn't have." He looked up at her and gave her a small smile.

"I can't believe you." She shook her head, but she didn't actually look upset.

"He was going to get himself killed. He was making a rash decision because he was upset. There was no way he actually wanted to go through with it."

"And how would you know that without talking to him about it? You can't meddle in people's life decisions. We've already talked about this. A few times."

"If something had happened to him, you never would have forgiven yourself. I couldn't live with that. Not when I knew I could stop it." He stood up and put his arm around her shoulders.

"Thank you." The words spilled out of my mouth before I could even stop them. I knew Tyler was tough. But I had been so worried too. And it seemed like he had enlisted for the wrong reasons, despite what he had said.

James smiled at me.

Penny shook her head but she still looked more unbelieving than angry. "Is that why you gave him the car? To make up for what you did?"

"I was being nice." He kissed her temple.

She sighed. "Well I'd say I hope he's happy, but clearly he's not since Hailey is here and not with him." They both turned back toward me.

"I know I messed everything up by sending him away. But I just thought...I assumed the worst. I shouldn't have. It's been a tough week for me and I wasn't exactly in a good place. He left a note explaining everything though. And I need to see him. I just...I love him so much and I need him to know. Please, you have to help me. I didn't know where else to go. There's hundreds of Tyler Stevens just in New York alone."

Penny smiled up at James. "Everyone deserves a second chance."

James nodded.

She grabbed a piece of paper and started writing down some information off her phone. "Here is his number, his mom's number, and a couple of his friends' numbers. Also, his address is on here, but I doubt he's there. It kind of seemed like he wanted to be as far away from New York as possible." She pressed her lips together again, like it pained her because she knew the reason why.

From everything Tyler had said about their relationship, I thought she was a tease. Maybe it had been that way between them before. But from what I could see, she just cared about him. She wanted him to be happy. And it physically hurt her that she was causing him pain. I respected her so much for that. I didn't have any friendships that were that strong. But I could see myself getting along really well with her.

"I hope you can find him, Hailey," said James. "Tyler and I have had our differences, but he's a good guy. I hope that you two can make each other happy. Now, if you ladies will excuse me, I think I'm going to go lie down for a bit."

"Are you okay?" Penny said. "Did you need me to get you anything?"

"No, no." He kissed her temple again. "I just need to rest for a couple minutes." He nodded toward me and headed over to the beautiful staircase that twisted up to a second story. I hadn't even realized there was another story until that minute.

I noticed Penny watching him over her shoulder.

"Are you okay?" I felt this weird need to make sure she was okay. Like maybe Tyler would have wanted me to ask.

"I'm fine." She smiled. But there was something sad in her eyes. She looked over her shoulder again as he disappeared into a room upstairs.

I could tell she wasn't. "Is he doing alright?

"I don't know. He should be taking pain killers, but he doesn't want to..." she let her voice trail off. "I mean, he's just trying to cope without them. For health reasons. He keeps saying he feels fine, but I can tell that he's not. I don't know why he's pushing himself. And I don't know why he feels the need to tell me he's fine when clearly he isn't. It's so hard to see him in pain. He's my rock, you know?"

"Yeah. I get that."

"And then I keep getting sick. So he's trying to take care of me. Which is the last thing he should be doing. I'm sorry that I'm going on and on. Really I'm just so sick of getting morning sickness." She smiled.

"Tell me about it." I hadn't even realized what I said before it was too late.

The worry was momentarily gone from her face. "You're pregnant?"

There was no point in lying about it. I smiled. "I just found out a few days ago."

"Tyler is going to be so excited."

"You think? I'm worried he's going to freak out."

"I mean, I don't know for sure, but he's a family guy. I think he's ready for that. Just give him a second to process it. He's definitely going to be an amazing dad."

"I just hope he's willing to give me another chance."

She smiled. "If there's one thing I know about Tyler, it's that he has the biggest heart. And he loves you. You should have seen the way he looked when he talked about you."

Talking to her did give me a little bit of hope. "I guess we'll see."

"Maybe our kids can play together." She smiled as we walked toward the door.

"I'd like that." I stepped out into the hall.

"And Hailey?"

I turned around.

"Please don't break his heart. I...I'll never forgive myself for how much I hurt him. I just so badly wanted to hold on to our friendship. I never meant to hurt him. He deserves the world. And..."

"He forgives you." I stepped forward and gave her a hug. I wasn't sure why I said that. I was just in a forgiving mood. But it felt like if he was here, he'd say the same thing.

She was going through enough. The worry was all over her face. She didn't need to worry about Tyler. I was going to take care of him. She looked a little more at peace when I released her from my hug.

"Good luck with the baby. And getting James to take it easy."

She smiled. "Thanks for letting me ramble. We're going to be okay. It's just been a little overwhelming."

I had no doubt that they'd be okay.

"And good luck with the baby yourself. And with Tyler. But you won't need it. He's going to be thrilled to see you."

"Thanks, Penny."

I stepped back into the elevator feeling so optimistic. I looked down at the piece of paper Penny had handed me. Josh's name was on it. For some reason it seemed like it was going to be a lot easier to talk to Josh than Tyler. And maybe he could tell me where Tyler was. My conversation with Tyler needed to be in person, not over the phone.

CHAPTER 64

Tyler

Tuesday

I watched Josh inhale the plate of brownies I had brought him.

"I seriously love your mom," he said with his mouth full. "Just because of these brownies, she's a total MILF."

"Don't make me beat you up."

He laughed. "You know you couldn't take me."

"Wanna bet?"

He shrugged and shoved another brownie in his face. "Maybe you could take me if you had actually gone through basic training."

I lightly shoved his arm and he pretended to fall off the kitchen stool.

He laughed as he sat back down. "Want to go out to-night? A new bar just opened down the street."

"I don't think I'm up for it. I'm a little jet-lagged."

"Come on, it's going to be awesome."

"Not tonight." I wasn't sure when I'd be up for it, but it wasn't anytime soon.

He shrugged his shoulders. "Fine. We'll just wait and see what the night brings." He pulled out his phone and started texting someone.

"You can go out if you want though." I wanted to read through the letters Hailey had written to me. I had been putting it off. At first it seemed like it would torture me for no reason, but now I just wanted to feel close to her. It was all I had left.

"Nah." He pushed the empty plate away from him and shoved the phone back in his pocket. "Let's rent a movie or something. Then we'll see if you're up for visiting that bar later."

I laughed. "Trust me, I'm not. I'm actually pretty tired. I think I'm just going to go to bed."

"Anchorman?"

I laughed. I'm pretty sure we had watched that movie a hundred times in college. "Okay, yeah, let's watch Anchorman."

"Score. Grab some beers out of the fridge, I'll go set it up."

***

I picked up the final letter, even though it felt like I couldn't read anymore. Most of them seemed composed. Like she was holding back her true thoughts. But in the more recent ones, pain radiated off the pages. It was like she had given up hope. In me. In living. No wonder she had sent me away. I stared down at the final letter.

Tyler,

I need something to hold on to. It feels like I'm drowning and I don't know how I'm supposed to keep going. No one understands. But I know you will. I just need to hear your voice. I need to know I'm not crazy. I need to know you're okay. I need you.

If I've done something wrong, you can tell me. But I can't keep writing like this. It's too hard. You feel so far away and I'm lost. You promised that I'd never be alone. I've never felt more alone. Please call me.
-Hails

Reading about her pain made my chest hurt. It felt like I couldn't breathe when she couldn't breathe. I touched the smudges on the page where her tears had fallen. No wonder she hadn't forgiven me. I hadn't been there and she had slipped back into the darkness. I felt myself slipping there with her.

After talking to my mom, I finally felt like I was ready to forgive myself for what happened with my dad. But I wasn't ready to forgive myself for hurting Hailey. Not when I wasn't sure if she was okay.

I stared at the ceiling. What the hell was I doing in Texas? I should have stayed in Indiana and fought for her. But the truth was, I knew why I left. A girl like that deserved better than me. She deserved someone who had their life figured out. She deserved someone who wasn't such a fucking mess.

Josh knocked once and then opened the door. "Dude, I thought you went to the bathroom. What the hell are you doing?"

I slowly sat up. "I fucked everything up."

"Yeah. I know."

I hadn't been expecting him to say that. How did he know? I hadn't really told him anything besides for the fact that Hails and I didn't work out.

"Why else would you be lying in my guest room reading a bunch of..." he lifted up one of the letters, "handwritten notes like a little bitch? Should we watch The Notebook instead of Anchorman?"

That was harsh, even for him. "I'm not..."

"Get out of bed."

"Seriously, Josh, I just need some sleep."

"No, what you need is something stronger than beer."

"Okay, fine. Your bar is completely stocked though. Let's just finish the movie."

"No. We're going out. And change into something less wrinkly or you're going to scare away all the ladies. You're killing me, man."

I looked down at my t-shirt that I had been wearing on the plane. He was right, it was ridiculously wrinkled. However, I didn't care about scaring away women. I didn't care about anything.

"Look, we'll stay there for five minutes. And if you aren't having fun, we'll leave. Deal?"

Jesus, he was not letting this go. "Fine." I stood up.

"Shirt. You look like a bum."

I changed into a new shirt to humor him and followed him downstairs. "How far away is this place?"

"Just down the street." He opened up the front door and basically pushed me outside. "It's karaoke night. It's going to be a blast."

Karaoke night. I pictured Hailey singing her heart out in Kansas. That's where she said she had fallen in love with me. This was going to be worse than just hanging out at a normal bar. Would everything always remind me of her?

"Do you want to talk about it?" Josh asked.

"There's nothing to talk about."

"Really? Because you're acting like a love sick puppy. It's like the Penny situation all over again."

"It's nothing like that."

"Sure."

"I never loved Penny. I just liked the idea of her."

Josh laughed. "It's about time you realized that. So if you love Hailey, why aren't you trying to win her back?"

"I promised her that I wouldn't break her heart, and I did. There's no fixing that. She thinks I'm a liar." *I hurt her.*

"I don't know, man, she seemed like a pretty strong girl. I don't think being love sick would keep her down that long."

He hadn't seen the letters, though. But he was right too. It wasn't just the grief of losing her dad that had beaten her down. It wasn't that she thought I rejected her. Either one of those things would push a normal person down. She had only crashed because it was both at once. Maybe if I gave it some time. She needed to grieve for her father. She needed to start to heal again. Then maybe, just maybe, there'd be room in her heart to forgive me.

I opened up the door of the bar and walked inside. There was some guy on the stage singing a country song I had never heard of before. The place was packed. Hailey and I seemed to thrive in places like this. We were so easily able to shut out the rest of the world when we were together. But it wasn't the same without her. It was too loud. There were too many people. I just had to wait five minutes before I made a run for it.

"Find a table. I'm going to grab us some drinks."

I found a table as far away from the stage as possible and sat down. The music. The noise. If I closed my eyes, it was almost like she was here with me. I'd do anything to turn back time and be in Kansas again. I wanted a do-over. It was like I could feel her presence. I was starting to lose my mind.

"Stop falling asleep, man," Josh said and slid a glass of whiskey toward me.

"It's already been at least three minutes."

"Cheers," he said ignoring me, as he clinked his glass against mine.

I took a sip. The burn down my throat felt good.

"Do you think she's the one?" Josh yelled over the music.

That was a shitty question. Especially because of the answer. I downed the rest of the whiskey. "Yes. It's been five minutes." I set the glass down on the table.

"One more song. Then we can go."

"Fine. I'm going to go get another drink." The country music was driving me crazy. It was all about love lost. I waved down the bartender and waited for another whiskey.

The beat to Beside Me by the Cigarsmoakers starting pumping over the loudspeakers.

Damn it. Our song.

"Babe, I thought I was good before I met you. I drink a lot which is an issue, but I'm alright."

I was out of my mind. Now I was imagining I could hear her singing it. I downed the whiskey the bartender handed me and turned around.

And there she was. In that little red dress we bought in Vegas. Our eyes locked.

She smiled as she brought the mic closer to her lips. "I know it hurts your heart. Fled to the suburbs in a really old car. And six months, no calls." She shrugged and winked at me.

She's here. I started pushing through the crowd of people.

"We're never getting older. We're never getting older."

I couldn't believe she was here. *Why were there so many people in our way?* The bar was more crowded in front of the stage. "Excuse me," I said a million times as I pushed my way closer to her.

"You look better than the day I met you." She pointed at me as I made my way to the stage. "I forgot why I left you, I must be crazy."

I was almost there. I tried to get on the stage but a bouncer was blocking my path.

"So, baby, get beside me in the backseat of your Audi." She starting laughing into the mic when she saw me trying to push past the bouncer.

"We're never getting older!" She yelled, even though it wasn't the right part of the song. She dropped the mic, ran to the edge of the stage, and jumped down into my arms.

The music came to a sudden stop as I wrapped my arms around her waist. And even though we were in a crowded bar in the middle of Texas, it suddenly felt like I was home.

"You always seem to be there to catch me when I fall." She smiled up at me as she laced her fingers behind my neck.

"Hailey, I'm so sorry. I never..."

"Tyler Stevens, nothing you say is going to change my mind," she said, cutting me off. "I love you. I don't want to spend another second apart. You're the only thing in my crazy life that I'm actually sure about. All I know is that I need you."

I pressed my forehead against hers. "I need you too."

"Ow, ow!" I heard Josh yell as people in the crowd starting clapping.

I glanced behind her. The mic had rolled over near us so that the whole bar could hear our conversation.

But who the fuck cared? Nothing in the world mattered except the girl in my arms. I grabbed the back of her neck and brought her lips to mine.

Everyone was still cheering when she pulled back to look up at me.

"And I need you to know that I wasn't too late. I got to say goodbye to him, Tyler. And I'm okay. Now that I'm with you, I know that everything's going to be okay." She tried to blink away the tears in her eyes.

I put my hand on the side of her face. Just like that, the pain I felt seemed to disappear. With her forgiveness, it felt like anything was possible again. For the first time in five years, it didn't feel like anything was weighing on me. She had healed my soul.

CHAPTER 65

Hailey

Tuesday

I woke up with his arms wrapped tightly around me. I hadn't been this content since I was sleeping in his arms in Santa Monica. When I tilted my head up, I was surprised to see that he was already awake.

A smile spread across his face as he looked down at me. "It feels like I'm dreaming. I still can't believe that you're here."

I pressed my hand against his chest. "I'm here. And I'm not going anywhere."

We stared at each other in silence for a moment. We had talked until dawn, filling each other in on the missing pieces of our time apart. I told him about forgiving my mother. And about realizing that all my dad ever wanted was for me to be happy. He told me that he was finally at peace with his past. We were both starting over. Nothing was holding us back from being together. Except one thing.

The smile on his face grew even wider. "Are you still a fan of fast and crazy?"

"Since everything we do is fast and crazy, absolutely."

He tucked a loose strand of hair behind my ear. "I think we should get married."

It was fast. It was crazy. And I so badly wanted to say yes. But he didn't know everything yet. Even though we had talked for hours, I hadn't gotten the courage to tell him about the baby. I had wanted to know that he needed me just as much as I needed him. His answer was in the way he looked at me. The way he kissed me. The way he held me. He needed me as much as I needed him.

"Hear me out." The smile on his face was contagious. "I'm in love with you. I want to spend every morning for the rest of my life just like this, with you in my arms. We're both starting over. And we're choosing to do that together. We can make a life for ourselves wherever we want. Here. We can go back to Indiana. Anywhere, Hails. The only thing I care about is that we're together.

Yes. A thousand times yes. "I need to tell you something."

"Nothing you say is going to make me change my mind, Hails."

Maybe. "It actually does change things. Quite a bit." I sat up and pulled the sheet around myself.

"Hailey." He sat up. "I know that I hurt you. And I can't apologize enough times. I just need you to give me one more chance. Because I can't live without you. When we're not together, I don't feel whole. You saved me."

It was like he was saying everything I should be saying to him. I shook my head. "I just showed you the way I see you."

He smiled. "Then I don't see what the problem is."

"I'm pregnant." It sounded harsh in the silence. I knew he wasn't expecting it, which maybe made it sound even harsher.

He didn't say anything.

"I found out a few days after my dad's funeral. And I don't know, it almost felt like I needed this baby. I felt so alone. I was all my dad had. And it was like I had this gift that made it so I wouldn't be alone anymore either." I was rambling, but I couldn't seem to stop because Tyler was completely silent. All I wanted to do was tell him everything I couldn't the first time around. I needed him to know that I loved him more than life itself. He was the world to me. The sun rose and set with his smile. I smiled to myself, remembering my father say that to me. "The ironic part is that this baby actually gave me strength to do what I needed to do all along. Find you. So really, it's not the same situation as me and my dad at all. Almost the opposite, really. I knew in my heart that we were supposed to be together. But I've always been so scared of love. Petrified really. Now it seems like I have this whole new perspective. I'm not scared. Not of what we have. I love what we have."

"You're pregnant?"

It was like he hadn't heard anything I just said. "Yes."

More silence.

"It's yours, if that's what you're wondering..."

"No, that's not...you're pregnant?"

I slipped my hand into his. The spark whenever we touched coursed through me. I could tell he felt it too, because the smile slowly came back to his face.

"Then it's possible that I love this baby even more than I love you." He leaned down and kissed my stomach. "It brought you back to me. And I'm nothing without you, Hailey."

I pressed my lips together and shook my head. "I'm nothing without you."

He smiled. "You still haven't answered my question."

"Are you still asking it?"

He placed his hand on my stomach. "Hailey, I love every part of you. This baby is a part of you. Of course I'm still asking. Will you marry me?"

Together we had grown so much. Together we were better than we were apart. Together we made sense. It felt like a new page had turned. It felt like I was finally free to be me. "Yes."

His kiss made me feel utterly complete. All of this was fast. It was crazy. But if it wasn't for him, I would have spent my whole life searching for myself. The version of myself that I saw in his eyes was everything I aspired to be. I had been broken my whole life without even knowing it, and he had made me feel whole.

"Thank you for taking a chance on me." He pressed his forehead against mine. "Thank you for climbing into my car and driving me absolutely crazy."

I breathed in his exhales. Somehow that was all I needed to survive. "You were worth taking a chance on, Tyler Stevens. You just hadn't found the right person to take the leap."

He closed his eyes. And I knew he was feeling it too. It was beautiful. It was pure. This feeling was better than anything anyone could see. We both felt it in our bones. It consumed us. We weren't broken anymore. When we were together, neither one of us had any missing pieces.

ABOUT THE AUTHOR

Ivy Smoak is the international bestselling author of *The Hunted Series*. Her books have sold over 1 million copies worldwide, and her latest release, *Empire High Untouchables*, hit #10 in the entire Kindle store.

When she's not writing, you can find Ivy binge watching too many TV shows, taking long walks, playing outside, and generally refusing to act like an adult. She lives with her husband in Delaware.

Facebook: IvySmoakAuthor
Instagram: @IvySmoakAuthor
Goodreads: IvySmoak

Made in the USA
Columbia, SC
21 April 2021